ELGAR
ON THE JOURNEY
TO HANLEY

ELGAR
ON THE JOURNEY
TO HANLEY

A NOVEL BY

Keith Alldritt

ANDRE DEUTSCH

First published 1979 by
André Deutsch Limited
105 Great Russell Street London WC1

Copyright © 1979 by Keith Alldritt
All rights reserved

Printed in Great Britain by
The Anchor Press Ltd
Tiptree, Essex

British Library Cataloguing in Publication Data

Alldritt, Keith
　Elgar on the journey to
　Hanley.
　I. Title
　823' .9'IF　　　　PR6051.L533R/

ISBN 0-233-97064-9

For Miranda and her mother

Does the imagination dwell the most
upon a woman won or woman lost?
W. B. YEATS, 'The Tower'

Go to your spiritual brides – but don't come to me
as well, because I'm not having any, thank you . . .
A clear look had come over Birkin's face. He knew
she was in the main right. He knew he was perverse,
so spiritual on the one hand, and in some strange
way, degraded on the other. But was she herself any
better? Was anybody any better?
D. H. LAWRENCE, *Women In Love*

1

THE short passenger train with its black squat engine and its three brown and yellow coaches and a guard's van stood waiting at a small country station in the northern part of Worcestershire. The October morning was bright but chill. Leaves fell onto the ends of the wooden platform from the trees on the dense green banks above. Rooks flew over the train and among the trees. The morning was very quiet.

Alone in one of the compartments of the train sat a youngish looking man and an older woman who regarded him anxiously. The man was in a paddy.

'I cannot for the life of me understand why I too must go to Wolverhampton. Smoky hole that it is! It would be far more convenient for me to go directly to Hanley.'

He sprawled forward sulkily so that his lower back rested on the seat cushions. The trousers of his heavy brown woollen suit were crumpled and worn at the knee.

The woman answered him pleasantly and tenderly.

'But you have been well pleased on previous visits, have you not? Remember how well *The Black Knight* was received at the Agricultural Hall.'

She spoke her words very slowly and distinctly like a teacher of young children.

'I tell you I am weary of trains and travelling and visits.

Gloucester, Leeds, London, Manchester. On and on. On and on. And to no avail.'

The last words he uttered with a slightly hysterical shrill that suggested both reproval and self-pity.

The lady would have none of this. She faced him more rigidly. She studied very carefully the bright, petulant eyes that had now turned away from her to look through the window. She wore a small, somewhat quakerish hat of dark red and a handsome travelling coat of heavy navy blue linen that reached down to her boots. It was shiny and worn at the elbows and the waist. She was a heavy woman, much stouter than her companion who was quite slim. She was nearly fifty but looked older. Her eye-sockets were wrinkled and a little discoloured. But the deep blue eyes searched his face energetically and unrelentingly. Her large handsome jawbone had set against him.

She cleared her throat quietly and with a characteristic gesture touched her blonde, greying hair where it swept up into the great topknot under the hat.

'Edward,' she began, 'I have every confidence in *King Olaf*. I know that it will be a success.'

He turned to look at her with a sarcastic sneer.

'My dear, you had confidence in all the other oratorios. You had confidence in everything else that I have written. You had confidence that I could go to London and become established and successful.'

He did a bitter unpleasant laugh, showing his discoloured teeth.

'And didn't we come back with our tails between our legs! To teach the fiddle to the young ladies of Malvern Wells!' His lower jaw hung down quivering. There was a nasty expression on his face.

'Edward!' she interrupted.

But his loathing was unleashed. He turned to her again with a snarl.

'And look at us! Look at us! Next door to beggary. Yes, that's what we are, beggars.' His mouth and jaw were twisted uglily.

There was a silence. Bitter and unseeing he again looked

through the window at the autumn day. He was nearly ten years younger than his wife but looked younger still. Within his long narrow face the deep-set eyes were intense and ever moving. His hair, which was just beginning to recede from his large brow, was of a very fine brown. Beneath the heavy moustache his lips were pink and moist. The top frontal lobes of his ears were unusually fleshy. They made his skull recall the skull of a fish or an animal.

Compartment doors were slammed. He could see the station-master surveying the platform. A whistle was blown and the train set off with a jolt.

The motion appeared to renew the man's bad temper. He sat up and brought his face closer to the woman's. His hands moved restlessly on his thighs.

'By the way,' he began in a tone of mocking courtesy, 'are your prosperous, ecclesiastical friends aware of my poverty? Do they know that without your money we should in fact be paupers? Do the Rector of Wolverhampton and his good wife know that we are maintained by your inheritance? That without it, we should be paupers? Do they? Do they?'

The last few words he whispered into her face with an ugly hiss. Then he threw himself back on his seat and again stared out at the countryside that was already moving past. He had triumphed. Bright teardrops hung between the woman's tired eyelids.

'Mrs Penny is your friend, not mine,' he continued rhetorically and unpleasantly. 'Surely you can understand that it is painful for me to visit your elegant friends. I am a tradesman's son and a beggar. What have I to do with Mrs Penny or any of the other gentry from Hasfield Court?'

He was beginning to whip himself into a lather of anger. The large brow started to glisten with the beginnings of perspiration.

'Hasfield Court! Hasfield Court! I am sick to death of hearing it. And of having to do with those who are associated with it. What are they to me? Or I to them? Do you hear? Do you hear?'

As he shouted these words, the Worcestershire burr in his speech increased markedly.

'You have not always felt this way, Edward. You know you have not. Think of their great generosity to us.'

The woman's voice quivered. But she clung desperately to the vision that she had of him and for him. From her reticule she produced a lace handkerchief and dabbed at her eyes.

Now that he had made her weep, he had expended himself and his irritation abated. He turned again to the mellow landscape of deep green and yellow fields.

After some time when the woman had recovered her composure, she said quietly, 'Perhaps, Edward, it would be for the best if you were not to accompany me. You could get down at one of the earlier stations and I could proceed alone. I could make your excuses to the Pennys and you could resume your journey to Hanley on a later train.'

He thought about this for a while.

'No,' he said at last wearily and with a hoarse grudging magnanimity. 'I will accompany you.'

He turned once again to the window and watched some great wooden farm-carts labouring over the darkening yellow stubble, carrying in the late hay. The rose hips were already out in the hedges. The leaves on the opulent trees surrounding the rich harvest fields were all on the turn to gold and brown. A parson in a dog-cart could be seen intermittently as he hurried along a deep lane.

As the man looked out onto the world, his companion continued to watch him solicitously. It made him irritable that she watched over him in this understanding, forgiving way. He fancied he could even feel the weight of her glances.

The train started to run more slowly. It was now passing tiny gardens at the back of artisan row houses on the edge of Dudley. The man stood up and craned his head at the compartment window to catch a glimpse of the ancient castle and the familiar thick round towers of the keep. He often travelled on this line to his various engagements and he would always try to snatch a view of this castle on its wooded hill. He thrilled to his images of the great nobles who had once lived there, the Duke of Northumberland, the Earls of Dudley.

The train entered the smoky station and came to an abrupt,

bumping halt. There was a smell of coal and of stagnancy. People left and entered the train. There was much slamming of doors. Then they were on their way again, moving into Staffordshire. The countryside and its smells were now quite left behind. The train ran among blackened factory walls and chimneys. The man watched the angular, unpredictable course of the canal that lay alongside the railway. The water in it was soiled. The many iron bridges that crossed it had decoration that was long obscured by the soot and the dirt. A large horse stumbled and strained at a rope to pull a long barge laden with heavy industrial porcelain that showed a brilliant white through its straw packing. The stout, red-faced bargee smoked his pipe complacently as the horse scrambled perilously and sickeningly along the towpath to pull the load.

To the right appeared the long, sweeping hills of the Black Country with their harsh lines of red, squat, row housing, and plumes of bluish-white steam from the low factory buildings and trails of dense black smoke from the high stacks. He caught the dull glow of the proving houses and the vast soiled warehouses of the stockholders of finished steel. There were Tipton and Ocker Hill and Coseley and Bradley and Deepfields and Bilston. The man could hear all the sounds of these places, the heavy regular thud of the drop forgings, the rather lighter chuff of the steam-engines, the repeated, insistent skirl of metal cutting against metal.

He turned away from it. The woman looked at him with a quick, ready sympathy.

'That is the way to become rich,' he said with an angry snarl. 'These Staffordshire ironmasters are all worth a king's ransom.' There was a contemptuous twist to his mouth. His lower jaw hung down so that his large tongue and teeth were visible. He looked to the woman to accompany him in his sneering, panting smile.

He sat back grumpily in his seat. It grew shadowy and dark in the compartment. They had lost the sunlight. The train was running along the bottom of a deep gorge of factory walls. Water trickled down them in furry green runnels falling into black, dead pools. For an instant they were out again in the sharp

October sunlight and then, again unexpectedly, they found themselves in the warmish fetid light under the glass roofs of the station in Wolverhampton.

The man stood up to remove his hat and his worn leather music-case from the netted rack. The tired-looking woman eyed him surreptitiously and speculatively as they prepared to leave the compartment.

They descended from the train and walked across the wide stone platform and gave up their tickets. The man breathed heavily and irritably.

In the high booking-hall beyond, two ladies rose from the long, light oak seats as soon as the man and the woman appeared. They looked more prosperous than their two visitors. The older lady wore a full-length grey coat of wool, black gloves and, by the standards of those times, a plain black hat. There was a certain nun-like simplicity to her appearance.

The younger woman, who looked about twenty, wore a blue coat with large lapels that were scalloped and braided in a darker blue. She also wore a creamy blouse with a very high collar to which was attached a cameo. She carried a muff of light brown fur. As she tripped along, the points of her strikingly small black shoes appeared and disappeared under the hem of her coat in a noticeable, fast, delicate rhythm. She was an extremely attractive girl with large light blue eyes, fair, almost blonde hair and finely shaped features with full, small, protruding lips.

The older lady hastened forward in ungainly strides. Her face was round and candid; the expression was one of great kindliness.

'Oh, Alice, how very good to see you . . . And Edward. I am so happy that you were able to visit us.'

The two older ladies embraced carefully and kissed each other. The lady in grey then turned and shook the man's hand warmly.

'Oh it is such a pleasure to see you both again,' she cried excitedly. Their visit was a genuine pleasure, a relief even, to her.

Then she turned to the pretty young girl with the muff who hung back, diffidently.

'Dora,' said the older woman, 'allow me to introduce you to

two very old and very good friends of mine. This is Mrs Elgar, my friend Alice, of whom you have heard me speak so much. Alice, this is my new stepdaughter, Miss Penny . . . Dora . . . Dora Penny . . .'

The characteristic homely graciousness of the lady in the grey coat could not accommodate all these names. She ended her sentence a little helplessly.

Shyly the young girl removed her small hand from her muff and stepped up and shook hands with the stout visitor.

'I am v . . . v . . . v . . . very happy to make your acquaintance.' Her voice was remarkable. It was very melodious and yet startlingly low and throaty.

'And this,' persevered her stepmother in her pleasant matronly way, 'is Mr Edward Elgar. I am sure Dora will not object to my saying that she is a great admirer of your work, Edward, and has been greatly looking forward to meeting you.'

A pink flush rose quickly from the girl's neck into her face. Elgar stepped forward gallantly and shook her warmly by the hand.

'That is most kind of you, Miss Penny, most kind.'

There was now a bright flicker to the eyes which only moments before had been dull and sullen. His whole being was suddenly changed.

The two older ladies appeared a little taken aback by the genial directness of his attitude to Dora. There was a brief silence.

'How long shall you be able to remain with us?' enquired the lady in grey helpfully. 'I recall from your letter, Alice, that Edward must proceed to Hanley for an important rehearsal and that his arrangements are very uncertain.'

'We may not stay long, I fear,' said Alice guardedly. 'The rehearsal is very much on Edward's mind . . . Just an hour or so perhaps . . .'

The man interrupted loudly. 'Stay as long as you wish, my dear. No need to rush off.' He smiled charmingly at the three women and rocked back upon the heels of his boots. His deep eyes radiated an adventurous, devil-may-care cheerfulness. He encompassed them all in his good spirits.

'I trust that you will be able to stay for luncheon, at least,' said the lady in grey with an anxious movement of her head. 'Our housekeeper, Mrs Bayliss, has prepared for five. And she becomes rather cross with us if her arrangements are upset, does she not, Dora?'

'Yes, mother, she does. But I think we should g . . . g . . . give her very straight answers upon such occasions.'

An expression of practical, commonsensical determination came over the girl's delicate features. It was just as unexpected as the sound of the voice.

Stepdaughter and stepmother glanced at each other sympathetically. Clearly some important but shared difficulty was here being alluded to.

The girl turned her finely poised head to the visitors.

'And if you c . . . c . . . could stay to l . . . l . . . luncheon it would be possible for you to m . . . m . . . meet f . . . f . . . father. He requested us to c . . . c . . . convey to you both his excuses for not c . . . c . . . .coming to the station to welcome you. It is his h . . . h . . . habit to devote Saturday m . . . m . . . mornings to the preparation of the s . . . s . . . sermon for Sunday.'

Her beautifully level eyes moved uncertainly from the face of the tall violin teacher to that of his wife, who was very small. Dora sounded slightly breathless as she concluded her little speech. The two visitors smiled but did not immediately reply. So Dora added by way of further explanation, 'H . . . h . . . his sermons are usually v . . . v . . . very l . . . l . . . long.'

Elgar's large, long face folded into an indulgent smile.

'But of course we can join you for luncheon,' he cried in a rush of enthusiasm. 'We shall be most happy to stay, shall we not, Alice? Stay to tea too, if you like.'

His wife glanced up at him disconcertedly. 'Of course,' she replied tremulously, attempting, but completely failing, to match his grand easiness on the matter.

The Rector's wife studied Alice's nervous eyes for an instant. They were very old friends and knew each other well. She also saw that Dora was blushing slightly after her speech. So she brought all these initial greetings and explanations to an end.

'Well, I am very glad that it is all settled. And very relieved. Let us now be on our way to the Rectory.'

With an abrupt, awkward movement she turned and led the way out. She moved her legs with a strange, heavy plodding movement. The other three followed on behind.

Outside the station, under the large glass awning, there was a great bustle of passengers, cab drivers and black-jacketed porters. The air smelled of smoke and of the manure under the horses that drew the cabs. There were wide, dignified four-wheelers and more dashing two-wheelers, their steel-rimmed wheels as high as the cab windows.

Purposefully Dora pushed ahead past her stepmother to where the green and yellow tram stood waiting. The two heavy, brown dray horses that pulled it swung their heads anticipating departure. All the time they moved their thickly-shod hooves delicately and neatly between the metal tracks.

'Do let us take the tram again, mother. It is s . . . s . . . such a fine day for a ride.'

'Well if you really wish to, Dora dear . . . Though we did come on the tram. And it is not so very far to walk. We ought perhaps to save the money and make an offering . . .'

The lady in grey looked helplessly to her two guests. But already Dora had climbed up on board the tramcar. And then with a quick movement of her skirt and a glimpse of white petticoat she swung up the metal stairs on to the upper deck.

The stepmother clambered slowly after. Then came Alice and at the last the violin teacher with his music-case.

Dora had chosen to sit at the front of the open-air tram. Her stepmother sat down immediately behind her.

'Miss Penny will forgive me,' said Alice Elgar, puffing quite heavily from the climb, 'if I sit by her new mother. I have had no opportunity to speak to her since she became a bride.'

But from the anxious way Alice continually looked around it appeared that she was even more interested to ensure that her husband should sit by the girl.

'It will be my privilege to accompany Miss Penny,' said Elgar obediently, sitting down beside her.

The two ladies to the rear chatted away energetically. But the man and the girl were silent for a while. Then Dora burst out.

'I g . . . g . . . greatly enjoyed hearing *The Black Knight.*'

'I am very pleased.'

Dora began again, her suppressed excitement fighting against a certain shyness.

'Father and I h . . . h . . . heard it at Hanley where you are d . . . d . . . due to go tonight.'

'Indeed.'

Her lively blue eyes searched his face to find some reason for this casual reception of her admiration. His apparent indifference confused her.

'Father was priest at Tunstall b . . . b . . . before coming to Wolverhampton. That is quite near to Hanley.' Her voice fell. This was not what she had meant to say at all. The full, prominent mouth quivered a little. She turned her muff over and over in her lap.

Elgar looked at her intently.

'Do you ever go to see the Wolverhampton Wanderers play football?' he enquired.

Dora was taken aback by his question. The deep eyes regarded her closely. His question was certainly frivolous. It was almost rude to change the subject in this way. But the eyes were direct and very kindly. A brother, had she had one, might have addressed her in such a fashion, she thought.

'I m . . . m . . . must confess that I am something of a fanatic of the Wolves,' she replied. 'But it is difficult for m . . . m . . . me to attend the matches, since father and mother, I know, would not wish to accompany me.'

'Is there a match today?' he enquired in the same slightly abrupt, growling voice.

'Yes, I believe th . . . th . . . there is.'

'Who is to play?'

She marvelled to herself at his interest and insistence. She was disconcerted by the mixture of gruffness and familiarity in his manner towards her.

'The Wanderers are to play the Stoke City team, I believe.'

'Should we go? You and I, I mean.'

'Whoa! Giddyup!' cried the driver coarsely and loudly. And the tram jerked forward with a whining and grinding of the metal wheels upon the tracks.

Dora suspected that the sudden movement of the vehicle had made her nod her head. She felt uncomfortable and flushed slightly. His question was utterly improper, of course. It would just not be possible for them to go out together unaccompanied. Though, of course, he was a very old friend of her mother's. And also he was a great deal older than herself. Old enough to be her father, in fact. But only just. Only just. And certainly she would like to attend a football match. She always thrilled to the mood of excitement that came into the town on match days.

'I should have to ask f . . . f . . . father. And m . . . m . . . mother also.'

'Of course. Of course you must. And I too shall appeal to them.'

His manner was utterly courteous as though there never had been, nor ever could be, any suggestion of impropriety. The girl was confused, but also excited.

Slowly the two straining horses hauled the tram up the incline away from the station. Away to the left down Horseley Fields and over to the right near the canal stood high Georgian factory buildings of small red brick with their many storeys of windows all with little white-framed panes. From within them came a perpetual, low rumbling rhythm of machinery. Immediately ahead was the great curving front of the Victoria Hotel. Its bright façade of yellow and orange brick shone in the morning sunlight. Its scale and colour introduced a town and a scale of building altogether different from that of the black and white villages of Worcestershire known and cherished by the country music teacher.

In Victoria Square a ruddy-faced young man in a brown frock-coat and jodhpurs cantered by, watching the tram warily. He looked to have come from the nearby Shropshire countryside to the west, into this alien, industrial place.

'Do you know where they hold the races in Wolverhampton?' asked Elgar, looking down from the brass rail of the tramcar upon horse and rider.

19

Again the girl was surprised by the question. 'The racing c . . . c . . . course is near Dunstall Hall,' she replied.

'If I come again to Wolverhampton, could we go to the races, do you think?'

On this occasion the tone and the manner were those of a courteous old gentleman, almost childlike.

'I sh . . . sh . . . should enjoy that too, if f . . . f . . . father and mother were agreeable to the idea.'

Dora was much intrigued by these possibilities. She glanced at the older man quickly, a faint smile of pleasure on her dark red lips.

The tram jangled noisily along Lichfield Street. How elegant all the fine new buildings of the last ten or twenty years seemed to Dora. She liked to be upon this street. She loved its wideness, its bazaars and all the people walking to and fro in fine clothes. She looked to her companion to see what he might think of it. On their left was the Grand Theatre built just a couple of years before. It had a long handsome canopy of glass on red metal columns covering the pavement in front of the bright white doors. And on the upper storey was a large loggia of arcading. Contained within the building was an expensive chocolate shop which Dora very much liked to visit.

'What is being performed presently?' enquired Elgar, inclining slightly over his companion in order to see the posters.

'It is a m . . . m . . . musical play entitled *His Excellency*,' replied Dora. 'Mother and I saw it two nights ago.'

'Indeed.' His voice expressed a courteous interest.

Dora continued. 'The b . . . b . . . book is by Mr Gilbert and the music by Dr Carr. It is about a practical joker who is himself, finally, the victim of a practical joke. It is a jape within a jape.'

Dora was surprised to discover how forthcoming she had been. The man turned to look at her. There was a flicker of laughter in his eyes. Her enthusiasm amused him.

'I know it well,' he said.

Dora returned his glance directly, even a little pertly. She would not be laughed at in this way. She would not. The man's face resumed a more serious expression.

The conductor came for the fares and sold the man four pink tickets from his long wooden rack. Then it was time to alight. They walked across the busy, broad street with its many carts and carriages to the large and ornate new art gallery. This had low relief panels in stone and a grand porch held up by pairs of pink granite columns. It was a building very much in the Italian style and was an important part of the stylish improvements made to the old borough during the last few years. To the left there rose up the graveyard of the medieval church of St Peter. This was the high point of the sprawling hill town.

The four people made their way along a path immediately to the east of the high church. Dora led the way through the old gravestones and they left the churchyard through a wooden gate on the northern side. Here was an altogether different quarter of the town. They were in a twisting cobbled street that had some old trees and only a narrow footpath. It was quiet and had something of the atmosphere of a close. On the further side, within a walled garden, stood the Rectory. It was a large handsome house built of the small, rich red brick of the seventeenth century. It had a steep roof. Dora pushed open the gate and walked on the uneven stone path to the door. She opened it and led them in.

They found themselves in a low narrow hall of old wood panelling. The hall was dark and smelled musty. The four people stood for a moment in a close group.

'Let m . . . m . . . me take your coats,' said Dora brightly. She slipped off her own blue top-coat and hung it on the high coat and umbrella stand by the door. Underneath she wore the creamy blouse with the high collar, a brown leather belt and a long well-tailored brown skirt reaching to the floor. For all her beauty she looked, at this moment, above all capable, energetic, practical. She could conceivably have been a nurse or a stenographer.

Her guests delivered their coats. Dora took them with easy confidence. Her stepmother handed over her grey coat uneasily but helplessly. She wore a grey dress beneath.

Then a door banged loudly at the back of the house. The tread of heavy footsteps approached and a loud, coarse voice called out, 'Right you are, Miss Dora. I'll take them coats.'

From the gloom at the end of the corridor there appeared a very large breathless woman in later middle age. She wore a black serge dress with a white lace collar. Two or three heavy keys hung from a leather thong at her waist. She was sufficiently fat that her flesh shook slightly upon her. She had a thick neck and double chin. Her fair, greying hair was hacked quite short around her head so that she had a slightly demented look.

'Right you are!' she insisted menacingly as she came among them. 'I'll see to them.'

'That will be all right, Mrs Bayliss,' said Dora. The girl was pleasant but firm.

But Mrs Bayliss did not hesitate even for an instant. She plodded up to Dora, seized the coats from her and, with a great shake of her meaty arms, thrust them up on to the wooden pegs. She was ruthlessly, almost brutally proprietary about her function.

'And now, if you'll just follow me,' she said, ignoring Dora and speaking to the group as a whole. She moved off down the hall, stopped and then, most unceremoniously, threw open a wooden door to the right.

'Just goo in there,' she ordered. 'And sit you down. And I'll bring you yer barley drink. Ah've got it all ready on the tray.' Her throaty imperiousness allowed no argument. Obediently they filed through the door and down a stone step into the low-ceilinged drawing room with its window of old glass through which slanted the bright cool light of the October day.

For a second or so the four people merely stood uncertainly upon the turkey carpet in the middle of the room. No one knew what to do. Dora regarded her stepmother with raised eyebrows that suggested more irritation than amusement at what had just happened. But the Rector's wife did not respond.

'Do sit down, Alice, Edward . . .' she said quietly. She was not ready to allow that the situation was in any way abnormal.

The musician and his wife sat down on an old settle of cherry wood. Brightly embroidered silk cloths hung down from the back and the two wings. Dora and her stepmother seated themselves on two chairs that looked very much out of place in this close, wood-panelled room of the late Stuart period. The chairs were of very dark black wood and inlaid with a complicated, sinuous design in ivory. Set into the wood here and there were small bright stones of red and green.

Alice Elgar noticed the chairs with happy recognition.

'Oh, the Indian chairs from Hasfield!' she cried out. 'How very well they look here!' She spoke in a kindly way but always a certain slow unctuousness in her voice made her statements sound not altogether genuine.

'And the cupboard! And the great table,' said Elgar, examining the room with interest. 'Both were at Hasfield, were they not?' He stared wonderingly at the two dark and ornate pieces of Indian furniture that looked so large, even sinister in the old, very English room.

'Yes,' replied his hostess. 'It has been a great pleasure to me that Alfred and Dora wished to make use of these things.' She smiled affectionately at Dora. 'I like very much to see them here. They have been a part of my life for as long as I can remember and in many places, ever since I was a child in Lahore.'

'You bring a dowry from the great Moguls!' said Elgar, looking down indulgently upon the ungainly figure in grey on the large, strange chair. His enthusiasm was growing. He moved around the room to look at other pieces of furniture. Dora smiled. She liked this informality of his.

'And here is another old friend!' he exclaimed, going near to the window. 'The black piano!'

It was a small handsome instrument of the Regency period, decorated chastely with slender swags and putti of silver.

The man sat down happily, and carefully lifted the lid. He was very much at home now. He saw Dora looking at him and smiled a little to himself. He did a highly exaggerated flourish with his hands that made Dora smile even more. Then he struck a great chord.

Immediately the door opened and Mrs Bayliss puffed in. She strode straight across the room towards Elgar, eyeing him most sternly and suspiciously all the while. She carried a silver tray with little pewter mugs on it. Her heavy chin shook as she walked.

Elgar stood up guiltily, apologetically. Mrs Bayliss thrust one

23

of the mugs heavily into his hand. He peered into it with some scepticism then looked up questioningly at the fat lady. There was a scarcely repressed snort of laughter from Dora sitting on her Indian chair.

Mrs Bayliss immediately scented and responded to the lack of decorum in the air.

'It's yer barley drink,' she explained grudgingly and gruffly, a strong suggestion of menace in her voice. It was clear that the look on the man's face was not acceptable to her.

'This is a temperance 'ouse now,' she explained slowly, as though speaking to one of distinctly lesser intelligence. 'The present Rector's not like the one before 'im. The Reverend Jeffcock always offered a glass of wine or spirits, or small beer or summat. But this one now is temperance. So this barley drink is what we 'ave now. It's very good for your innards and your daily 'abits.' This statement she delivered in an emphatic and queenly way. Her massive confidence was such that she managed to make the unexpected beverage appear normal, even fashionable. And the man was made to seem lacking in refinement and social grace. There was a power to Mrs Bayliss' truculent parochialism.

It was the same with her voice. Below her efforts at genteel speech lay a harsh Wolverhampton growl that could if necessary swear, rail and brawl. Yet she bore herself with the fine confidence of a queen or of a queen's chatelaine.

She moved grandly around the room handing out the barley drinks. They were accepted meekly. The Rector's wife sat up a little in her chair and enquired in a thin voice:

'May we assume luncheon will be ready at half-past twelve, Mrs Bayliss?' She added, smoothing down her skirt, 'That was, I believe, the hour that you had in mind.'

'Yes, Madam, I did. But I've been having trouble with Mrs Shinton again. 'Er's been on the beer, I don't mind telling you. Proper Willen'all 'er is. And 'er all but spoiled the meat. I'm not so sure as I can do with 'er in the kitchen much longer.'

'Perhaps we should discuss this matter when the Reverend Penny is able to be present,' said the Rector's wife pleasantly.

'Ar, I shall mention it to him, don't you worry,' said Mrs Bayliss in her harsh-voiced, calm arrogance. 'Any road, I'm not

24

too sure when your luncheon'll be ready. But I'll tell him to come into you now. It's about time, I should think.'

She gave one last look around the room to see that all was to her satisfaction and then closed the door behind her.

Dora moved restlessly upon her chair. 'Isn't she th . . . th . . . the utter e . . . e . . . end?' she cried indignantly. There were bright red patches on the tops of her cheeks.

'Now, now, Dora dear, do calm yourself. Mrs Bayliss means well,' said her stepmother in a low but urgent voice.

Dora tossed her head irritably; the topknot of fine brown hair shook and threatened to fall.

'I am most sorry if Mrs Bayliss was rude to you, Edward,' said the Rector's wife to the tall, shabby figure, still imprisoned behind the piano.

'Not at all. Not at all,' he murmured sheepishly. He touched at his round soft collar with his large, unusually broad fingers.

His curious abjectness made Dora laugh. Her anger suddenly left her and she laughed aloud.

The man was attracted by her laughter but disconcerted that he was the object of it. Her mouth was open and he could see her small silvery-white teeth. He wanted to share her mirth as an equal.

'I must confess,' he said, 'that I have never in my life before played a chord to such devastating effect.'

Dora's laughter sounded out again, more loudly.

'It surpassed anything that I have ever heard in Wagner,' continued Elgar. He was becoming eloquent and enjoying it.

Dora answered again with a laugh. It was hoarse, throaty laughter. It ended in a sputter.

'Dora!' whispered her stepmother with sympathy and anxiety in her voice. 'Do control yourself. Mrs Bayliss might return any moment.' She was obviously afraid of such a possibility. She was also made uneasy by the girl's laughter. Dora hastily seized a small handkerchief from her belt and held it to her mouth and eyes.

Alice Elgar watched her husband and the girl alertly from behind her faded eyelids. Her husband had been about to say something else to make the girl laugh again. But at the wish of his hostess he subsided. With a careless elegance, he plucked up the knees of his trousers and sat down again at the piano stool.

Dora had not fully composed herself when the door was opened once more. The lady in the grey dress stood up.

'Oh, Alfred, it is you,' she cried relieved. 'Here are our guests. Pray allow me to introduce you to them.'

The Rector of Wolverhampton stepped down carefully into the room. He was a tall, heavy man and the low door proved difficult for him to negotiate. When he had entered, he stood and beamed around at his family and guests. He was a ruddy-faced, handsome man in his early fifties. He had a sweep of greying black hair, pronounced sideboards and a full beard. In his arresting blue eyes you could recognise Dora's own. Yet his always appeared to look beyond or alongside the person he was speaking to.

'I bid you all most welcome,' he said in a booming, theatrical voice which was too loud for the room.

His wife presented the two guests and he shook each slowly and heavily by the hand. But he paid no real attention to them; his mind was elsewhere, on the sermon perhaps which he had come from writing. When the introductions were completed, he continued to stand on the same spot near the door, smiling falsely and foolishly at them all.

Dora was agitated on his behalf. She finally jumped up from her chair.

'D . . . d . . . do sit here, f . . . f . . . father, whilst we await luncheon.'

'Ah, yes, Dora my dear,' boomed the Rector, turning his handsome, empty smile upon his daughter.

He was preparing to lower his stout form into the black Indian chair when Mrs Bayliss bustled back into the room. Her fleshy face had grown much redder. Her manner indicated that she was put out and disinclined to accept any interruption.

'Luncheon is ready, Reverend,' she called, ignoring everyone else.

'Ah, yes, Mrs Bayliss,' said the Rector, responding immediately and submissively. He rose up from the chair he had not quite sat down in. Perhaps it was his emotional and mental

absence that made his body an unpleasantness and an embarrass·
ment in the room. He looked uncertainly at his two guests.

'Mrs . . . Mrs . . . Mrs . . . Elgar,' he murmured, not really
addressing her but rather struggling to remember a name from
the distant past. 'May I invite you to accompany me to the
dining room?'

Elgar fell in with the rather pale, slightly simpering Mrs
Penny. As he did so he exchanged a quick, quizzical smile with
Dora who followed in at the last.

The five place-settings around the long table in the dining
room were plain and simple. The Reverend Penny stood with
bowed head behind his chair at the top of the table and his
daughter unobtrusively indicated to the guests where they should
sit.

'Let us pray,' called out the Rector peremptorily in his
resonating voice. And the grace began.

The Rector prayed for a blessing on the food, on those who
had prepared it and on those who were forgathered in the Lord's
name to eat, for those who had tilled the land and cultivated
the good vegetables, for those hinds and shepherds who had
tended the animals whose flesh was today eaten as a sacrifice, for
all those who broke bread and ate food in the service of the
Lord, for all those in the parish of the Collegiate Church of St
Peter in this town, for all those in the mother diocese of Lichfield
and in the see of Canterbury, for all good Christian folk in the
lands beyond the sea . . .

On and on he went. His voice grew louder and assumed a
strange threnodic beat as he continued to pray.

Elgar swayed a little as, like the others, he stood with his
head bowed and his hands clasped together in front of him. He
suppressed a yawn. He opened his eyes stealthily. He was shocked
to discover that at that very moment Dora was opening hers too.
Despite herself she smiled. She controlled herself only with a
slight but audible sucking noise.

Her stepmother, with her eyes still shut, swayed her head
towards the girl reprovingly. But the Rector continued, oblivious
and undeterred.

He was praying now for all those of the Christian fellowship

27

in Melanesia, for the soul of good Bishop Selwyn who had first brought the faith thither, for all those diligent labourers in that hot, stony, dangerous vineyard, and especially for those dwelling on the south-eastern corner of Norfolk Island who had only recently come to know and serve the Lord, for Charles Sapibuana, Abraham Baulee, Hugo Gorovaka, Kalekona, Halembosa, Tambukoru . . .

The door opened with a bang and Mrs Bayliss entered bearing a large brass tray. She brought it down with a resounding crash upon a serving table immediately to the rear of the Rector. As she stooped and rested her large quivering arms on the table, she accidentally nudged the Rector with her big bottom so that his voice quavered for a moment as he prayed on.

He prayed now for those upon Norfolk Island who had gone out to testify to their faith with only a loincloth to wear, only the smallest of garments upon them, for those who had danced their dances for the Lord in the purple light of evening, for those who for their faith had submitted their beautiful God-given bodies to spears, tomahawks, knives, hammers, axes . . . The voice pulsed on.

Unreverently Mrs Bayliss ignored the prayer. Life in the Rectory for her was primarily a logistical matter and only incidentally a theological one. In her heart she was coarsely sceptical. She ladled soup noisily from a tureen into the bowls. And these she placed irritably in front of those at prayer.

Mrs Penny was flushed in the face. She cleared her throat twice. But the prayer still proceeded. She coughed loudly. The Rector continued rapidly to intone.

But then he was again carelessly buffeted by Mrs Bayliss as she picked up her brass tray. She set things on it heavily so that the ring of it interrupted the prayer. The Rector at last paused. He tried to look at her. He was a little shaken. She nodded heavily at his bowl of soup.

'Ah. Ah,' he intoned understandingly. He gabbled to a conclusion with a rapid listing of the Trinity and then sat down.

The large blue eyes once, open, benignly encompassed the whole table. But he said nothing. He gave the impression of waking from a deep sleep or of reviving from a state of unconsciousness.

His wife nodded anxiously to the others to begin and herself started her soup. The Rector took up his spoon also but drank his soup only slowly and jerkily. The blue eyes looked beyond them all and beyond that room as if to distant places and to distant seas.

'Mr Elgar will be travelling to Hanley later today, Alfred, to rehearse his new oratorio,' ventured Mrs Penny.

'Ah yes.' The eyes sought to concentrate.

'My husband's former parish was in North Staffordshire,' continued Mrs Penny, turning hopefully to Elgar.

'Yes indeed,' recalled the Rector in his loud, musical fashion. 'I held the living of Christ Church in Tunstall for some years. After my return from Melanesia, that was.'

After this very brief social exchange the Rector gave signs of relapsing into his reverie. But just then the door was flung open again loudly and Mrs Bayliss re-entered the room with some cold-looking lamb chops and vegetables on her serving tray.

A few seconds later she was followed by a rather thin, bilious-looking woman with unkempt hair. Unsteadily she carried a plate with three more chops and these she scraped on to the serving dish.

'Thank you very much, Mrs Shinton. That'll be all. Thank you very much.' The large lady pushed the thin one through the door. Then she thrust the plate of chops on to the table. The Rector gazed at them in some astonishment.

'You must have found a good deal of difference between Staffordshire and Melanesia,' resumed Alice Elgar in her crooning, thoroughly understanding voice.

'Ah yes,' replied the Rector, dwelling mooningly on the two syllables. 'God's work is of an altogether different order here.'

Mrs Bayliss waddled round the table. She dropped serving spoons noisily and inelegantly into two of the large dishes. The Rector's wife regarded her with a hurt expression.

'You have only recently come to Wolverhampton, I believe.'

'Yes, yes,' said the Rector. 'It was a year ago I think, was it not, Dora?'

'Yes, father. You remember. It was a year last August that you were inducted.'

29

'Yes. Yes.'

'It was quite an eventful t . . . t . . . time,' said the young girl brightly and sociably to the two guests. 'Father was inducted on the very day that the trial of Mr Oscar Wilde came to its c . . . c . . . conclusion. I can remember the sidesman looking at the *Express and Star* on the sly in the vestry.'

She looked smilingly to the others to share her amusement at the memory. Elgar regarded her blandly with a slight movement of his large lips. Alice and the Rector's wife looked at each other in some uneasiness. Was the girl utterly innocent and candid or was she not?

'That was indeed the time, Dora. You are quite correct,' mused the Rector in his distant unworldly way. There followed a silence. Then the Rector bestirred himself. 'I never did read any of that unhappy man's books, you know.' A light of enthusiasm came into his eyes. 'Have you read any of Mr Conrad's books, Mr Elgar?' he enquired.

'No, I do not believe that I have,' replied the musician, chewing his chop with difficulty.

'Oh you should, Mr Elgar, you should. I greatly recommend them.' The eyes again stared into great distances. 'Mr Conrad has sailed the seas off Melanesia, has he not, Dora my dear?'

The girl smiled a little uncomfortably but had no reply.

'Did you accompany your father to Melanesia?' asked Alice Elgar in a voice of lingering, wondering curiosity.

A frightened look came briefly into the fine young features.

'N . . . n . . . no. Mother and I stayed in England. We lived in a house together until mother died. Then I was b . . . b . . . boarded at school for a while. And then father returned from the east and I lived with him at Tunstall.' The girl spoke in haste.

'Yes, yes,' boomed the Rector, remembering. 'And now we must all labour together for the Lord on this stony ground of Wolverhampton. Where the nonconformists revile the Church and hate her. Where the nonconformists own the newspapers and use them to malign us. Where, I now find, they manufacture the very tomahawks that our poor Christian brothers in Melanesia employ to destroy each other!'

Mrs Bayliss set before them the dessert of stewed plums. She was as oblivious to these criticisms of her native borough as to everything else that the Rector ever said.

'You know, Rector, I think you may grow to like it a little better,' said Elgar, with courtesy and charm. 'There are some kindly folk here and, as I well know, some good music. The church group is very fine. They sing their hearts out. And the working people conduct themselves in a very decent way.' He looked pointedly at Dora for a moment. 'I have often noticed this seeing them on their way to the football match in the town. They're a pretty decent crew.'

He glanced at the girl, calmly challenging.

She was provoked. Of course she would do what she had promised. Her face became purposeful. Her responses were always utterly overt and never camouflaged.

The Rector mused away to himself.

Dora moistened her lips with the tip of her tongue.

'Father,' she began, 'I understand that Mr Elgar w . . . w . . . would be interested to attend the football match that is to take place in the town this afternoon. Do you have any objection to my directing and accompanying him there?'

The large head was inclined away from her, distractedly.

'No, my dear, not at all, not at all.'

But Mrs Penny was most alarmed. Her eyes fluttered in dis-belief from face to face. 'But, Dora . . . Edward . . . are you sure?' Her eyes rested on Alice Elgar as the most likely ally.

Alice was looking at her husband very thoughtfully. She said, 'Do go if you would like to, Edward and Dora dear. Go and enjoy yourselves.'

Mrs Penny was astonished at her friend's acceptance of this highly unusual arrangement. She gazed at her uncomprehend-ingly.

Elgar cleared his throat. 'I'd quite like to see the game, you know.'

'Off you go then, my dears,' said Alice. 'Minnie and I will keep each other company. We never were athletically disposed, were we, Minnie?' There was a note of steely calculation in the languid, patronising voice.

Mrs Bayliss entered and announced, 'Ah've put the coffee in the parlour.'

Instantly, as though obeying an order, they all stood up.

Dora consulted the little gold watch in a locket that hung by a gold chain from near her bosom.

'Father, perhaps Mr Elgar and I should forgo coffee, if we are to be there for the beginning.'

'Very well, my dear.'

'Shall we be on our way then, Mr Elgar?' enquired Dora, turning to him shyly and vulnerably and for the first time in public.

'Very well.'

'Let us fetch our c . . . c . . . coats then,' said Dora. She hurried out, smiling rather self-consciously at her father, her stepmother and the man's wife.

As Dora was putting on her coat, Mrs Bayliss emerged and surveyed the couple.

'Aye ye stoppin' for yer coffee?' she demanded gruffly.

'No. Mr Elgar and I are going out for a while,' replied Dora firmly. Unlike her stepmother the girl could summon some of Mrs Bayliss' own aggressiveness when dealing with the house-keeper.

Followed by Elgar, Dora tripped back to the sunny parlour where the older three sat dutifully awaiting their coffee.

'We shall be back for tea,' called Dora. There was excitement in her voice.

Goodbyes were called.

'Enjoy yourselves,' crooned Alice Elgar.

After a moment of hesitation, Dora led the way along the hall and opened the front door. They made their way down the path and went through the garden gate into the street.

Each was now astonished to be actually alone with the other.

They were together in the street. They walked a few paces in thrilled, shocked silence. Then the man took the girl's arm and placed it confidently under his own.

2

HORSE FAIR was busy now, with men in groups of two and three and four walking along unhurriedly but purposefully to the match which would take place a few streets away. Most of the men were drably dressed. They wore dark, thick woollen jackets and trousers and heavy worsted caps. A few who wore the Wolverhampton team favours of old gold and black gave the march something of a festive look. And here and there swaggering along were a few sports in bright or check trousers, brown bowler hats and loud waistcoats.

When the tall man and the young girl from the Rectory joined up with these groups of marchers, some of the men turned curiously, but not blatantly, to look at them. How different those two were from all the others in the crowd! The man, in his old brown suit, looked every inch a countryman. He could have been a country doctor, or perhaps a lawyer. There was a slight nervous arrogance to his bearing. He stood out conspicuously in this factory town. And on his arm was the nimble, bright-faced girl in her stylish long blue coat. Amidst all the sombre, shabbily dressed men in that narrow street she showed up as a brilliant patch of peacock blue.

The procession tramped along down the steepening gradient of Horse Fair with the great mass of the collegiate church and its large crossing tower to the left. It was a high, proud tower of the Tudor time. The marching men continually nudged each other and looked surreptitiously over their shoulders at the pair who had joined them. This persistent attention and the slight self-consciousness which it eventually created in the couple caused them at last to resort and to speak to each other.

'You do know the way to go, eh?' His tone was avuncular.

'Well, y . . . y . . . yes, if we f . . . f . . . follow the crowd, we shall come to the f . . . f . . . field.'

Dora was embarrassed. She looked at him hopefully in half profile. The small provocative mouth was slightly open. She was most anxious not to fail as hostess of this daring expedition.

'But you have visited the grounds before, have you not?' This was more than a straightforward question. It was bullying, in the manner of an older brother.

The blue eyes were distressed. Dora blushed. 'No, I have not been to a f . . . f . . . football match before, but . . .'

'Well you're a fine one!' The deep-set eyes turned on her, mocking her, chiding her.

Dora hastened along beside him as he strode out, her glance cast down. Then she looked up and said, 'Well, I don't see that it matters. I know where the grounds are. There should be no g . . . g . . . great difficulty if we only f . . . f . . . follow along with these men and use our s . . . s . . . simple wits!'

The soft, prominent mouth had contracted into a firm common-sensical stubbornness. She would not be chaffed in this way, nor would she be overcome by supposed difficulties. For all her fineness of face and figure there was a practical, powerful energy in her.

She looked up at the man defiantly. 'See,' she said as they turned out of Horse Fair into North Street. 'This is right. That is Giffard House over there.'

She pointed to a handsome early Georgian house with segment-headed windows and drainpipes with interesting baroque tops. The house stood behind wrought-iron gates. It was apart from the crowd of football spectators.

'Yes,' said the man, intrigued by the building. 'That is one

34

of the old settlements of the Faith at Wolverhampton, is it not?'

'Yes,' replied Dora thoughtfully. She found it difficult to accept that the man was a Catholic, though her stepmother in her many talks about her friends had told her so several times. Dora recalled her father's many careful arguments and sermons on the doctrinal differences between the Roman Church and the English Church. But this man was not the sort to be troubled by such difficult, abstract scrupulousnesses, she thought. He was more at home here in this crowd than behind the wall of the Rectory garden. And the same was true of herself, she realised. Outsider though she was, by her voice and her dress, she was excited by this crowd and by the occasion and the ritual to which it went. And the man beside her had a fleshy horsy quality to him that made him belong with these men rather than with her father and all the pale curates and the opinionated, pompous parsons who shared his doubts and uncertainties and endless discussions. Glancing up at the man whose arm held her arm, she noticed now his large bony brow and muzzle. It reminded her of the head of the cod that Mrs Bayliss had bought the other day to make a fish pie.

They continued along North Street. Here the crowd was becoming more dense. Before them stood the Molineux Hotel, another of the large Georgian buildings in this quarter of the town. It was more stolid than Giffard House and had heavy stone quoins and a hooded porch with gaslight brackets of wrought iron on either side. On the roof was a sporty-looking clock tower that had been erected only recently. In front of the hotel were groups of men on horseback and others holding horses by their bridles. They all held glasses or pewter beer mugs in their hands. From a brake drawn by two black horses there alighted a succession of tidily dressed working men. They appeared lost as they looked round the congested inn yard.

'Huzza for the potters!' cried one of the local sports in a loud check waistcoat, raising his mug to them.

The crush intensified and Elgar and Dora felt themselves jostled.

'Make way for the lady and the gentleman there!' cried the sport loudly. He had clearly drunk quite a lot and there was a certain rhetoric in his manner. But his concern was genuine. He raised his arm to ward off the crush.

'Thank you,' said Elgar mumbling.

Dora was surprised to see how aloof and formal he was with this well-meaning man. They passed on around the side of the hotel towards the football grounds.

Very old residents of the borough could remember a time when the grounds had been known as Mr Molineux's Close. They were once the spacious, beautiful grounds of Molineux House and had contained orchards, long lawns, flowerbeds and a lake in the style of the picturesque. When the family died out and Molineux House was sold for a hotel during the Regency period, the new owners exploited the gardens as a place of entertainment and pleasaunce. Some seven years ago, in 1889, they had given the land over to the fashionable, new entertainment, association football. The ancient gardens were levelled to make a pitch for the popular and successful town football team to play on.

The tall countryman and the young girl took their places in a queue of men under the old, lichened garden wall. Here it was dark and chill. There was a stagnant smell of beer and spirits. The queue moved forward very slowly. Dora stood on tiptoe and peered ahead in eager anticipation of being in the grounds. At last they came to the gate in the wall where a fat man with a leather money bag hung around his neck received the florin which Elgar offered. He politely returned the change. They passed under the garden gateway, clambered up an earthen bank and suddenly found themselves in the sunlight again.

They were both exhilarated. They were released into light. The pitch was a brilliant green. The great crowd of six thousand muttered expectantly. Dora was very much excited by this atmosphere. Eagerly she threaded her way through the men down to the white rope which ran round all four sides of the pitch to mark off the area for the spectators. The men made way for her, and for her companion, with respect and also with wonderment in their eyes. At last the two were in a position in which they had a clear view of the whole field. Dora smiled up at her companion. They both stared at the lush green field as though mesmerised by it.

The murmuring undercurrent within the crowd suddenly intensified into a deeper rumble.

'Hooroo! Hooroo for the Potters!'

Dora looked up to her right and saw the Stoke players coming out of the pedimented doorway of the hotel. They filed out slowly and modestly. They were toasted and applauded by men who leaned out of the large Regency window on the north side of the hotel. The players made their way carefully down the steep walkway of the old garden on to the field. They did not wear the red and white shirts of the Stoke City teams of later years but shirts with vertical stripes of red and black. The football which they brought to practise with was much larger than that which would be used in a later period.

Another, far louder hooroo from the crowd greeted the Wanderers when they emerged from the hotel. Almost all the players had close-cropped heads and large moustaches. The gold of their shirts shone and flashed brilliantly as they congregated around the white goal-post nearest the steep path from the hotel. A chorus of spectators called out the name, Malpass, Malpass, several times. This was Wolverhampton's stocky, robust centre-half who had been the hero of the team's victory against Everton in the Cup Final just a few years before. Dora was anxious to identify this player. He bustled about, blowing out his cheeks and breathing hard. He was quite indifferent to his admirers.

The match that day was fast and eventful. Gradually Dora and Elgar became as involved in it as was most of the crowd. A great moan went up when the referee in his striped shirt and trousers indicated that Clare, the Stoke right-back and captain, had won the toss of the guinea. Wolverhampton kicked off but immediately the ball was taken from them and passed down to Schofield, the visitors' small outside-left who ran around man after man in a very fast dribble. The ball spun greasily along the moist grass just inches from Dora's feet. She stepped back in some alarm but her companion held her arm the more firmly. She was shocked to be reminded that he held her. Schofield shot cleverly at the Wanderers' goal and the right-back, Bunch, was only just able, very clumsily, to kick it away.

37

'Go at 'im, Bunch. Try 'arder, Bunch,' cried some of the home spectators in shock and dismay. They shouted out the poor full-back's name with that peculiarly harsh Wolverhampton pronunciation of the vowel that made their dissatisfaction sound yet more contemptuous.

An old man in a long shabby coat and greasy black bowler, who stood just to the rear and to the right of Dora and her companion, was slowly and systematically pulling a lobster apart, eating the flesh and dropping the red shell on to the earth at his feet.

'Up the 'omesters! 'Urra for the 'omesters!' he called out, regularly and mechanically, between mouthfuls.

There was a gasp from the crowd. After another clever run, Schofield had actually run around the great Malpass himself. A large, stout man in a brown frock-coat was jotting down comments in a thick, leather-bound notebook. A small, pale man standing nearby said very respectfully, 'He's a good 'un, aye 'e, sir?'

'Dashed good.' The man in brown spoke wheezingly as an acknowledged expert. He could well be a reporter for the newspaper. He took a pull on his large, thick cigar. Dora enjoyed the smell of it.

' 'Oo is 'e, sir? Do ye know, by any chance?'

'That's Schofield. They call him the Stoke Flyer.'

' 'E's a good 'un, no doubt.'

'I don't think that you'll ever see a better on this meadow,' commented the large man loftily, returning his attention to the game and dismissing his neighbour.

After twelve minutes Schofield achieved what he had promised from the beginning of the game. With a beautiful, long, curving shot he beat the Wolverhampton goalkeeper and scored the visitors' first point. The little player trotted back up the field thoughtfully and somewhat bashfully. There were some scattered hooroos from the small minority of spectators from the Five Towns but the local people stood in a shocked, disappointed silence. The man in brown muttered what he was writing into his notebook.

'Schofield . . . banged . . . the leather . . . home.'

For some reason Elgar was greatly entertained by this idiom. He turned to Dora laughing silently and secretly, his big mouth open in a grimace. She herself was not so amused by the words but was intrigued, affected even, by the intimate physical fact of his laughing in this way. There was something familiar and not at all proper about it.

The Wanderers were now making a lively effort to draw level. On one occasion their inside-left, H. Wood, had an open goal before him. But he kicked high over the bar as though to hit the clock tower on the Molineux Hotel. The crowd groaned mockingly.

'Up the 'omesters! 'Urra for the 'omesters!' called the lobster eater, unperturbed.

In the next attack, Pheasant, one of the Wolves forwards, was charged in the back and fell. There was much argument on the field and finally Maxwell, one of the Stoke players, was sent off back to the hotel, and the Wanderers were awarded a penalty kick from which Owen scored. The incident caused much angry discussion among the spectators.

' 'E fell, I tell you. 'E fell. Pheasant fell.'

'No 'e daye. 'E never did. 'E was upset, Pheasant was. 'E was upset.'

The lordly reporter shook his jowled head gravely as he wrote again in his notebook. He appeared shocked by the whole affair. Elgar and Dora smiled at all the arguments and anger. The responses of the crowd were to them a part of the entertainment of the afternoon.

In the second half, as sometimes happens at football matches, a certain staleness came over the game. The sunshine was disappearing and it was becoming colder. The players were more lethargic than they had been earlier and seemed to have agreed tacitly to settle for a goal apiece. Members of the crowd looked up to the clock tower on the hotel to learn the time. There was much shuffling of feet. Even the mechanical, stupid cry 'Up the 'omesters' came less frequently.

Then, unexpectedly, there was a passion of activity from the red-clad Stoke players. They made run upon run at the Wolverhampton goal, the tiny steel-headed forward Schofield again prominent in all the attacks. Time after time, in one way or another, the Wanderers managed to beat the ball away. Dora, like the other spectators, found herself becoming involved again in the game. She was associating herself with the unsteady Wolverhampton team. After each attack was fumbled away, she would turn to her companion with an anxious grin of relief. The rest of the crowd sighed deeply every time the Wanderers escaped.

Still the attacks persisted. The Stoke players would not give up. The ball was swung right across the Wanderers' goal-line but no one was there to kick it in. The crowd cried out in fear and then relief. But back again came the Stoke forwards. Again and again. Then there was a large number of players struggling together in the Wolves' goal-mouth.

'Ain't it a scrimmage!'

And then suddenly the ball could be seen in the back of the home net. The crowd was much cast down by this. There were groans of disappointment.

Dora looked at Elgar sadly. He smiled down at her disappointed face. She looked away.

The players on the field argued. Some of the Wanderers ran after the referee, politely remonstrating with him. The crowd discussed the goal feverishly.

'Who scored? Who was it? Did you see? Ah must 'ave blinked me eyes and missed it. Who was it?'

'Did you see who scored, sir?' asked the little man of the reporter. The latter wrote away steadily in his book.

'I shall give Arthur Wood the credit for giving the leather the final touch,' he replied casually, not troubling to address his questioner directly.

Then the Wanderers' energy revived. They struggled desperately to avoid a defeat. They kicked the ball around determinedly but without the subtlety and method of the Stoke team. Down the pitch they ran, time after time. Dora jigged up and down excitedly, hoping that they might score.

At last there came an attack that looked genuinely dangerous. Malpass and Owen brought the ball down the field, passing it rapidly to and fro between them. The crowd roared appreciatively and expectantly. But then, just yards from the goal, Owen collided with the Stoke centre-forward, both fell over and the ball ran slowly and infuriatingly out of play.

There was a snarl of anger from the home spectators and then another louder one when it was seen that the referee would penalise the Wolverhampton player.

'He was hocked,' called out Dora shrilly, looking around for support. 'I saw it most d . . . d . . . distinctly. Owen was h . . . h . . . hocked.'

Men nearby looked at her in some surprise They were disconcerted by her enthusiasm and by the indignant, educated lady's voice.

Dora looked to Elgar very directly.

'Er . . . I did not see the incident very clearly,' he responded, shuffling a little.

Dora regarded him suspiciously. She thought this might be a subtle tease. A scowl possessed the beautiful face.

'You cannot have been looking,' she cried loudly. 'He was d . . . d . . . definitely hocked.'

She stepped back a pace from him, confrontingly. Her stammer now revealed the intense energy and wilfulness that were within her small frame.

Dora had her sympathisers.

'Ar. Owen was 'ocked, definitely 'ocked,' muttered voices nearby.

'The 'omester was 'ocked,' cried the figure with all the lobster shells at his feet. He took a large pleasure in his new sentence.

The reporter also shared Dora's view. 'Owen was most certainly the victim of a hocking.'

Elgar glanced around; his eyes were wary. 'Perhaps you may be right,' he conceded prudentially.

Dora's indignation collapsed into a spurt of throaty laughter. She had stuck him out and won. Her blue eyes moved merrily as she looked at him.

The free kick awarded against Owen was easily cleared. But the setback had demoralised the home team. They no longer displayed any ambition to score. The match drew slowly and dully to a conclusion and then the whistle shrilled out over the ground announcing the end. The spectators moved off quietly. They said nothing about the game; they looked rather depressed. How different it had been before the kick-off.

Elgar and Dora stood and watched them go. They both now realised how tired their legs were from the hours of standing. It was chill now that the crowd was dispersing. The brightness and excitement had gone out of the afternoon.

Elgar turned to leave. 'Very good. I greatly enjoyed that. Thank you very much for accompanying me,' he said in his courtly fashion.

They regarded each other for a moment as they set off. In her eyes there was still some unspoken satisfaction remaining from the hocking incident. In his, as he looked down upon her, there was a quizzical, piqued interest.

They followed the last of the crowd up the steep slope past the hotel. A group of Stoke supporters were calling to their team through one of the windows, cheering them and singing a song of admiration. Dora and her friend passed quietly on.

Ahead of them at the top of the hill they could see the great west window of St Peter's shimmering coldly in the falling rays of the late afternoon sun. Under this window the market people were beginning to close up their stalls. Some had already lit lanterns in order to load their carts and wagons. On the cobbles below the church were big baskets of apples and pears, sacks of potatoes, and fine, plump brown fowl clucking away in their cages. The market wagons bore the names of the Shropshire villages from which they had come. The people in the market moved in their twinkling, lantern-lit haze as if in another element.

There was already a smell of winter in the air. The man and the girl felt content now to be returning to the warm interior of the Rectory. As they approached, each was aware of the strangeness, the utter unexpectedness of their being together. But it was not to be talked about. A little weary, but content with their afternoon together, the man and the girl walked on up Horse Fair in the darkening, smoky air.

As they entered the dimly lit hall of the Rectory, they could hear the voices of the ladies, as the two old friends conversed companionably. Alice Elgar's voice was slow and pedantically emphatic; Minnie Penny's more shrill, hesitant and anxious.

'Ah, my dears, have you enjoyed yourselves at your football match?' Alice regarded her husband and the girl pleasantly but intently as they entered the room. 'Edward,' she continued, without waiting for an answer, 'I wonder what you think. Minnie has kindly suggested that we spend the night here and return to Malvern tomorrow. Would you like to do that?'

'Would you, my dear?'

'Well, yes . . . it might perhaps be more convenient to await you here, since you will be so busy in Hanley.'

'Then let us by all means accept Minnie's kind and generous invitation.' He looked around from one to the other, grandly presiding. He smoothed down his moustache.

Alice appeared pleased. But there was also some scepticism in her face at his ready acceptance of the proposal.

Minnie Penny said simply, 'I am so glad that you will be able to stay with us, Edward. Alice and I have so many more things to say to each other.' She sounded gratified and relieved. She continued, with some hesitation, 'I am afraid that Alfred has had to attend a meeting of the British and Foreign Bible Society. Unfortunately this will necessitate a later tea than we had expected.'

'I have consulted the Rector's railway timetable,' said Alice very capably to her husband. 'And I discover that if you are to have any chance of arriving at Hanley by seven-thirty, it will be necessary for you to leave within the next hour. There are two trains . . .'

'But, Alice,' cried Minnie, agitatedly twisting her fingers together on her grey lap, 'I thought that I had made it clear that there is no possibility of Alfred returning until after six o'clock.' The kindly, apple-faced woman looked very afraid.

'Then I fear that Edward will have to do without his tea, or at least wait until he arrives in Hanley. The folk there are most hospitable and will undoubtedly offer him some refreshment. In

43

any case, it will not be the first occasion upon which Edward has had to forgo his food in order to discharge his responsibilities. We are quite accustomed to such eventualities, are we not, Edward?'

The steely, bullying insistence of the slow voice had not been heard before in this room. It created a silence.

Then Dora said brightly, 'I shall be happy to p . . . p . . . prepare some food for Mr Elgar. There is time, I believe.'

'But how shall you do that, Dora?' enquired her stepmother, her mouth atremble.

'Why, go down to the kitchen and make s . . . s . . . sandwiches of some kind.'

'But Dora, you know that Mrs Bayliss insists that no one enter her kitchen uninvited and that it is now her rest period until the Rector returns. That is precisely the difficulty.' Her face quivered with fear and some irritation as she spoke. Dora was being obtuse, or reckless.

'But this is an emergency,' said Dora. She would have no truck with her stepmother's delicacies and weaknesses. Her capacity for single-mindedness was asserting itself. There was again that characteristic set to her fine mouth and jaw that suggested not only wilfulness but a headlong energy.

'Come, Mr Elgar,' said Dora. 'Come and show me what you would like to take with you.'

'But, Dora, I really don't think that you should!' The Rector's wife rose from her chair in a panic.

When this kindly, once placid lady had married the Rector some months before, she had fancied herself more capable than he. His unworldliness was greater than hers, she knew. She could be of service to one of God's priests. But that realisation had come to her in the summer woods and hayfields of Redmarley d'Abitot, the quiet Gloucestershire village where she had grown up. In this brutal, manufacturing town her belief was radically challenged. The quiet, pious middle-aged lady felt undermined by the peculiarities of her husband, by the harsh manners of the people, by the parish, by the old Rectory and its staff.

But Dora was not to be stopped.

'If it becomes necessary, I shall explain the position to Mrs

Bayliss and she will understand. Never fear.' The throaty voice was calm and utterly determined. The slight stammer had disappeared.

'Come, Mr Elgar! I shall make you a railway picnic.'

She left the room beckoning. Elgar glanced at his wife who very readily nodded her permission for him to go.

Dora led the musician down some narrow stairs covered with brown oilcloth. The kitchen had a stone floor with heavy old benches up against the whitewashed walls. The atmosphere was chill and unfamilial. Dora looked around for something with which to make a sandwich. She was very much the stranger down here.

In an alcove at the furthest, dimmest end of the kitchen the two intruders were taken aback to come upon Mrs Bayliss fast asleep on a shabby, brocaded armchair. Beside her on a brick ledge lay the fatty remains of several lamb chops and an empty bottle of India pale ale. Dora looked up at Elgar. She was greatly shocked. But almost immediately her face relaxed into a smile. The large figure slept on. The double chin was sunk into the chest. Mrs Bayliss belched very slightly as she snoozed.

At the sight of her Elgar's face had contorted in exaggerated dismay. He now shambled away slowly on tiptoe. This made Dora want to laugh. She twirled around and hurried after him to the area nearest to the stairs. For a while they stood and made faces as they tried to subdue their violent mirth and slightly hysterical sense of trespassing in a forbidden place.

When they had become calmer, Dora explored the kitchen and its cupboards. In a corner larder she found a round, flour-dusted loaf that smelled new and appetising. And from a cupboard she produced a large uncut ham. In a whispering dumb-show, with Dora giggling slightly, the two agreed that this would make a satisfactory sandwich.

Dora carved the ham inexpertly. Her small hands held the large knife at a difficult angle and left jagged edges in the pink meat. Her small body shook with suppressed mirth. Occasionally tears of laughter and nervous apprehension would come into her eyes and she would have to pause.

Elgar, trying to help, dropped the loaf on to his foot. Dora

45

was now shaken with repressed convulsions as he stood looking at it. She had to lay down the knife on the bench.

Then came the coarse, threatening voice from behind them.

'Miss Dora, may I ask what you are doing in my kitchen?'

Dora hastily dabbed at her eyes with the thick cuffs of her blouse. Then she turned around. She was utterly self-possessed.

'Mr Elgar is compelled to leave us at short notice. I have come to prepare some food for him, since, as I understand, tea will not be available here until later.'

Mrs Bayliss swelled slightly with anger. 'You know as it's been agreed as I and nobody else is to come in 'ere without me knowing to it.'

'That is quite true. But this is s . . . s . . . something of an emergency.'

'I don't see 'ow it is.'

'But of course it is.' Despite her youth and physical slightness, Dora quite matched the stout housekeeper in presence and determination. She gave the impression of hastening on very purposefully to some end.

'Well, I reckon as I shall 'ave to complain to the Rector about this!' Mrs Bayliss would not stoop to argue the matter any longer. Her chin shook; her voice was harsh.

'I trust that you will not find it necessary to trouble m . . . m . . . my father, Mrs Bayliss. But that is your affair and your decision. And now I should like to finish Mr Elgar's sandwich. Mr Elgar is a very well-known composer in these parts and must travel to Hanley tonight to conduct a choir and an orchestra.'

From beneath her badly cut hair Mrs Bayliss' eyes followed Dora's as the girl looked admiringly at the musician. The older woman's hostility suddenly lessened. Did she realise that she had met her match? Or was there for a moment a motherly sympathy in the large fleshy face as she considered the girl and the man?

In any case she no longer spoke in her usual style of bullying, mimic gentility. There was an unexpected flicker of kindliness in her voice.

'Finish what you'm doing then, Miss Dora. And try not to ruin that ham. It cost a lot of money. And please to give warning in future.'

Dora was astonished at the change of tone.

Behind them the door opened. And there stood Alice peering from the light into the dim underground room.

'Ah, Edward,' she called melodiously, scrutinising the scene.

Mrs Bayliss returned instantly to her former self.

'Can I be of any assistance to you, Madam?' she enquired weightily and unpleasantly. 'I'm rather busy in 'ere. I shall be doing the teas in a bit.'

'I only came down to remind my husband that it is almost time for him to leave for the station,' intoned Alice, completely unaffected by the resentment of the big woman.

Dora wrapped up the sandwiches in brown greaseproof paper and put them in a bag.

'I believe we are ready, my dear,' said Elgar a little sheepishly. He and Dora followed after Alice as she slowly made her way upstairs.

'I could accompany you to the station, should you w . . . w . . . wish it,' said Dora in the hall. She was anxious to do this. She was still full of their secret, intense camaraderie of minutes before.

'No, I shall find my way all right. Stay here and rest and enjoy your tea.'

Dora was disappointed by this refusal.

He stepped into the drawing room and said a courteous *au revoir* to his trembling hostess. Acting on his own the man moved differently. He was quick, lithe, nervous.

In the hall Alice said, 'Edward, do accept Dora's offer to accompany you to the station.' Alice Elgar smiled her encouragement. There could be no doubt that she wished the girl to go with her husband.

'No, that is neither fair no necessary. But thank you for your kind and generous offer, Miss Penny.'

After a moment's hesitation he stepped forward and shook the girl by the hand. Awkwardly he went and kissed his wife on the cheek.

Then, in a couple of rapid, tense strides he had reached the door and disappeared into the hazy acrid dusk of the town.

'Do let us go in and sit down, my dear,' said Alice pleasantly, taking the young girl by the arm. The older woman's attitude suggested that she might be the hostess.

'I should very much like to hear about your afternoon at the football ground.'

3

AFTER high tea on that Saturday afternoon the Rector and his wife and daughter entertained Alice Elgar in the shadowy, gaslit drawing room. Mrs Bayliss bore in a large bamboo tray with four beakers of rich fatty coconut drink prepared after a recipe from the Solomon Islands and much enjoyed by the Reverend Penny, who sipped at it insistently. Alice could not drink it at all. Nor, she remarked, could the other two ladies. She followed their example and unobtrusively placed her drink on the floor behind her chair.

The Rector then spoke of the use of coconuts as currency in the various parts of Melanesia. With his plump hands folded on his lap and his eyes gazing at one of the plopping gas mantles at the far end of the room, he soliloquised musingly on the monetary system of the islands.

'Porpoise teeth and dogs' teeth are also employed as currency, you realise. But dogs' teeth are more valuable in the ratio of one to five. A porpoise tooth represents the smallest sum in use; its equivalent value is ten coconuts. A dog, as I am sure you will know, has only two teeth available for this purpose, those on the lower jaw immediately behind the large fangs. Only those two may be used in commerce.'

His words and his interest quickened.

'In the historical criticism of recent years the age of these island races has, as you will know, been much debated. Bishop Selwyn studied the matter a great deal. But in my view an irrefutable proof of the antiquity of these peoples is the fact that though there are very few dogs, yet the teeth possessed by chiefs and persons of wealth may be numbered in their thousands and tens of thousands.'

The Rector turned to his listeners with a look of triumph. There was a pleasurable gargling sound in his throat. The blue eyes moved confidently from face to face seeking out the slightest hint of reservation or opposition which, it was clear from his expression, he would crush with great energy. The three ladies nodded politely.

The Rector cleared his throat. He was about to begin again. He had other theories to advance.

'Alice . . . Alfred,' said Minnie Penny swiftly, 'Dora and I have been practising duets for quite some time now. And we have agreed that we might ask if tonight you would consent to be our first audience. We should account it a great honour if you would agree to hear us play.'

'But of course,' answered Alice, her face brightening. 'What a kind and interesting suggestion. It would be a privilege to hear you.'

The ladies' eyes were now upon the Rector. The suggestion had dislocated his train of thought.

'Er . . . er,' he said. He looked like a man struggling to awaken from a deep sleep. 'Er . . . yes . . . yes. That would be most entertaining, I am sure.' But his words could not conceal his painful disappointment.

Without a moment's hesitation, Mrs Penny arose and seated herself at the piano. She rubbed her hands together purposefully. A plain, frugal figure of a woman, she looked out of place at the exotic instrument in that shadowy room. From a nearby low oriental chest decorated in heavy brass marquetry Dora brought out her violin-case. She took out the instrument and placed her music upon the stand. Smilingly her stepmother helped her to tune the strings.

Then in an instant the room reverberated with the shock of

the music of the two instruments. The two performers were away, playing attentively, occasionally exchanging brief, confirming glances. They played passages from Handel, country airs and folk songs such as 'The Ash Grove', 'Sweet Lass of Richmond Hill' and 'Sweet Polly Oliver'. Then followed a few items from Gilbert and Sullivan and some adaptations for violin and piano of famous Verdi arias.

Dora swung her upper body enthusiastically as she bowed. The shimmering gaslight shone upon the old brown wood of her violin, on the delicate creamy flesh of her cheeks and small ears and on the puckered drapery of her blue sleeves. Her head of upswept hair glimmered nacreous in the shadows. Her stepmother smiled happily as she struck the piano. All her earlier anxieties had now fallen from her. She looked a merry little figure. The two ladies played together confidently, if not finely.

To conclude the performance Dora took a pace forward and announced that the two final pieces were by the husband of their honoured guest and were offered as a tribute to Mr and Mrs Elgar.

Dora stepped back and immediately began playing 'Bizarrerie' and 'Mot d'Amour'.

At the close Alice Elgar applauded with genuine enthusiasm.

'Oh very good, very good,' she exclaimed. 'You play quite excellently together. I do wish that Edward had been present to hear you. He would have greatly enjoyed it.'

But from her manner it was apparent that it was simply the idea of her husband's music and of its being performed rather than this actual performance which fired her so.

'Bravo,' she called again, inclining her head to one side and pursing her lips in an emphatic smile.

The Rector, slowly bestirring himself, judged it necessary to follow Alice Elgar in applauding. He had, after all, enjoyed hearing the music. He usually did, though his taste was very conservative. Music provided a condition in which he was free from the requirement of social exchanges and thus able to pursue his memories and remoter sequences of thought undisturbed.

But he was also slightly bad-tempered. He sensed that the ladies were somewhat dissolute and undiscriminating in the pleasure which they took in this entertainment. With something of a military brusqueness in his voice he pronounced the concert to be at an end.

'It is now time,' he called, his voice resounding impersonally, 'for us to attend to our devotions. It is the evening before the sabbath day.'

From a drawer he took a large leather-bound copy of the *Book of Common Prayer*. He plucked up his black trousers at the thigh and got down upon his knees. After a long opening prayer he slowly read the collect, the gospel and the epistle for the approaching Sunday. His voice was too loud for the room. The three ladies sat in their chairs, their hands folded in their laps, their heads bowed and their eyes shut. The light flickered on the linen fold of the ancient oak panelling.

There came at last a long silence. The Rector rose to his feet and announced dramatically to the seated figures, 'The hour grows late. I shall retire now to my private devotions and then to rest.'

'I hope that the lateness of Edward's return will in no way inconvenience you, Rector. I fear he spends many hours at rehearsals. He works so arduously.'

Alice Elgar was embarrassed and apologetic and yet proud. The Rector reached down and shook her by the hand.

'Never fear, Mrs Elgar. It is merely that I must rise early to officiate at the Holy Eucharist.'

Mechanically he kissed his wife and then his daughter on the brow.

'You will bolt the door, my dear?'

'Oh yes,' replied his wife, anxious to reassure him. 'I have told Mrs Bayliss that she may go to bed and that I will take the responsibility. There will be no need for difficulty in that respect.'

'Dora, you are going to sit up too?' The Rector sounded surprised. There was a suggestion that she might be too young to do such a thing.

Dora's mouth clenched irritably. 'Yes, f . . . f . . . father, I shall sit up with mother and with Mrs Elgar until our guest returns.' She was definitely not to be prevented.

'Yes. Yes indeed,' agreed the Rector vaguely as though his

mind had now moved on to other matters. He looked around the room unseeingly. But he did not leave, as he had said he would. He stood pondering. The ladies said nothing. Dora and her stepmother glanced at each other in some embarrassment. Still he did not leave. He was like someone who had completely forgotten what he was about to say. Or do.

There came a knock at the outer door of the Rectory.

'It cannot be Edward already,' cried Alice standing up disbelievingly but with a vulnerable expression of hope on her broad face.

'Perhaps it is,' replied Minnie Penny. 'It is quite late really.' She hurried down the passage followed at a little distance by Alice.

Minnie opened the door to reveal Elgar standing in the porch, a dark stooping figure. The two women welcomed him in and helped him off with his coat.

'How did they perform, Edward? Did they understand their parts properly?' asked his wife immediately. She was in a flurry of agitation.

'They sang most effectively, my dear. They are a most excellent Midlands choir. It was a privilege to conduct them.'

There was a throb of suppressed excitement in his voice that had not been there earlier in the day.

He followed his hostess into the sitting room. He bowed to the Rector and smiled at Dora. There was a blatancy in his pleasure at seeing the girl again.

'Oh I am so glad, Edward,' pursued his wife, not noticing. 'Was anything at all amiss, anything at all?' she enquired insistently. She expressed her anxiety and solicitude as though they were in private. She was oblivious of the other people in the room. Her voice was now without that condescending suaveness that was usual with her.

'No, as I say, they are a grand North Country choir. Just what was needed for the cantata.' The depths of his pleasure and satisfaction with the rehearsal could not be fully expressed.

'Did you see Dr Swinnerton Heap?'

'Yes, my dear, I did. He asked me to convey to you his warmest regards.'

'Did you encounter Whewall?'

'Yes, he was there.'

'Was he as . . .?' Alice Elgar paused. Her curiosity was mixed with a spitfire readiness to attack the person alluded to.

'Was he as . . . arrogant as usual?'

'No, he was very kind.'

Elgar glanced around at the others in the room. He sought to escape from his wife's urgent monopoly of him. He looked to Dora. He wanted especially to converse with her.

'James Whewall is one of the choirmasters in Hanley,' he explained, directing his words to the girl. 'And a most ambitious one. It is his ambition to take his choir to the Welsh Eisteddfod and to defeat the Welsh on their own ground.'

Alice interrupted to supply what she judged to be the necessary comment on this.

'A commercial and speculative approach to music that must inevitably vulgarise the art. But then Whewall is a most vulgar man, flashy and insolent, and with no real training in music. These competitions are quite pernicious.'

'It is rather like our football teams of this afternoon, is it not?' remarked Elgar, smiling attentively at Dora. He would not be cut off from the girl.

She was struck by how pale and drawn he looked. The shadows of the room made his deep eye-sockets look dark. His worn woollen trousers were deeply creased at the groin from sitting on the train.

'Whewall is really rather an interesting fellow,' he continued, speaking to the girl, 'though a trifle flamboyant. He is a miner who was once nearly drowned in the sump of a pit-shaft when the cage fell. He barely escaped with his life and considers himself to have a special mission on this earth. He is something of a prima donna and quite the dandy. His suit is a most expensive one from London and he always wears a rose in his button-hole. But he is dedicated to music. Genuinely dedicated.'

Dora was aware of a quivering intensity in Elgar as he spoke of this other man's zeal for the art.

'But you will perhaps know the man, Miss Penny, and you also, Rector. He was born in Talk o'th'Hill and spent much of his

54

life in Tunstall where, I understand, you resided previously. He is a very well-known character in the area.'

'Is the man a churchman?' enquired the Rector indifferently, his thoughts still elsewhere.

'No, he is choirmaster at the Wesleyan Chapel, I do believe.'

'We knew only churchmen in Tunstall,' observed the Rector, standing aloof and faintly offended that he might be expected to have known anyone else.

Dora was embarrassed.

'Father's work at Tunstall was most demanding. We were unable to make the acquaintance of as many people as we would have wished.'

She spoke apologetically and trustingly to Elgar. She felt drawn to him in sympathy and he to her. For despite his tiredness there was a vitality in him that affected and attracted her. It was born of his successful experience of working with the choir and the choirmaster at Hanley. To her he was now someone other than the slightly patronising elder man that she had known earlier in the day. There was a powerful excitement in him that created an exhilaration in herself.

Alice intervened to establish a necessary perspective.

'Dr Swinnerton Heap is, of course, the real leader, the true leader of the musical life of Hanley and its surroundings. He studied at Leipzig and holds a doctorate from Cambridge.'

'I have met Dr Heap on more than one occasion, w . . . w . . . when he came to conduct the choral society here in Wolverhampton,' said Dora. She was polite but it was clear that further information on this subject would not be required. Dora was always anxious that her knowledge of the world should not be underestimated.

Quietly arrogant, Alice looked past the girl.

'Did Madame Reymond attend the rehearsal?' she enquired of her husband. She was taking him to herself again. Her question was pointed, suspicious even.

Elgar smiled widely. 'Yes, she was there.'

Again he broke away from his wife and turned to Dora.

'Madame Reymond is Danish and the widow of a Frenchman. She is the lady patroness of John Cope, a working lad from

55

Milton. It is her intention to create a North Staffordshire symphony orchestra with her protégé as conductor.'

Dora was incredulous. Elgar regarded her with a quiver in his lips. He wondered if he had been, however slightly, indelicate.

'He is an extremely talented young man and . . . Madame Reymond has a great deal of money . . .'

Dora nodded but uncomprehendingly. Her large blue eyes looked at him doubtfully, swimmingly. Her face could have a beautiful candour.

'It is a little like Svengali and Trilby,' added Elgar in a helpful, worldly way.

He glanced for a moment at his wife.

'Do you know the play?' he asked Dora blandly.

'Oh yes, I saw it not so long ago, here at the Grand Theatre,' replied Dora offhandedly. She would not allow herself to be credited with that sort of naïveté.

The man's patronising half-smile disappeared. His thoughts returned to the people at Hanley.

'It is rather like some of the passages in my cantata, you know . . . the ladies, I mean.'

Dora looked at him, stirring with curiosity. She very much wanted to hear some of this latest music. She wanted to be affected, washed over by that tense thrilled preoccupation within him. And she knew that he was passionately eager to re-live some of his rehearsal.

He contemplated her as she looked at him.

'Would you like to hear one or two parts of the score?' he asked.

'Oh yes. Yes.'

Dora turned and appealed to her stepmother. 'That would be all right, would it not, mother?'

Mrs Penny looked helplessly to her musing husband. Still deep in thought he did not speak.

'Why yes . . . yes, of course . . . that would be a great privilege.'

Alice's stiff complacent expression confirmed that it was indeed a privilege.

Elgar rose diffidently and went to the piano. Dora recalled

the incident earlier in the day. How she had wanted to laugh! Now she felt in awe of him. He was the artist her stepmother had told her so much about. She felt sensitively how large, hunched and intent he was.

He opened the piano and was about to play. Then abruptly he rested his large hands on the top of the instrument and said hoarsely, 'I should tell you that this is a setting of a work by the American poet, Longfellow. It . . .'

Alice interrupted him enthusiastically. 'Some sections of the text are by Mr H. A. Acworth, a good friend of ours at Malvern Link who is a civil engineer and also a poet.'

Elgar waited politely for his wife to finish, suspended upon himself. Then he began again.

'It is the tale of King Olaf sailing into Trondheim to avenge his father and to convert heathen Norway to Christianity. The performers have to be looked upon as a gathering of skalds . . .'

His voice fell and he lost confidence as he surveyed his audience of three in that old drawing room.

'All the singers take part in the narration of the saga . . . but really you know, you should hear the thing in full, with all the voices. It can hardly be done at the keyboard.'

His large hands dropped to his sides. There was a sulky throb of disappointment in his voice, almost falsetto, as he spoke these last words.

But Dora was on her feet. 'Oh no, do play for us. Do play, Mr Elgar. We would love to h . . . h . . . hear it . . .'

She stood there, a slim, dramatic, insistent figure. She held her hands towards him in a way that might have been considered histrionic, but was not. Her firm young breasts showed up thrustingly under her tight blue dress.

She was in a passion of anticipation to hear his music. And slowly her emotion infused him. His body became rigid, his pale, tired face was again intent.

'After the introduction we have the challenge of Thor,' he explained, 'who is the heathen god.'

For the first time Elgar played some notes on the piano. They were the opening lines of the chorus.

'Oh you should have heard how the Hanley choir sang that!'

57

he exclaimed happily, as though the sounds had restored the memory of the rehearsal.

And then he was away, playing the violent, rhythmic music with its *ostinato* bass part. He played the piano heavily and emphatically without any of the care that Minnie Penny had taken earlier in the evening. The slap of his fingers on the notes could be heard distinctly. He also made the old instrument sound much larger than it was. It resounded with a peculiarly orchestral rumble.

Dora watched him with still, liquid eyes. He looked to her from time to time and then would turn his eyes upward as though returning to his own concerns with the playing of the score.

Then he began to speak some of the words of this noisy tempestuous music. Or rather to chant them. For there was a reserve, a shyness in him that made him reluctant to sing the words. But the passion in the music and the words prevented him from merely reciting them. So he intoned them, occasionally interrupting himself briefly to comment on the way the singers at Hanley had delivered particular passages of Thor's challenge to the Christians.

> 'Force rules the world still,
> Has ruled it, shall rule it;
> Meekness is weakness,
> Strength is triumphant.

'How well that was sung! How clear and strong they were! And then the conclusion.

> 'O Galilean!

'All beautifully enunciated!

> 'Unto the combat,
> Gauntlet or Gospel,
> Here I defy thee!'

The music came to a conclusion with a crash in the always violent bass part. For a second or so, in the pronounced silence that followed, the pianist looked abashed, as he returned his attention to the drawing room. But unexpectedly the Rector came to his assistance.

'What fine music, Mr Elgar, how very fine. How powerfully you evoke the pagan spirits!'

The usually placid, unresponsive clergyman was powerfully roused by the music. The violent rhythms had made him breathe heavily. His large, broad face was flushed.

'What comes next?' enquired Dora in a low voice. Her figure was intent and immobile, her eyes glaucous in that shadowy light.

'Olaf fights with Ironhead, a worshipper of Thor. He kills Ironhead and shatters the image of Thor.'

The composer turned to the instrument again and struck it heavily and rapidly. The small black piano *appassionato* reverberated again through the room. Within the straightforward melody of this new passage there came a harsh insistent drumming. The Rector crossed and re-crossed his legs but only to readdress his attention the more thoroughly to the performer.

Elgar shouted over the music, 'Then, as he travels on his quest, Olaf encounters three ladies. The first is Gudrun. She is a very dangerous lady, a destroyer. Olaf marries her as an atonement for murdering her father, Ironhead. But on their wedding night she attempts to stab him. But he awakes.

> "What is that," King Olaf said,
> "Gleams so bright above thy head?"'

In a different voice the composer chanted Gudrun's airy floating answer,

> ' 'Tis the bodkin that I wear
> When at night I bind my hair.'

For all the drama, the music had become slight and tinkling. The Rector had slowly relapsed into a slumped position. The battle had engaged him more than the love story. And the two older ladies had the look of those who are consciously listening and responding to music. Only Dora remained captivated. She craved to have yet more of the man's music in her ears and in her nerves, beating against her shoulders and her arms. Her attention and feelings were polarised upon him, as in his chanting recitation he spoke out the words (and she fancied directly to her):

> 'Underneath the fairest hair!
> Gudrun beware!'

The musician's cheeks were pallid and preternaturally large; they glistened with a bright film of perspiration. He proceeded with his summary: 'Then comes the pagan queen, Sigrid. When Olaf proposes to marry her, she refuses. For this he curses her and then strikes her.'

He paused apprehensively for a moment before speaking Olaf's words.

> 'Thou has not beauty, thou hast not youth,
> Shall I buy thy hand at the cost of truth.'

As his hands made the piano sound out the striking of the old woman, Elgar glanced covertly at his wife from under his thick eyebrows. But she took little interest in this section of the work. Her attention was directed at her fellow auditors to be sure that they heard and appreciated her husband's music fully.

'Mr Acworth inserted the next passage at my husband's special request,' she said, quite loudly, to the Rector who now showed signs of drifting away into sleep.

And yet she remained unmoved when her husband played and spoke this section, Queen Sigrid's cry of revenge against the man who had humiliated her.

How could she not feel it when her husband felt it so acutely? Dora decided that it was all a confused dream involving people in that very room in which some assumed the roles of others. But she wondered how that could be, when Elgar had composed the music before he and she had met.

Only when the music grew quieter and a song of spring was played to introduce the third lady, Thyri, did Alice attend at all closely. Blithely she said, 'This is a most beautiful passage to my mind. He finds his love at last and promises to win back her dowry which she has lost in coming to him.'

Quietly she recited the words with her husband as he spoke them, accompanied by the now subdued piano.

> 'Sweet are thy words, but O! meseems,
>   A sweeter gift would be,
> The boon that haunts Queen Thyri's dreams,
>   Her dowry over sea.'

His wife's participation provoked the composer. He slapped at the notes irritably and then, without notice, moved ahead to another section of the cantata. Alice was abandoned in mid-sentence, her mouth still open.

After some dozen bars, Elgar explained curtly that this was the victory of the heathen Svithiod's forces over Olaf. His hands struck hard and decisively at the notes now. The tingling strings boomed sonorously. Dora was completely captivated. She could do nothing but give herself to it, so that it was her. She could feel it moving in her body as in her mind.

Then, to her chilled amazement the man called out to her as he struck vehemently at the piano.

'Would you come and turn the pages for me?'

The voice was harsh and compelling. It was a command more than a question, almost like a bark.

All through the performance he had been snatching awkwardly at the pages of the score, sometimes turning two or three in error. Now he wanted to devote both hands unencumbered to the finale of the work.

Dora rose obediently. At this moment she felt quiveringly susceptible to the man. She was driven by him and by his music. She went swiftly across the room and stood by him. She attended closely to the music. There was a panic at the base of her stomach for fear that she might not turn the page at the correct moment. But no, she had managed it! Her body warmed with pleasure. She was a true acolyte. The relationship of the afternoon, that of an uncle and a pert niece, was now transformed.

Her stepmother held back from the music. The simple face of the gentle, devout lady puckered anxiously at the sight of the girl's distraction.

The music mounted to its conclusion. Dora felt herself to

be in some heightened state of consciousness. The old, familiar drawing room was a phantasmagoria. She was hearing the prophecy that St John would continue Olaf's work. She thought of the performance of *Tannhäuser* that had enraptured her at the Prince of Wales Theatre in Birmingham just a year before. The rhetoric of the religious emotion in the music she was now hearing could easily have made her sob.

There came a brisk heavy knocking at the drawing room door. Elgar ceased playing. The Rector bestirred himself and stood up. Either as a result of one of his own reveries or of the visionary quality of the music he had been sitting with his eyes shut and his legs stretched out, revealing large expanses of black woollen stocking. He now marched solemnly across the room and arrived at the door before his wife, who had also risen to answer it.

Mrs Bayliss' voice could be heard chuntering. Her words were muffled. She sounded pretentiously polite but also hard and coarse. Her bullying contralto rasped like a file. The music was ruined. The gathering mood in the room was shattered.

The Rector could now be heard replying. He was being melodiously reassuring in a practical but unhearing way. The woman complained again more briefly and less loudly this time. And again the Rector confronted her. After two more of these diminishing exchanges he shut the door with a firm click and returned to the centre of the room where he addressed the company.

'I fear that our little concert has been disturbing to Mrs Bayliss in the room below and keeping her from her proper rest. I have informed her that since the hour is late we will bring our entertainment to a conclusion. I should like to express our thanks to our guest for allowing us to hear something of his most excellent composition. I now ask that we join together in a last prayer before retiring for the night.'

Dora seethed with anger at her father's humiliation by this bullying, uncouth woman. How could he defer and obey in this abject manner? Yet he heard the woman and did her will without appearing to be personally involved. He gave the impression that the woman's wishes chimed perfectly with his own. Perhaps

62

they did. At the end he had lost interest in the music. And he was as indifferent to Mrs Bayliss' desire that the music should end as he was to Dora's that it should continue. How Dora hated that blithe, egotistical indifference that was mitigated only by his inexplicable obsessions.

The sing-song prayer began. Dora was hot with anger. She tried to bring herself into the right state of mind for prayer. For she was a sincere member of the Church, took its principles seriously and endeavoured to employ them. But her bitterness and humiliation at her father's humiliation would not easily abate. The prayer at last ended and the five people began to take leave of each other for the night.

There was a tremor in Elgar's voice, Dora fancied, as he spoke his goodnight to her. Certainly the deep eyes lingered upon her before he set off upstairs with Alice, led by the Rector's wife. The score was now put back in his music-bag and this was stuffed awkwardly under his arm so that the pages were bent. From the back he looked stooped and threadbare. Dora experienced a sharp, almost painful, feeling of protective sympathy for him.

That night the girl slept very little. In turn, the music, the anger and the compassion throbbed and burned in her head and in her body. She wondered if she were ill. Feverishly she found herself returning to that hectic state she had been in whilst listening to the music. For some time she dozed and dreamed of some strange ceremonial among Grecian columns in which she swore to serve the man in his high calling. After she had sworn her oath, she felt the man's heavy moustache sweep her brow in a chaste kiss of acceptance. She stood between the man and his wife in flowing robes. Alice held her delicately at the waist and by the arm as the rite was performed.

Dora awoke with a start to find it dawn. Over the nearby row houses and over the countryside beyond there was a chill silvery light. She was restless and uneasy. Her sleeplessness, like the music, made her feel that she was no longer herself.

She washed herself and put on her new green dress. She combed up her hair. She put on a broad bracelet of old silver given her by her real mother. She pondered the texture of the

63

metal against the light golden down on her arm and wrist. She sat and waited.

As the time for breakfast at last approached, she grew fearful about how they would encounter each other after all the intense exchanges of the previous evening. The old, normal courtesies could no longer apply.

But in the event both Elgar and his wife were cheerful, formal and distant. They were just guests eating their meal and preparing to hasten back home to proceed with their many responsibilities. On this morning as on any other Elgar was in haste. The moment was of no particular significance to him. (Though more than thirty years later, when rich, famous and much decorated and much alone, he would, as an act of commemoration of this time, set out on another journey to Hanley to conduct *King Olaf*.)

Dora could have wept at his indifference. Had there been no contact between them last evening? Had not things been said, intimated? Was she imagining it all? She could not believe that.

Breakfast ended, as it had begun, with a lengthy prayer. The Rector then strode off in his stately way to return to the church. Alice and Minnie were dawdling, talking to each other at the far end of the room. Alice wished to fetch something she had forgotten from upstairs. Then they would go, she said. Dora hung back, hoping that both women would go. Yes, her stepmother was going too. The two ladies made their way with tantalising slowness out through the door, talking all the while. The man had stayed with her.

He turned and strode up to her.

'I will write to you,' he said thickly. 'Will you write to me?'

'Oh, yes.' She could have broken down with the excitement and the relief.

He did not look at her as he spoke.

'You will not forget?'

'No.'

'Will you send me the newspaper account of the football match?'

'Yes. Yes, if you would like t . . . t . . . to have it.' She was

64

in an ecstasy of relief to have something to do in the service of her feeling for him.

The door opened silently and there was Alice in her worn travelling coat saying, 'I am ready to set off now, Edward dearest.'

The girl flushed. She turned aside awkward and ashamed. But Alice was not at all upset with her. On the contrary she came over and kissed Dora's cheek as she bade her goodbye. Indeed she appeared very approving of the girl's private conversation with her husband. Dora was much intrigued by this. Alice even asked her, pressed her, to come to stay with them at Malvern. The man now smiled at her cheeringly. Dora expressed her gratitude and said that she would discuss possibilities with her stepmother.

And then the man and his wife were gone. Dora was left alone in the empty dining room. She could feel her heart beat. She gazed lovingly at the bacon rinds that lay on his plate. Her head was in a fever of loss and of hope.

4

On the following day, by the afternoon post, Dora received from him a letter in code.

It came in a sealed envelope within another in which Alice had posted her formal note of thanks for the hospitality at Wolverhampton. Minnie brought it up to Dora, who was in the small library and writing room completing a letter to one of her maternal aunts in the south. Minnie held out the envelope without speaking and Dora took it wonderingly. The words 'Miss Penny' were written on the outside. She opened the envelope carefully and took out a small slip of paper. Her breath quickened as she surveyed the three lines of squiggles. Then she grew vexed that she could not understand the code.

'It is in cipher,' she exclaimed to her stepmother, who was watching her with close attention.

Dora bit her lip. She wished that she had not said this. The message contained in the letter might well be a very private, intimate matter between herself and the musician. She folded up the paper protectively and clutched it in her lap.

'Oh, Edward always was a one for jokes and riddles and puzzles and the like.' The stepmother spoke laughingly, to set the girl at her ease. But the kind, brown eyes studied the girl's face in undisguisable anxiety.

Dora now placed the note on her writing table and regarded it with some puzzlement. She thought that if it were just a simple joke, she should pass the paper over to her stepmother to see if she could decode it. But Dora could not do this. The letter made her arms and shoulders tremble.

'Why, I remember one evening when we were at Bayreuth, the three of us . . .'

The Rector's wife set off on a long account of one of the composer's cleverly managed mystifications. Minnie's voice tinkled with merriment as she spoke, even while her nervous eyes suggested some puritanical guilt at the amusing memory. There was something very innocent about her; she would be easily susceptible to a trick, Dora thought. But at this moment the young girl was not at all interested in yet one more story of that German holiday to which the generous lady had treated the Elgars, some five years before, when they had been virtually impoverished. Dora knew for sure that there was more to this letter than the comic puzzles and the trick solutions of which her stepmother was now speaking.

When the story was finished, Dora jumped up abruptly and announced that she would go out for a few minutes to post her letter. It was to an aunt in Tite Street, Chelsea, who had written to say that she had sent Dora a bicycle for her birthday and a dress for Christmas. (It was the habit of this lady to forget about Dora for years at a time and then, unexpectedly, to send her expensive presents.)

Minnie Penny followed her stepdaughter downstairs and watched her put on her plaid cape and gloves. The older lady was in a state of intense nervous anxiety. She was always uneasy about Dora's habit of making unaccompanied excursions into the town. Also, concerning the musician, she felt that Christian duty required that she say something to the girl. But the words would not come to her. Her mind dithered ineffectively between facts and suspicions. Her thick, capable but small fingers that were dominated by the heavy golden wedding-ring played restlessly with her own letter.

In some preoccupation Dora turned and kissed her stepmother and sped off into the town.

On her way, outside, at last, Dora could allow her excitement to run. She moved eastward, her mind in a hot blur of intoxication. At the top of Broad Street a red-faced drayman reined his two great horses urgently and bellowed at her to look out. People stopped and stared and this made her pay more attention to her circumstances. She continued down Broad Street. To her right, a few feet below a metal rail, ran a cobbled gully with decayed old houses, a couple of them with thatched roofs. Dirty, half-naked children called up to her from the gully but Dora was oblivious. On she went, past the Quaker burial ground and the old meeting-house. At the bottom of the hill she came into Cann Lane and crossed over to the grand cast-iron bridge with its array of bright heraldic ornament that had been built just twenty years before. It spanned the canal which a century before Telford had here brought close into the centre of the town.

Dora stood on the bridge, took out the letter and laid it on the parapet to look at it again. Still she could not decipher it. Perhaps she could when she was less disturbed and could bring her simple wits to it. Above her loomed the canal warehouses of sooty, maroon brick. She looked down into the sombre, shadowy canal basin and studied the brightly painted cabins of the barges. The bargees and their families were eating their midday meal from their gaudy crockery. The immense barge-horses snuffed and tossed their hay-bags in the air. Men were bringing foaming jugs of beer down to the boats from the little public house across from the bridge. It was all part of that other Wolverhampton which Dora found at times intriguing and at other times frightening. There was a lively clatter of noise and activity in the basin below. Presently the barge people became aware of the well-dressed girl looking down upon them from the bridge. Some nudged each other and stared back at her. They grew less noisy. This brought Dora to herself again. With a start she turned away and hurried off up the hill towards Victoria Square.

A flash of anxiety went over her and she realised that she had completely forgotten her other errand. She had as yet been unable to obtain a copy of Saturday's 'pink 'un' to send to the musician as she had promised. Mrs Bayliss had agreed to ask her brother, a foundryman who lived in Old Brickkiln Street; unfortunately he had not bought a copy that day. But Dora had another idea.

She hastened past the smart façade of the Victoria Hotel and then turned into Queen Street. On her left were the Mechanics' Institute and the old Assembly Room and library, all quite debonair classical buildings in white stucco from the Regency period. To Dora, at this time, this street had a dated rakish quality. The buildings she associated with the tales of the ne'er-do-wells in her family which her own mother, a deeply religious woman, had related to her years ago. Sharing her mother's admiration of the architectural ideals of Mr Ruskin was for Dora a way of being in touch with her.

At the western end of the street Dora entered a shop with fluted metal columns at the door and broad, high glass windows behind which were displayed two grand pianos, an old spinet, two or three cellos and several violins which were placed upon low white pillars draped in green velvet.

This was Haywards. The shop had been opened some thirty or forty years before by Henry Hayward when he had retired to Wolverhampton after a triumphant career as virtuoso violinist and composer. In his day he had been known as the English Paganini. A country fiddler from Brosely in Salop, he had gone to London and become the pupil of Spagnoletti and had subsequently performed his original compositions at the Philharmonic Society in the presence of the Prime Minister, Sir Robert Peel. The English Paganini had died some twelve years before and now the business was carried on by his son, Mr Charles Flavell Hayward.

Dora entered the shop breathing heavily from her haste. A black-suited young man stepped forward from the gloom of the shop to attend to her. He bowed.

'I wish to speak to Mr Hayward,' announced Dora with a confidence that was unexpected in one as young as she.

The young man was deferential.

'I regret to have to say, Miss Penny, that Mr Hayward may not be here. I believe he went out to give a lesson. I am almost

69

certain that I saw him leaving in the trap. But I will endeavour to make sure. If you would be kind enough to be seated for a moment or two . . .'

Gracefully Dora seated herself upon one of the large plush chairs by the counter and waited. She always enjoyed the sombre coolness and silence of this shop after the bustle of the town streets.

A pale, diffident lady who was two or three years older than Dora appeared from the back. To her long navy-blue skirt there clung two small children of about four and five, the boy in a sailor-suit and the little girl in what looked like a miniature ball-dress.

'Oh, I came to speak with Mr Hayward,' said Dora, rising disconcertedly.

'I am afraid that my husband has had to travel to Sowick to give a lesson,' replied Mrs Hayward.

The young woman had a thorough Black Country accent which she was at great pains to try to conceal. The two children peeped out shyly from behind her skirt.

'Is there anything that I might do?' continued the young woman uneasily. For all her respect for the Rector's daughter there was a hint of suspicion, of defensiveness in her somewhat sickly, anaemic face.

Dora was in fact greatly disappointed to discover that Charlie Hayward had gone out. He was a good friend of hers, a comrade in music, a fellow enthusiast. It would have been so much easier to deal with him.

'There are several things which I wished to say to Mr Hayward,' answered Dora in some impatience, but attempting to sound pleasant. 'But I have one very particular request with which you might be able to help me. I have promised to send a c . . . c . . . copy of last Saturday's "pink 'un" to a friend of mine in the country. I know that Mr Hayward takes the paper regularly and I am wondering if y . . . y . . . you still have a copy which I might beg.'

Mrs Hayward's apprehensive expression relaxed into a smile. This was so much more human and understandable than the grand and sometimes abstruse conversations between Miss Penny and her husband which she had happened to overhear. A happy sympathy came readily into the pretty face.

'I believe we do, Miss Penny. And if it is not thrown out, you shall have it. Come, children, let us look in the parlour. Kindly wait here, Miss Penny, and I will try to find it.'

She turned and thrust the folds of her full skirt behind her. The children were completely revealed. They turned away their faces bashfully. They were much in awe of the grand lady from the church who came to speak to their father. Dora, seating herself again by the dark oak counter, was, as usual, indifferent to them.

After several minutes the young mother returned to the shop carrying the newspaper. She was delighted to have found it. She was shyly eager to protract the visit. There was a tenuous, hopeful impulse in her to speak to Dora as herself and not as her husband's wife. But the handsome blonde girl with the slightly dazed expression was quite uninterested. Politely, unhesitatingly, she expressed her thanks for the newspaper, announced her intention of visiting Mr Hayward in the near future and then hurried out leaving the shop bell jangling briskly behind her.

She moved swiftly down Market Street, turned the corner and entered the fashionable new post office building of loud yellow and red brick. Inside she prepared a band of brown paper. Trembling she wrote the composer's name and address on it. Then she wrapped up the parcel and took it to the wire wicket. As she waited to hand it in, she thrilled at this contact with him and at the thought of continuing this cryptic correspondence. A clerk suddenly took the little packet and it was gone, out of sight. Dreamily she left the post office, not noticing people at all, her mind looking forward to and imagining how he would next communicate with her. When would he write? What would he write?

In the event Dora was greatly disappointed. Months went by without any genuine word from him. He and Alice merely sent her their regards in letters directed to her stepmother. Occasionally these would contain joking allusions to her. Otherwise there was nothing.

When Dora's violin teacher, Mr Clarence Grainger, moved to Worcester, she insisted on travelling there on the train to continue her lessons. Worcester was near to Malvern, as Dora knew, and this was a prime reason that she determined to continue her course of instruction. To her great excitement, when Elgar heard of this, he wrote and suggested that he take her on a tour of his native city and show her the cathedral. But on each possible occasion it turned out that he was travelling to some engagement and finally nothing came of the idea. The weeks went by emptily.

Yet Dora never gave up her faith in this secret relationship. She never for a moment doubted it, even while her life was taken up with other people, other activities. Dora sang in the choir, helped her father and stepmother with the daily running of the busy, prosperous church and joined its societies. She practised hard at her violin. (This could be a special bond between herself and the musician.) And she grew friendly with the family at the vicarage at St George's, the large ashlar church up on the Bilston Road. Dora's father was disturbed by this. For the Reverend Danks had frequently spoken in a way that showed him to be perilously close to the Roman faith. But Dora would not listen to him. She enjoyed the company of the five impoverished brothers and sisters and their sad, wan mother who had so manifestly come down in the world. Dora became their leader. Since the members of the family were all very musical, she decided that they should form a small string ensemble. The Danks, much impressed by Dora's energy, wilfulness and position, quickly agreed. Dora organised many lengthy rehearsals.

But her pleasant habit of intimacy and ease with the family was disturbed at the Christmas of that year, when during an evening of fellowship the eldest of the Danks' sons, who was reading theology at Cambridge, engaged her in an intense private discussion of certain issues of transubstantation that quickly betrayed something more than an interest in Dora's doctrinal position. After this there was for several weeks some strain in Dora's relationship with her little orchestra at St George's.

And then in the early spring of the next year the Rector's wife received a letter from Alice Elgar, asking if they might come to Wolverhampton for a visit. Elgar was tired and in need of a change. He had been wishing to return to his friends at the Rectory and Alice was sure that such a visit would be most beneficial. He also had some bee in his bonnet about wishing to visit Boscobel House, where Charles II had hidden from his pursuers in an oak tree. Alice would be grateful if this latest enthusiasm could be catered to; the place was not very far from Wolverhampton.

Guilelessly Minnie Penny read out this letter to Dora as they sat in their painted Indian chairs in the library. When she had finished, Minnie slowly pondered the contents of the letter: what Alice had said, what Elgar had said through Alice, and what Alice might be saying about her husband.

Dora remained silent but a secret excitement surged through her. Minnie glanced up at Dora doubtfully. The innocence of her look was almost foolish. She was happy at the prospect of seeing her old friends again but had such obvious and definite misgivings about Dora.

During the next two or three weeks the girl was tense, almost sick, with anticipation. Some nights she could not sleep and would walk about her room composing sentences which she would say to him. Yet at the dawn of the day the Elgars were due to arrive she felt so feverish and confused that she feared she might not be able to utter a word to him.

It was a bright but gusty spring day. The clouds scudded past the high pinnacles of the church tower. The winds shook the white blossom on the west wall of the Rectory garden.

On the station platform were rows of empty milk-churns.

'I always think that there is a smell of the West Country on this particular platform,' said Minnie Penny in a little flutter of homesickness. In her way she was almost as excited as Dora. She kept taking deep breaths as though preparing for some intense effort.

The train came into sight. It moved slowly, grindingly, leaning perilously to one side on the curving rail. Both ladies cleared their throats. The train edged past them and, at last, stopped. The doors were thrown open and there, first off, was the musician, looking back into the compartment, to assist his wife. But what-

73

ever was he carrying? It looked like a large brown paper parcel about three-quarters the size of himself.

'Whatever has Edward got there?' exclaimed Minnie, a nervous yet intrigued laugh in her voice.

'I think it's a k . . . k . . . kite,' suggested Dora, disconcerted by his manner of arrival.

He was striding towards them, followed by Alice who looked more threadbare, more harried than when they had last seen her. The man, from what could be seen of him, looked a little smarter, more prosperous, more energetic.

Minnie shook his hand and then kissed Alice enthusiastically. She was always happy to be with her old friends. Purposefully the musician came up to Dora and shook her hand. But there was more to it than the formal gesture. There was an extra pressure of the hand, a quick significant squeezing of her fingers that gave Dora confirmation (had she needed it) that her faith in their secret, subterranean relationship was not misplaced.

'I am so happy to meet you again, Miss Dora,' he said huskily, the intense eyes lingering upon her.

Minnie unceremoniously interrupted this silent exchange.

'But, Edward, whatever have you got there?' she demanded playfully.

'Oh, Minnie,' exclaimed Alice in great irritation, 'I did try so hard to persuade him not to bring it. I know that it will cause inconvenience.' She spoke like a tired mother who is close to losing her patience.

'Not it, Chicky, not it,' said the man with much confidence. There was a slightly bullying cackle to his voice. For some reason he had the upper hand over his wife now.

'It is not at all polite to bring such a thing on a visit,' persevered Alice naggingly.

'Miss Dora and I shall fly it at Boscobel, shall we not?' he chuckled coarsely.

There was some ribaldry in his eyes. Dora had no memory of him being like this. This was a new side to him. There were so many sides. She was provoked but also wary of becoming involved in this difference between the man and his wife.

'Miss Dora will not take part in such an activity. Kite-flying is no pastime for adult persons,' insisted Alice in a weary magisterial fashion. But even as she spoke these words, Dora was persuaded that Alice would really not mind, might indeed be encouraging their flying of the kite together. Often neither one of them could be relied upon to say what they meant. They were engaged combatively and self-regardingly in some strange game.

The large box-kite was difficult to carry on to the tram. The other passengers watched with great curiosity. The man handled it with delicate skill. Walking through the graveyard to the Rectory with the kite over his shoulder, he looked like some large, comic bird, Dora thought. The angular struts and brown paper looked like a grotesque wing and his moustached mouth thrust energetically forward resembled a beak. She could have laughed aloud and was surprised at herself, for she had not thought to laugh at him during the days and weeks of anticipation.

Luncheon was eaten quickly, because the brake that was to take them to Boscobel was to come early so that they might have as much of the light as possible. Mrs Bayliss handed round the various courses. She eyed Elgar suspiciously and was especially alert to any exchange of words or glances between him and Dora.

Then they were in the brake and away down the long incline of Darlington Street and into Chapel Ash with its many fashionable shop windows decked out with cast-iron Corinthian columns. On the road to Tettenhall they passed large Georgian row houses with handsome, pedimented doorways and then more recent villas of red brick. At the bottom of the cutting which Telford had made through the high sandstone Rock at Tettenhall they turned lurchingly to the right and were quickly out into the open country. They went through the tiny village of Codsall and on down a tree-lined road where there was an occasional glimpse of one of the large new houses of the ironmasters, usually named for the Queen's houses, Osborne, Balmoral, Sandringham.

As the brake lumbered on in a slow, pleasant rhythm through this lush green countryside, the Rector was giving the company an account of what he called the 'barbarous obsequies' of a

75

heathen headhunter of his acquaintance. He spoke as if by rote, in a strident, trance-like recitation. Sometimes his voice faltered as though he were engaged in some inner, spiritual struggle.

'The dead man was placed upright in a deep grave,' the Rector was saying, 'and the earth filled in till it reached his neck. Fires were then lighted round the head from which the scorched flesh soon dropped, leaving the skull bare. This was then carried to the canoe house, to be sacrificed to as a Tindaloo. A Tindaloo is a spirit, of course. The dead man's young wife and child were next dragged to the open grave and strangled there . . .'

The effect upon Alice Elgar was pronounced; she looked increasingly as though she might be sick.

'What house is that, Alfred?' enquired Minnie suddenly, pointing through the window. She was more concerned to spare her guests any more of this obsessive recitation than to discover the name of the mansion.

The Rector shivered, sat up and peered out. On the right was a large gatehouse of buff stone and an avenue leading away under tall oak trees.

'Ah, that is Chillington . . . The family is of the Church of Rome, of course.'

'Ancient upholders of the Faith in this country,' agreed Elgar quietly.

The Rector regarded him with his empty smile. He appeared puzzled by the enthusiasm in the musician's voice. Perhaps he had not realised that his guest was a Catholic.

Dora remembered the day of the football match. She was taken aback by this religious fervour that occasionally revealed itself in the man. Strange that it was the pagan passages rather than the Christian which had sounded the more strongly in his music. But he was very conscious of his Catholicism. It was a part of his vital tissue. Her father's spirituality she found, in her heart, to be perverse and complacent. But this other man's with its dangerous exoticism, its traditions of outlawry and adventure caught her imagination. There was a feeling also of playing with danger. For though Dora knew herself to be stable and robust, she could recall many people, young, intently religious girls of her own age and young curates especially, whose

76

intensifying sympathy with the Roman view had been accompanied by illness, breakdown and madness.

Dora was again aware of this alien, possibly menacing side to the man when they went on their tour of Boscobel House. Upon arrival the Rector and the two elder ladies resolved to sit for a while under a tree and drink a glass of the fruit cordial which they had brought with them in a hamper. They arranged themselves carefully upon the grass and prepared to enjoy this early sunshine of the year. Elgar carefully propped the kite up against the bark of the tree.

'Miss Dora, should you like to come and visit the house with me?' he enquired unexpectedly.

Dora found it difficult to accept the invitation in front of the company though she wanted to.

'Oh do go with him,' said Alice Elgar. 'Edward can never sit still. Do go and look after him. The rest of us would like to sit for a while.'

Dora saw not only acquiescence in Alice's eyes but also a purpose. For reasons of her own Alice definitely wanted her to go with her husband. Dora felt accepted and contained within the calm egotism of the tired, shabby little woman. Dora was made uneasy by this thought but she decided that she would consider it later. For the moment she was agog to accept the invitation.

'Yes, I should like very much to see the house,' she replied, struggling to sound calm, indifferent. She turned to say goodbye to her father who was looking away, a glazed expression on his face, and to her stepmother whose brown eyes quivered fretfully.

The two set off together. As they walked across the grass to the Jacobean farmhouse, she placed her arm in his. She wondered what they would say to each other when they were no longer in sight of the others.

They came into a lavender garden of the seventeenth century, the light purple herb smelling pungently in the blustery spring air. On the western side of the house was a projecting chimney-stack built with six windows and window slits which, when looked at more closely, proved to be only painted on.

'Whatever are they?' exclaimed Dora, troubled by the harshness of the black lines.

'They have always been there,' replied the musician quietly. 'They are there on the oldest engravings of the house and have remained there throughout all the changes and additions and rebuilding.'

'But what are they?' persisted Dora.

'Some say they are the marks of a safe house. Others say they are a version of the mystic marks.'

He looked down at her kindly, indulgently, invitingly. But she said nothing more. She would not ask him what he meant by these things. She felt that he wished her to. And she herself would like to know, but she feared that she might in this way become susceptible to what she now thought the sinister icons of his alien spirituality. In these matters she now felt afraid of him and would keep her distance.

A stout, bonny, red-faced farmer's wife met them at the door of the house. She and her husband were the custodians; they were the tenants of the Earl of Bradford, of nearby Weston Park, who owned the place. There was flour on the woman's heavy arms from the baking and her broad face shone with perspiration. She asked if they would like to see the place and led them in. They went into the small parlour, walking carefully on the old timbered floor. Their guide dutifully pointed out the plaster frieze with its interlacing pattern and the dark Jacobean panelling. The kindly woman waited for them to admire it. Elgar examined it all intently while Dora herself was taken with the echoes of history in the low-ceilinged room.

'Should yo like to goo upstairs and see the secret places? That's what most folks am interested in.'

'Secret places?' repeated Dora.

'Yes,' answered Elgar throatily, his voice thrilled but muted. 'The secret places of the house. The hiding places for the priests.'

Dora was disconcerted by his manner.

'It's where King Charles hid after his day in the oak and where the Catholic priests hid during the time their religion was outlawed.'

78

The farmer's wife spoke in a practical, down-to-earth way that was reassuring to Dora.

The large woman led them up a narrow winding staircase. At the top of the old attic stairs was a trap-door giving access to a cramped cube of space measuring about four feet in every direction. Elgar inspected the secret hiding place very carefully. Dora was surprised that he could be so interested in what was little more than a large box. She could almost have laughed, such an anti-climax it was. Why must he take it so seriously? She was becoming tired of the house with its cramped rooms and its fusty-smelling darkness. She was relieved when the farmer's wife led them down again into the bright spring sunshine and the fragrant lavender garden.

On a nearby wall of old small bricks in Flemish bond five or six fan-tailed pigeons sat trilling and cooing. They had all spread out their brilliantly white wing and tail feathers in the sunshine.

Dora cried out in admiration.

'Ar, they am pretty, aye they?' agreed the stout woman, still panting from the climb up all the stairs. 'And they'm always in love, like they say. We 'ad two to start, and now we've got 'alf a dozen or more . . .'

She stopped herself, surveyed the two visitors and wondered whether, in the circumstances, this piece of information had been indelicate.

'Shall ye goo and see the Oak now?' she resumed.

'Yes. And perhaps do a spot of kite-flying in the field, if that is permitted,' answered Elgar.

'Yo goo and enjoy yourselves,' said the woman with a broad, ready smile of encouragement.

The two set off to fetch the kite. There was a new energy in the man's step as they walked. That hieratic mood which had disturbed and, at moments, amused Dora, was now altogether gone. He hurried along with boyish enthusiasm. Occasionally Dora had to lift her skirt above her shoes in order to quicken her pace to keep up with him. They came upon the tree by which the kite had been left to discover that the others had set off. In fact they could be seen on the other side of the field, making for the house by a roundabout way. Again, Dora could have laughed at the sight of those distant figures, the tall, batlike clergyman in black striding along the hedgerow unheeding and the two small, plumpish ladies in their bonnets trailing along behind him.

Elgar took up the kite with great care and they set off for the open space around the ancient oak in which the young Charles II was said to have hidden during the Civil War. They stopped by the high, circular iron palisading around the tree. The man examined the tree closely. Dora thought he might become preoccupied with it. Such a royalist he was, she knew. But no, he turned away and began to unwind the string and to unfurl the box-kite. Then they went along a narrow path through the silvery spring wheat that was rippled by the wind so that it swished gently, silkily. Dora felt that the wind caught her in the mouth and the throat. She was exhilarated by this high place with its long, extended views over fresh green fields and woods right across to Lizard Hill and the Wrekin itself.

'Here we go then,' shouted Elgar suddenly, the wind catching his words and his breath. And he started to run with the big brown kite. Slowly it rose behind him. He ran more quickly and Dora ran along after him, her knees smack, smacking against the inside of her long, narrow skirt. She caught up with him. Now the kite was head high and the man stopped, breathless, and pulled in the string so that it immediately rose higher still, with a surprising, pretty buoyancy. Then gusts caught it and he played out the string again so that it rose two or three times his own height. Dora's heart beat heavily from the run and from the excitement of seeing it rise.

But then the wind turned about and abandoned the kite so that it suddenly fell to half its height. Then after some moments of uncertain hovering it fell yet again, precipitately.

The man and the girl were shocked, sickened even, as they watched the descent. The man started to run again, pulling abruptly at the string. But still it fell, in brief, quick stages. Pathetic and inadequate he looked as he struggled unavailingly to raise it. Coils of string lay around him on the grass. At last the kite dropped a final six feet to the earth and struck a grassy mound with a loud impact.

'Oh,' cried Dora as though she herself had been struck.

The two of them raced over the bright green turf to where the brown object leaned gracelessly on one end. They dropped down on their knees beside it. Anxiously, rapidly, Elgar felt over it with his fingers, seeking, and yet passionately hoping that he would not find, a fracture in the struts or the paper.

He looked up at her at last in a passion of relief and happiness.

'It's not damaged, you know. Nothing is broken.'

'Oh, I am s . . . s . . . so glad,' breathed Dora, utterly at one with him in excited sympathy.

'Your turn now!' he barked suddenly. He was holding the kite and the ball of string towards her.

Dora hesitated. 'I don't think I could. I . . .'

But he would not listen to her. He was like an elder brother or an intolerant schoolmaster.

Uncertainly she took the bulky kite in her small hands. With considerable irritation he took it back and thrust the string and the struts into different hands.

'Good,' he cried. 'Let us run then . . .'

And off he set, Dora following unsteadily and without confidence. But surprisingly, after a minute or so, the kite started to lift. She felt its gentle tugging, tugging motion in her hands and arms.

'Capital!' he cried. 'Capital!'

Up and up it went. Dora's blue eyes shone with pride in her accomplishment. Higher and higher it went. It was now further from the ground than when the man himself had flown it. Dora could feel her breath burning in her lungs as she panted from running and the excitement. The kite rose still higher.

But then, just as before, it started to fall.

'Run faster . . . to lift it . . .' gasped the man urgently. 'Come on. Off we go . . . Faster . . . Do not let it . . . fall again . . . as before . . .'

They struggled on as fast as they could go, breathless. But still the kite fell, in abrupt stages.

'Don't slow down . . .' insisted the man gasping. Dora raced as fast as she could in her inconvenient skirt and still the man urged her on.

Then suddenly her foot struck something hard and she fell full length to the ground with a dizzying, sickening blow. She felt the grass strike up at her body with a hard thud that drove all the breath out of her. She had lost her footing in a hidden rut.

Within seconds she was struck again, this time upon the top of her body. It was the man's head hitting her shoulder just above her breast and his arm or his leg beating into her stomach down by her thighs. The man had tripped and fallen too. On top of her. For some moments they lay together on the grass, he upon her. In each of them consciousness all but flickered out. But throughout Dora remained aware of holding on to the kite-string whilst the kite itself fluttered about in the air, innocently, some three or four feet above their heads.

After the shock started to pass away, Dora found herself laughing, but without mirth, at their upset. The man removed his limbs from her body in a slow, stunned way that was almost like a caress. Dora's laughter became a hoarse, choking sound.

'Are you all right?' he asked her weakly. He could see the pink inside of her mouth, the small tongue and the white teeth.

'Oh yes. I hope you are.' The words came in gasps.

He sat up and moved away from where she lay. Dora also sat up. She saw that in the fall her skirt and her pale blue petticoat had risen a good way up her leg so that the leathern top of her boot and much of her white woollen stocking was revealed. She was embarrassed. Her laughter subsided as she replaced her skirt. The man watched her do this. Then he looked away guiltily.

They remained there for some time looking stricken and ill. Dora felt a throbbing in her leg and side where she had struck the ground. It became increasingly painful. She must be heavily bruised. Her brow and neck were becoming hot. She let her head fall forward in a feverish drowse. The man also looked to be dozing, although breathing heavily, almost convulsively.

Dora had no idea of how much time had elapsed when she became aware of the blackbirds hastening around purposefully. With increasing interest she followed the dart and flash of the yellow beaks that showed up so brightly against the glossy black feathers. She was beginning to feel better. Wearily she raised herself up and saw the man in a kneeling position looking down on her.

'How do you feel now?' he enquired in a soft manner.

'Recovered, I think.'

'That was a very serious fall.'

She saw him looking at her skirt down the side of which there was a slither of muddy red earth.

'Shall you be able to walk?' he continued. He spoke quietly but solicitously. His treatment of her was altogether different from what it had ever been before. He spoke to her as though to an invalid but at the same time there was also a delicate gallantry in his tone. He was affected by the hurt to her as a woman.

Dora jumped up but stumbled. She felt the pain in her body again. Elgar went towards her as though to support her but at the last instant held back from touching her.

'I shall be all right,' gasped the girl, trying to smile. She hobbled around for a while as though practising walking. At first she limped heavily. The man watched her in great anxiety. Gradually her walking became easier. She bent down and tried to brush off the soil from her skirt.

'Are you able to return to the others now? Pray take my arm.' He surveyed her intently.

She turned towards him. There was a quick flash of hurt in her eyes.

'Let us not return yet. Let me recuperate a l . . . l . . . little longer. My mother will become upset if she sees me like this.'

'Should . . .?' The man was excited by some possibility but then right away shy of voicing it.

'Yes?'

'I fear that walking is painful for you.'

'Not at all. That no longer presents any difficulty.'

He sensed that there might be some bravura in this. But he would voice his suggestion nevertheless.

'I wondered if you might like to walk to White Ladies. It is not very far from here, I believe. It would give us an opportunity fully to recover ourselves . . .' His voice trailed away. He looked somewhat abject as he stood there. A sensitive diffidence showed through his large shaggy exterior.

'What is White Ladies?' enquired Dora, her face lighting up with interest.

'It is the remains of a Benedictine house near here. It was built in the twelfth century, I believe. It is only a ruin now. I have not seen it. But I have read about it.'

He looked to her. 'Are you sure that it is not painful for you to walk?'

'Oh do let us go there,' she cried with her old lively enthusiasm. 'I should very much like to see it.'

For all her youth, she spoke now in a queenly way. She had every confidence that her wishes would prevail with him. She stepped forward and unselfconsciously placed her arm in his and they set off across the field.

She helped him pick up the fallen kite and fold it. They leaned it against a tree. Then they went on, coming to a narrow lane where rabbits spurted out before them and the big clouds driven by the bluff spring wind made the sunlight appear and disappear, flickeringly before their feet. In the hedge pheasants scuttled and clucked.

They walked and walked but did not arrive at the place. Yet neither was at all perturbed. It was a pleasure merely to be walking together slowly and without speaking, allowing the last eddies of shock to have their way. Dora felt dreamily content as the throbbing worked itself out within her. Almost physically, through his arm, she could feel the man's concern and devotion. They had drawn close to each other, as, during all those weeks before, she had known that they would. Soon they would be able to speak about it.

Seeing a sign, he led her from the lane on to a dirt path that led through a copse. As they walked among the trees Dora thought momentarily that this was what was meant by a compromising situation, but the idea neither interested nor affected her and her contented reverie floated on.

They came into the open and there was the old priory on an incline below them, its large romanesque door illuminated by the silvery spring light.

They entered and walked between the high walls quietly and respectfully, as though remembering the dead that had once lived there.

'The nuns, the white ladies, are said to have been well known for their kindness hereabouts. The only complaint against them was that they had a taste for luxuries and were said to keep hounds.'

Dora smiled at this. Then they stood and listened to the country silence which the ruins made them feel as something ancient. Dora remembered the time she had gone with her father and stepmother to Uriconium, on the road to Shrewsbury, and her father had declaimed a poem about it that had been published just a year or so earlier. How rhetorical and out of place her father's reciting had been! How it spoiled the place for her!

But now all was delicately silent as they stood there. The man's words led her to think of the white ladies, the dead nuns who lay buried in the grassy earth beneath. She was aware that she was cultivating a mood of sadness and reverie. The man and the silence of the ruins assisted her. She knew that she and the man were sharing it together. His face turned half way from her was intense, rapt.

But part of her stood aside and judged. She knew that she was inducing a feeling. She wished that she were more abandoned to the feeling, as he was. But she could not be. For her there was a falsity in it. She could go no further with him in this fine melancholy.

Then one of the big glossy blackbirds fled by with something dangling from its shiny yellow beak to build a nest with. It flew only inches from her face. They had been standing so long and so quietly.

Dora laughed. The man stared up, pained.

'We should be going back now, I think,' he mumbled.

They turned and set off without saying any more. A relaxed contentment returned to them as they walked through the woods. When they came to the lane they could hear the farmer calling to his large brown horses as he worked away at the spring ploughing. Dora and the man walked ever more slowly, as though they wished that their walk would not come to an end. All was changed between them. What would happen next?

When at last they came in sight of the tree where they had left the kite, they saw their three companions waiting for them.

The clergyman and the two ladies stood like people at a railway station awaiting a train that is long overdue. They stood stiffly and tensely, fidgeting with gloves or hats or collars. They did not speak to each other. Occasionally one of them would go up to the kite and examine it suspiciously.

When they saw the man and the girl trailing towards them over the grass, the three hurried up to them in a way that suggested irritation as much as anxiety.

'Are you all right? Are you all right? We were wondering what had happened to you,' panted Minnie. The small appleface was aquiver with vexation and responsibility.

'Wherever have you been?' called Alice Elgar who came up second, her slow speech sounding like that of some stern and suspicious headmistress. 'And whatever has happened to you?' added Alice, surveying Dora's soiled skirt and her crumpled blouse and coat.

Dora ignored the question.

'Mr Elgar and I merely went a walk, when we g . . . g . . . grew tired of the kite-flying,' she replied casually. There was a confidence, a grandeur even, in her manner that completely halted the flurry of questions. She held her head to one side imperiously. What a princess she could be!

The two older women were silenced. After a while Minnie started to mumble that it had grown very late and that the Rector was expected at a meeting of the Borough Conservative Party. But that was all.

The Rector himself said nothing until they were all seated again in the brake and had set off on their return journey. By then everyone else was preoccupied with his or her own thoughts. But the Rector was moved to speak.

Polygamy, he announced, was the subject that was on his mind, at this moment, polygamy as he had known it in Melanesia, of course.

He continued ruminatively: 'Bishop Selwyn made it a *sine*

qua non that a polygamist shall put away all but one wife before he receives baptism. That is the only Christian way. That this is the right course in Melanesia I cannot for a moment doubt, though,' and here the Rector cleared his throat hoarsely, 'the case of the woman put away is in some respects a hard one. She loses the protection of the common husband, and, if a chief's wife, a certain amount of dignity.'

The Rector sighed heavily to himself and struck his knee. His anthropological musings were clearly problematical. He was racked with confusion. But none of the others took any interest in the subject. Politely they ignored him. They were hungry and weary from the activities of the excursion. It was the fag-end of the day. The spring air had got over them.

But the Rector struggled on.

'All the women are bought and sold in marriage in Melanesia. But oh the evils of polygamy! A chief's daughter seldom marries young because the parent demands such an exorbitant price for her. Then when the chief dies at last, his daughter is bought for an old song by some middle-aged polygamist . . .'

The Rector continued his halting discourse, citing many examples known to him. But he elicited no response. It was the Rector's misfortune that he could never talk about matters that were important to him in terms that others could readily understand. A certain scrupulousness, a certain squeamishness prevented him. The voice sang on in its familiar suave fashion but there also developed an unaccustomed note of angry, self-pitying railing. On and on he went. The visitors, especially Elgar, nodded agreement occasionally in order to humour him. But no one took any real interest in the difficulties that had confronted, and continued to confront, this former missionary.

At last, from the sound of the factories and the smell of the air, the party knew that they were returning again into Wolverhampton.

5

ON the following day, the Sunday, Dora awoke in some agitation and for some moments could not discover the reason. Then at last she knew that she was afraid lest what had occurred between her and the man yesterday should be cancelled or forgotten today. She rose, and still in her light nightdress gazed out of her bedroom window high up among the gables. The town had the stillness of Sunday but looked sombre in a warm grey mist. It was a dull wet day. Heavy spring rain beat into the grimy, sodden brickwork of the factory buildings.

During the first half of the day Dora was kept in suspense. The morning was taken up with church-going. When Dora judged it late enough to go downstairs she discovered that the man and his wife were already on the point of leaving for Mass. Dora scarcely had an opportunity to speak to either of them. It was a very difficult moment. For Alice was enquiring of Minnie the whereabouts of the nearest Catholic church and Minnie, to her great embarrassment, did not know. The Rector's wife touched at her lips with rapid nervous movements of her tongue. She looked to Dora who was then just entering but decided to ask Mrs Bayliss, who was placing the chafing-dishes for breakfast on the oak serving table.

Mrs Bayliss wore a black dress and despite her girth looked a very puritan figure.

'The nearest Roman church to 'ere is in Westbury Street, I reckon. St Patrick's, isn't it?'

Mrs Bayliss' scepticism and suspicion were only barely controlled. They pulsed in her. They seemed to affect her very breathing. And they were directed not only at the two visitors but also at the Rector's wife, who was responsible for bringing such questionable and possibly subversive people into a Rectory of the Church of England. Mrs Bayliss was beginning to have grave doubts about the new Rector and his wife. Such people would not have been seen here in the Reverend Jeffcock's day!

The man and his wife hurried away, both of them looking constricted by their Sunday clothes. Dora was struck by the thought of them setting off from here to that small, towerless church. It was a squat church built by Pugin only some thirty years before and its red brick walls still shone with newness. It stood in an area of narrow, dirty streets and low row houses with pathetic vestiges of the classical orders at the windows and doorways. The area was one of the slums of the borough. The people who lived there were mostly Irish navvies and foundryhands and their families. There was much drunkenness and fighting in those streets where the children often ran about naked. Dora had never before known anyone who had gone to church in that place.

Before the Elgars returned, Dora herself crossed over Horse Fair to the ancient Collegiate Church that dominated the town. The rain still fell heavily; it left black patches on the deep red sandstone of the proud upsweeping tower. Today, as was her custom on a Sunday, Dora attended Holy Communion, helped to rehearse the choir and remained for Matins. On this day she was perfectly aware of how hard she had to struggle to keep her mind on her task.

By the time that she returned to the Rectory, the hour for luncheon was approaching. There were to be guests today: a visiting missionary, a churchwarden and his wife and the clergyman who had preached at the morning service. Dora found herself separated from the musician and his wife by almost the whole length of the table. Realising that her stepmother was responsible for arranging the places in this way, Dora felt an intense anger towards her. She could scarcely eat her food from upset.

When the slow meal had finally come to an end, the diners moved into the parlour and sat down. With determination and without the slightest thought for appearances Dora went and seated herself next to Elgar. He had the large armchair; the only seat for her was a low stool of black mahogany. This she took.

'I have wanted to speak to you all day,' she burst out, tremulously, almost like a child, her large blue eyes very bright.

'Well, here we are together again. What should we talk about?'

He spoke slowly and warily but there was a kindliness in his tone that sent a jet of happiness through her.

'What m . . . m . . . music are you writing at present?' she demanded with embarrassing abruptness. She was asserting her rights, desperately.

He was very much taken aback; to him such a question was a gross familiarity. Nevertheless, after a second or two, he answered.

'I am considering a composition to do with a very ancient Briton.' He regarded her gravely but there was a humorous movement to the deep-socketed eyes.

Dora remembered his refusal to talk to her about his work on that first occasion. This would be the test.

'Please tell me about it,' she continued even more insistently. Her candid face made a definite demand upon him.

He gave in. He spoke quickly and shyly, not looking her in the eye any more. He mumbled ineptly.

'It was my mother who suggested the idea, originally. One of the hills near Malvern, where we live, is called British Camp. There Caractacus fought the Romans. I think it should make a splendid subject for a cantata.'

'Who are the characters?' asked Dora delicately.

'There is the British king and his daughter Eigen and Orbin who is her betrothed. Orbin reads the omens for the king but he is overruled by the Druids. The king goes to fight the Romans.'

Dora caught the spirit of his words immediately.

'A magician who can read the omens better than the priests?'

she suggested, re-stating his words questioningly. Her eyes became alight with love for him. He was entrusting her with secrets.

'It *is* about reading signs . . . and reading the future,' he agreed, suddenly raising his head and looking at her directly.

Dora's body trembled with excitement.

'And it is about ancient truths,' he added, continuing to stare at her most pointedly. Then he looked away again, abruptly. There was a shiftiness in him now.

Dora could not think of words to say to him. She felt her inability like a pain. Perhaps he had said too much, more than she could receive. With all her sympathy she strained to understand him.

Through the window at the end of the room she could see the rain streaming down the factory backs. A few feet from her she could see the brightly polished black shoes of a rotund and prosperous Wolverhampton grocer. There was an unpleasant shine of perspiration on the man's florid face. He was listening with crudely feigned interest to one of the Rector's sonorous, mooning stories of the Orient. How false and pointless it all was! Dora longed for the musician's ancient truths in this dull, grey place with its ignominious gasometer and its ignominious grocers.

And yet what more could she say to the man now? How could this moment of closeness be protracted?

'Did the British win the battle?' she asked. Even as she spoke, she was aware of the silliness of what she said. The cheery question with its confidently implied answer made her sound like a schoolgirl. She blushed for the gaucheness of her tone.

But the man did not notice. 'No,' he answered, a trill of emotion throbbing into his voice. 'The Britons do not win and did not win. The Empire was victorious and rightly so.'

Dora was slightly shocked. For, though her family was High Church and High Tory her education had left her with the Whig liberal view of history that was so widely prevalent at the time.

'Why rightly?' she asked humbly. She was intrigued by the importance of this to him.

'Because the people of the hill forts must needs submit to the great ordering . . .'

He spoke with brisk confidence, almost pompously. His words

implied a sneer at any other view. There was in him this belief in orderings and in the need to subordinate himself. It made Dora uneasy. There followed a silence. She considered how they might return to that closeness that had briefly subsisted between them.

'Edward, Edward . . .' The deliberate voice came from the little group ranged beside the Rector. It was Alice Elgar, looking very much an old lady in the dull, rainy afternoon light.

'Did you tell Dora your good news? I imagine you did. Are you not happy for him, Dora?'

The man was uncomprehending. 'The march,' insisted his wife more loudly, as though irritated by his silliness. 'Edward's new march,' she said, calling across the room to Dora, 'the one he sent to Novello's, is to be played by massed bands at Sydenham, at the Crystal Palace. Massed bands. The concert is part of the celebrations of Her Majesty's Diamond Jubilee. And Edward's march is to be played. Indeed it is to be called the Imperial March . . . And there is even talk . . .' Alice attempted to lower her voice confidentially, but had to give up, when she realised that she could not now be heard across the room.

'There is even talk of playing it at the Royal Garden Party in the summer. Imagine!'

Dora could not help but be amused at the shabby little lady's struggle to converse with them from such a distance. But she was also touched by her joy and enthusiasm for her husband's achievements. For all her genteel propriety there was in Alice Elgar an unabashed, unselfconscious boastfulness on her husband's behalf. Dora respected it. But the man fell silent and looked away uneasily. Dora found herself wondering how an Imperial March played by massed bands could express the ancient truths. For some reason she kept thinking of the oompah bands she had heard in Bavaria. Even when they attempted something serious, she wanted, somewhere in herself, to laugh.

Alice Elgar talked on confidently from her distance. She listed other recent compositions, other performances and phrases that she remembered from occasional newspaper reviews. In her pride she was unaware that her voice was coming to dominate the room. She was also unaware of her husband; she spoke as though he were not there.

Dora realised that her opportunity to talk to the man was now gone. Not out of pleasure but out of pride the lady had made up her mind to join them and she was not to be ignored.

But Dora had unfinished business with the musician. Quickly she devised her own plan.

As the lady drew breath, Dora interrupted.

'I also have some news. I have a surprise w . . . w . . . which I quite forgot to tell you about yesterday.'

The man lifted his gaze from the floor. Dora noticed how far his thin fair hair was receding from the sides of his brow.

Alice faltered in her measured flow and, with obvious reluctance, fell silent.

'I am now the owner,' announced Dora, slowly, formally, drawing out the suspense, 'of a bicycle.'

As she delivered this announcement, Dora also thought of the unusual, daring, even perhaps rather shameless dress from the aunt in Tite Street, which had been delivered at the same time, some weeks before.

'A bicycle!' exclaimed the man with amused interest. He eyed Dora rapidly from head to foot as though imagining her upon it. His lower lip hung open slightly, under the thick heavy moustache.

'Can you ride it?' asked Alice from afar.

'Not very well at present. But I think that I am improving.'

'But, Dora, whatever do you wear, when you ride upon the bicycle? Knickerbockers and Rational Dress?' The last phrase came in a tinkling laugh. Alice was amused and a little scandalised that Dora should be a bicyclist and thus directly involved in the issue of proper dress and decency for lady riders which was such a prominent topic for discussion and debate in provincial England at that time.

'No, I wear a skirt, as for any other activity,' replied Dora with easy, lofty confidence. She was shocked to think how old and staid Alice Elgar was. Her notion of proper modesty was old-fashioned. Her maidenly simpering question came from an earlier generation.

The man continued to eye Dora keenly.

'May I enquire what led you to purchase the machine?' he asked.

'Oh, I did not buy it myself. It was sent to me as a gift by an aunt who lives in London.'

'Ah.'

'It is a very advanced machine, I believe, a Dursley Pedersen Royal.'

'Indeed!' There was a merry, affectionate interest in Elgar's eyes. He was young and his wife was old.

'Should you like to look at it?' asked Dora with well-managed innocence. But it was clear that this invitation had been the sole reason for introducing the subject in the first place.

Elgar glanced warily to left and right. 'Why yes . . . I would . . . I have never had an opportunity to inspect one of these safety machines at close quarters . . .'

He faltered, uncertain of what was socially possible.

'Should you like to come?' Dora asked Alice in a chilly voice, yet ridding the man of his difficulty.

The wife surveyed her husband and the girl for a moment or two thoughtfully.

'No, I think that I would prefer to sit a little longer. I fear that I do not greatly enjoy the crazes that we seem to have at the present time. Edward's pyrography is quite sufficient for me. But do take Edward and show him the bicycle, I know he will enjoy it. I shall be quite content to remain here. But Edward must promise not to attempt to ride it.'

Alice's words trailed off in a patronising trill of laughter. She watched them leave the parlour with evident satisfaction.

Dora led the way down the dark hallway into the yard at the rear of the Rectory. The rain still came down, though less heavily. It was fine, silvery, slanting rain now, and there was a greasy mist in the air.

The courtyard at the back looked as if it belonged to a farm rather than to a house in the middle of this smoky borough with its noisy iron industries. The area was laid with red brick through which grass and lichen grew. It had a Dutch look. On the left was a row of stables from which the Rector's two horses could be heard shifting their hooves. Directly in front was the high old wall of the kitchen garden. And to the right was the earth closet with its faint reek that mixed, in the wet air, with the smell of the horses' stale.

'It's in the far stall,' said Dora, pointing. 'Shall we run across or is the rain too heavy?'

'Not it!' exclaimed the man stoutly. 'We shall not come to hurt.'

They darted across the wet courtyard. He caught her hand as they ran. They came in under the pedimented eaves of the stable. He immediately let go her hand.

Dora turned to him. The rain had stuck a lock of fair hair to her face.

'Oh, what a relief to be out in the fresh air!' she exclaimed. 'Even in the rain. I was stifled in the p . . . p . . . parlour. All those dull people!'

Elgar smiled and then laughed, like a fellow conspirator or a lover. Panting slightly with his face close to hers, he was about to say something.

But then they saw Minnie tripping after them through the shining puddles. Dora laughed, for the lady who was carrying the Rector's large umbrella looked like some dark, plump mushroom on the move. At the same time the girl was vexed; she knew that her stepmother had come to play chaperone.

'Are you going to show Edward your safety bicycle, Dora dear?' twittered Minnie, being understanding and agreeable. 'I should so like to look at it again myself.'

With her busy, agitated goodwill she pulled open the door to the stable. The man and the girl exchanged a brief, rueful glance, then followed her in. But Dora was in no doubt about that continuing bond between them. They would be together later; she knew it for sure.

The bicycle was kept in its pale wooden packing-case from which one of the long sides had been removed. The machine was shorter than later models and had high handlebars. The tri-angular frame had a finish of burnished copper that gleamed in the dim light. The white felt handles also stood out brightly. There was a smell of felt and of the new rubber of the inflatable

95

tyres and of the oil that had dripped from the oil bath on the gear-case.

The three people regarded the bright new machine in silence for some time. They were each mesmerised by its lines, its engineering, its shininess and all that it promised of movement, travel, freedom.

'Would you like to give us a demonstration?' Elgar asked Dora gruffly. In front of other people he would generally adopt this bullying, avuncular tone towards her.

'Oh, Dora, do not! Edward, you shall not suggest such things! Goodness knows what might happen. Dora, I know, is as yet only a beginner. Perhaps later on when she is more proficient . . .'

But ignoring the older woman's agitation Dora calmly stepped forward, eased the cycle from its case and with a neat, pretty jump of a movement seated herself upon the saddle. Then, pulling herself along in a straddling fashion, with her black buckled shoes, she made her way out of the stable. Out in the yard she began to describe a circle with this ungainly, waddling form of propulsion.

But then, by the door to the kitchen garden, she increased her pace, lifted her feet and started to pedal. She completed almost half the circle, her black shoes and cream-stockinged ankles flicking out at slow, regular intervals from under her skirt.

Elgar watched her intently. He was utterly absorbed by the sight and oblivious of Minnie's cries of 'Oh, dear!' She had palpitations of anxiety as she watched. She twisted a lace handkerchief in her hand and feared every moment that some terrible accident would occur.

But Dora now slowed down, reverted to her treading motion, and at last brought the bicycle back to the very place where they were standing.

'There!' she breathed out triumphantly, carefully wiping the fine rain from her hair.

'May I congratulate you upon your skill?' said Elgar with a courtly bow.

'Would you like to try it?' asked Dora inclining the handle-bars towards him.

He was intrigued but said quietly, 'No, I fear I am too old.'

'Nonsense!' exclaimed Dora, completely forgetting her manners in her flash of irritation with him. 'You are not old.'

They eyed each other for a moment.

'How about you, mother, would you like to try?'

The lady stepped back hastily as though threatened by a large dog.

'Oh no, Dora. I dare not. I should be too frightened. Really, no. I cannot imagine how you have progressed so far in the short amount of time that you have had the instrument.'

'Mrs Shinton was kind enough to hold me up by the saddle some mornings . . .' began Dora.

'Mrs Shinton! Mrs Shinton!' Minnie Penny gazed around the walls of the yard, fearing that someone else might hear. 'But . . . but Mrs Shinton is surely most unreliable. Really, Dora, I think . . .'

'No, mother, Mrs Shinton assures me that she is quite capable, once she has caught her breath and eased her nerves with the proper mixture of stout and small beer. And I believe that to be true.'

Refusing to discuss the matter any further, Dora eased the machine into its wooden box. She took a duster and removed a few specks of drizzle from the mudguards.

She looked up to find the musician staring down at her with a curious smile. How he loved her wilfulness, her spirit, her independence! At this moment she sensed the strength of his interest in her and turned away with a quick, flirtatious smile.

Minnie was saying that it was drawing close to the time for the evening meal.

'Come along, shan't you now?' she kept saying, trying to shepherd them back inside the house. She considered things to be much more manageable inside the house than here outside.

Within, the guests of midday had departed and the members of the family were now retiring to wash and to change for dinner. Dora, slipping off her green serge dress in her bedroom, was afire with excitement from the activities and exchanges of the afternoon. She wondered what she might wear. She had not many choices. And the Elgars had seen most of what she had. The new dress was, of course, unthinkable, the one that had been delivered at the same time as the bicycle. She wondered when her aunt imagined she would be able to wear it. Dora would have liked to go to London to see how young ladies wore such dresses in society. Certainly she had not the confidence to wear it here tonight.

But she was determined to wear something different. There was an excitement in her that accelerated and intensified of its own volition, without her being able to control it. She was reminded of the occasions she had drunk wine.

From the ornate mid-Victorian chest Dora took out a dress which she had not worn for some time. She slipped it over her petticoat. It was of a light cream linen decorated with muslin and lace. There was some décolletage at the front and back. Deep, lace falls hung over the sleeves and there were butterfly bows on the shoulders. Dora examined her appearance carefully in the old pier-glass. Her own mother had bought her the dress some three or four years before for evening entertainments. Then it had appeared fashionable but not, finally, immodest; it was a young girl's dress. After some minutes of debate Dora resolved that she would wear it again tonight. For though it might not now be fashionable by London standards, it would still look most elegant here in Wolverhampton. And she so wanted to be done with all the sanctimonious dullness of that drawing room. She wished to do something that would help create that mood of glamour and magic which she and the musician craved.

She also put on a pair of black stockings embroidered up the front with dark red roses. And she wore her best shoes of soft white leather. At the last she combed up her hair. It shone golden in the weak guttering gaslight of her bedroom.

Excitedly she hurried down the stairs. There was a somewhat larger company for the evening meal than for luncheon. The new visitors were a solicitor, a clergyman, a prosperous outfitter, two aged widows and two of the vestrymen and their wives. They were all dressed in black and stood about uneasily, waiting to be summoned to the dining room. Minnie was talking to a fat, vulgarly dressed woman who blushed all the time. But when she caught sight of her stepdaughter, Minnie quickly excused herself.

'But Dora dear . . . you . . . you are in evening dress.'

'Oh, I thought I would, you know,' the girl replied offhandedly. She looked to the other end of the room and saw the musician and his wife had been left talking together, alone.

When the company proceeded to the dining room, Dora immediately went and sat down in the chair opposite to Elgar. She threw herself down on it so that her creamy skirts flew out. He smiled across the table at her and then winked.

Minnie hurried up, biting her lip. 'Dora . . .' she said, 'I had thought that Reverend . . .' But then she gave up. It would have been an embarrassment to the tall, sallow clergyman behind her to continue her attempt to enforce her seating plan. Dora was not to be tricked for a second time as she had been at midday. As her stepmother retreated, Dora gave Elgar a triumphant, emphatic nod and he smiled back with ill-concealed merriment in his face.

Throughout the meal Dora chattered away. She asked him about his recent compositions: the *Te Deum*, the *Benedictus*, *The Banner of St George*. She was indifferent to the mood in the rest of the room. Sometimes her voice could be heard ringing out whilst all the other stiff, sombre personages around that table were either mumbling or silent. Dora devoted herself to the man without a qualm and ignored the people seated to her right and left.

There was more than a hint of scandal in the room.

Mrs Bayliss, dressed in black from head to foot, bustling about serving the food and panting with all the exertion and worry of it, could hardly hold back her contempt for the musician. Every time she came near him, she quivered profoundly as though she could only just prevent herself from pouring out upon him her disgust and gall. An upstart she thought him, a nobody, a shabby little music master who had no more right to be waited on in this room than she herself. From what she had been told he came from nothing better than a family of piano-tuners who had kept a dirty little shop in the High Street in Worcester. And then his treatment of this foolish young girl without a mother! Mrs Bayliss caught a glimpse of his ugly, shameless eyes; she boiled inwardly with rage.

And the lights of that long dining room did make the man

look in some way shabby and unkempt. Earlier in the day his dress had looked that of a negligent country squire, although with a slightly histrionic touch in his primrose Ascot. But now the light fell in such a way as to show the many worn places in his coat and the dirt-spots on his trousers and sleeves. His shirt cuffs had been often darned and renewed. In this light he could have been taken for a poor clerk.

Dora was also displeased by her own dress. It was not that she feared at all to be conspicuous. But she was aware that this once very grand dress had faded in places, that there were brownish patches on the inside of the elbows and at the wrist and that generally the material drooped and lacked a necessary stiffness. Above all, as she sat there, talking lightly but increasingly falsely, she was strongly aware that this was a dress she had worn when very much a girl. Her choice had been a mistake. The dress made her look too young. It went with a former self. The dress was finished. She felt betrayed. She did not wish to appear younger than she was; she wanted to be older. Her poise was threatened.

Elgar sensed her disturbance and was affected by it. He began to feel remorse, physical remorse, that he desired her, that his eyes lingered so readily on the cream-coloured flesh of her neck, her bodice, her bosom and her finely downed shoulders. He remembered another woman, not his wife . . . At the end of the table he could see Alice conversing formally, politely, emptily to some indistinct personage. And he knew that this beautiful young girl could not be his. And that even if she were, there would have to be others. And he was more than forty years old. There was surely something foul and monstrous in him. And she was little more than a child, attempting to dress as a woman. How vulnerable and pathetic her youthfulness was in that dress! She could have been his daughter. He was sick with himself. Or at least he told himself he was. He also enjoyed his persistent desire.

He decided he should disengage himself from her. But he felt that in her present distress she was in some way throwing herself upon him, even as, actually, they merely sat among the others at that dark candlelit table finishing their meal. And he was aware that everyone else in the room was surreptitiously attending to them. The country fiddle teacher and the Rector's stately blonde daughter composed a scene that the visitors regarded covertly with a mixture of shock, bewilderment and fascination. Elgar wondered how he might subdue the highly audible exchanges between himself and the girl.

Mercifully, at the last, Minnie Penny's clear voice was heard suggesting that they all now move to the drawing room.

There was a scuffling of chairs being pushed back. The dark dresses could be heard trailing, slithering across the floor and through the hall.

In the drawing room Dora again stayed near to Elgar. Her brazenness was hectic. Minnie intervened.

'Edward, I wonder if I might call upon you to play for us? Most people here know and admire your work and congratulate you upon your recent successes. It would be a great honour if you would play for us.'

Minnie's voice was tremulous, lacking in confidence yet distinctly purposeful. It was up to her to take charge of the evening. Her husband gazed about as one of the local dignitaries chatted to him with much deference.

Gauchely mumbling in his thick moustache Elgar agreed to play. He went and sat at the piano. Dora went and sat near to him. She was quite unabashed.

'Play some of the music of Eigen and Orbin,' she said to him intimately. She wished to re-establish the mood of their conversation early that afternoon or of that other evening when his music had roused her so.

He gave her a quick reassuring glance of affection as he turned his eyes to the piano. But then to her surprise, he began to play a sequence of short, light, popular pieces. He played some of his own briefer compositions: *Sevillana*, the *Moorish Serenade*, *Shepherd Songs* and other trifles. He played some of the popular tunes of the moment by Paolo Tosti. These he performed with a slight mimicry of the Italian's expressive movement of the hands and shoulders. He was encouraged in this by seeing that his little audience was pleasantly amused.

They were also relieved. For politely and gently the pianist was managing to extricate himself from Dora's conspicuous monopoly of him. He addressed himself more to the whole room and not to Dora alone. From a distance, Minnie, much reassured, smiled to him encouragingly.

The man now started to play the short pieces that were to be known as the *Three Bavarian Dances*. Minnie relaxed all the more in her chair, happily remembering the Gluckstrasse, the Münchener Kindl, the Starnbergersee with the immense background of the Alps, the swimming in the green waters of the Isar, and all the talk about Wagner and Brahms . . .

Elgar was now playing the second of the two dances, the lullaby *Bei Hammersbach*.

And there, suddenly, was Dora, standing up, interrupting the concert and saying, so that she could be heard from one end of the room to the other, 'That's lovely . . . I sh . . . sh . . . should like to d . . . d . . . dance to that.'

The man stopped playing and was momentarily disconcerted. Then he said with polite uncertainty, 'I wish you would; I'll play it again.'

'No, wait a moment. Play something else. First I shall change my frock.'

Regally, energetically and full of herself, Dora walked from the room. She cared not at all for the disruption she had caused. She would not be subordinated to this dull, commonplace entertainment. She had her own idea.

There followed an episode which was talked about in Wolverhampton for many years afterwards.

Dora went up to her room, took off the dress that had so mithered her during the evening and took out the one which her aunt had sent her from London. While listening to the music, she had had the thought that this was a dress in which to do her dancing. One of Dora's interests was the expressive form of dancing which was becoming known in those years and that later would be associated with the names of Maud Allen and Dalcroze.

She unfolded the dress and draped it over her shoulders. The dress had on it a delicately coloured pattern of water-snakes and lily leaves. It was from a design by Mr Voysey who was a friend of her aunt's. The chief colours were heliotrope and eau-de-Nil. Wearing the dress, Dora felt, as she had felt before, both shocked and exhilarated. It was like a long Grecian tunic, very low and loose at the neck and even lower at the back. The short sleeves were so wide and loose that when she raised her arms the slightly matted blonde hair in her armpits was illuminated by the light.

Dora touched her body, wondering over the way in which the unusual primitive dress simultaneously concealed and revealed her form. The colour and the pattern and the art of it would surely surprise the people below. She hesitated. Perhaps she ought not to wear it. But no, she would not be bound by the dull social decorum of the place. She would infuse some life and interest into this banal, sugary entertainment.

She hurried down the stairs excitedly, her head held high. She could hear the man hesitantly playing one of the pieces he had played earlier. His playing sounded desultory and apprehensive. The girl smiled to herself, pleased at the sheer devilment of what she had done.

Dora strode into the long parlour. In the stronger light of this room the subtle, serpentine purples and greens of her dress could be seen rippling beguilingly as she walked. The people in the room looked to be sitting with a new rigidity in their chairs. There was utter disbelief and dismay on Minnie's face.

Confidently and with some haughtiness Dora made her way to the piano.

'Will you play that piece again, now, please, the lullaby?'

The man looked bemused. It was a moment or two before he could take his eyes from the dress with its unusual, decadent lines and colours.

'Oh yes,' he said. 'Yes, of course.' A hoarseness in his voice prevented his words from having the normality he sought.

He turned away to the piano and began playing the opening bars. In the music there could be heard the slow but pronounced lilt of a mountain stream in the evening light. Dora began slowly to move to this rhythm, undulating her body, trailing now her arms, now her legs. To and fro before the dark old panelling she wafted along, the lightly-coloured loose stuff of her dress flying out behind her. Her face looked white and rapt. She was given over to the music of the stream. Then the piano made the sound of some faint, distant horn. A-tiptoe, she listened, her head and body inclined forward so that the audience might have seen down the top of her loose dress.

Minnie flamed with embarrassment; the Rector looked on, only mildly interested, his head held to one side.

There came now a brighter mood into the music. This Dora met with a quick, pretty kicking movement. Her steps were abrupt but nevertheless graceful and they showed the tops of her white shoes and also several inches of the black stockings with their embroidered flowers.

Then the dance started to move towards its finish. The sound of the piano now rendered the slow extinguishing of the last twilight and the inexorable coming of the dark. Delicately, ever more delicately, Dora responded to this sensitive music, so that its motions could be seen and felt in her mouth and lips, her extended hands and her slim fingers and fingertips.

The sinuous lines of her dress, the flickering water-snakes and the movements of her slim body had completely captivated the audience. Temporarily they were beyond being shocked; they looked on fascinated.

On and on she went with her slow mimicry of the ending of the light. And then suddenly, with an almost comic plunk, the piano announced the very last moment of the light and of the composition and Dora fell to the floor in a bow, her dress spread on the floor about her looking like some large and exotic tropical plant.

There was a silence in the room. There was also some uncertainty and embarrassment about what would come next. But then slowly there came murmurs of appreciation.

'What artistry . . . a most charming surprise . . . an unexpected delight . . .'

Dora herself was intensely excited. She went over to the piano.

'Shall we repeat it?' said Dora to Elgar. The words were more a command than a question. He could not but obey.

He silenced the room with a ringing note. And the dance began again. On this second occasion Dora moved even more suavely. The man watched her closely. He made a few mistakes in his playing as he watched. Her dancing re-created a certain eeriness in his music of twilight. At the same time the dress and the lithe movements of her body within it gave him a new, rousing awareness of her womanhood. He was reminded of the way his senses had been startled when he first saw the Beardsley drawing of the dancer. He was much disturbed.

At the conclusion of this second dance there was more applause that was now confident and protracted. But Dora had no inclination to perform any longer. She rather disconcerted the audience by going and sitting by an old lady who chatted to her pleasantly, all the time staring and, in a motherly way, touching at the dress the girl wore.

The others in the room felt abandoned. The performance had ended as unexpectedly as it had begun. What was to happen now? Slowly they assembled into little groups and conversed.

After a while Mrs Bayliss brought in the tea service and started to pour. She was aghast at the sight of Dora reclining in a chair in her Chelsea dress.

Elgar was left alone at the piano. The confusion in his feelings increased. His mind and pulses raced.

Tomorrow, he knew, he and Alice would return to Malvern immediately after breakfast. There was little time to be lost. Abandoning all concern for the look of the thing he strode over to Dora and, stooping, spoke quickly and quietly to her.

'Promise that you will come to Malvern. And we will walk together to British Camp. You and I.' His eyes were shy and agitated.

She looked at him for a brief while before replying. She might have been assessing, savouring the effect she had had upon him.

But then came a rush of excitement to join with his.

'Yes,' she whispered swiftly, 'I will come.'

6

AT early breakfast on the following morning the Elgars made repeated invitations to the family at the Rectory to visit them in Worcestershire. Alice, Dora was surprised to notice, was the more urgent in this than her husband. Minnie was polite but non-committal. Yet when the guests had left, an idea occurred to her. The choirmen's outing from St Peter's was due to take place shortly and Malvern, she thought, would be an ideal destination. The men and boys could climb the hills and so on and Dora and herself could go to their friends' house.

Dora was dismayed. She had hoped to make the visit alone. But Minnie's mind was made up. She conferred with the choirmaster and wrote to her friends informing them of the date. Dora could have wept with frustration. She wanted to go alone. The man, she knew, expected it. Minnie's foolish arrangements were compelling her to break her promise.

The day of the outing was extremely hot. The sun shone brilliantly. As the two ladies emerged from the red brick Jacobean station at Malvern Link there was a strong smell of melting tar in the courtyard. In the newly built, raw streets of villas the heat was luminous and could actually be felt as something heavy. The two ladies with their parasols made their way through the estate slowly and perspiringly.

The house in which the Elgars lived was at the end of a cul-de-sac off a road named for the wife of the Prince of Wales. Dora was taken aback to see how very small it was, merely a semi-detached villa with just one bay, and a porch of creamy brick designed to give something of a Gothic effect. On the wooden gate was lettered the name 'Forli'.

The two visitors entered the small front garden and were surprised to see a brown bell-tent erected on the parched lawn. With blatant inquisitiveness Dora lifted the flap. Elgar was writing at a small camp table. He was in his shirt sleeves with his waistcoat unbuttoned. There was a large, dark patch of sweat under each armpit. The white shirt was soiled and the tent full of the smell of him.

'You can't come in here – it's private,' he snapped. There was more to this discourtesy than his usual gruffness. There was a suggestion of resentment and bitterness directed very much at her. He did not look up. She let the flap fall. She was hurt by this reception but guessed the reason for it.

Minnie looked at Dora sadly, sympathising uncomprehendingly with her in her rebuff. As they passed the front window and glanced into the small drawing room, Alice Elgar noticed them, jumped up from her chair and took the few paces into the hall to let them in. Small woman that she was, she appeared too large for this house.

Alice led her guests back to the drawing room and poured them glasses of Malvern water from an ornate crystal bottle that stood on an immense Indian serving table. It was surely meant for a much larger room and looked ludicrously out of place here, taking up the length of one whole wall. There were other large Indian pieces too, all in dark, richly patterned wood. There was a display cabinet with the most intricate filigree tracery and a table in the Mogul style with splayed-out legs. On this stood a mahogany vase full of scented Tonkin beans. And above, hanging from the dust-soiled wall, was a beautiful green silk bag with long tassels. It contained letters in graceful Hindu script and the bag had been used, Alice took pleasure in telling Dora, to send letters from one Indian prince to another. On the long table was a large, dark purplish bowl of what looked like Derbyshire

Blue John with nine oranges stacked up in it. The oranges were the brightest point in an otherwise sombre, gloomy room.

Dora felt ill at ease among all the old Indian furniture. She had never become fully accustomed to that in the Rectory. It made her feel very much the stranger. Alice and her stepmother both came from families once distinguished in the Indian Civil Service. This was one of the several bonds between them. Dora was the outsider.

Alice enquired with circumstantial, formal politeness about their journey from Wolverhampton. For all the slightly comic smallness of the room she presided with the air of a grand lady. She was far more sedate here in her own house.

Deliberately, punctiliously the slow voice proceeded with all the questions that social form required. Dora grew bored and the intense heat added to her discomfort.

Then Elgar entered. The energy of his step shook the little room and its contents. He had replaced his suit coat but still had a sweaty, disreputable look.

'I thought it would be time for luncheon, my dear.' He spoke deferentially.

'No. Ellen will come and announce when preparations are complete.' Alice Elgar answered him in a way that suggested a mere parenthesis in her pattern of exchanges with Minnie. And on she went.

Ignored, Elgar sat down. He regarded Dora frowningly. She knew he thought she had let him down. She tried to look away from him as though she were involved in the other ladies' conversation. But this was unconvincing, because she was sitting just a little too far away from them.

Glancing back at the man Dora sensed that his irritation had started to break up. Flippantly he took one of the oranges from the bowl, threw it in the air and caught it with a great smacking sound as its skin struck his soft white palm. He threw it up again and then again. Alice glanced over at him with irritation. He continued to throw the fruit up in the air, faster and faster.

And then he threw it at Dora!

The fruit flew high towards her chest. She was shocked. And

she only barely managed to reach up her hands and catch it. She held it in her lap regarding it with surprise. His action was a joke but there was also exasperation and malice in it. She threw the orange back gently. He hurled it right back at her, very hard. This time she put more energy into her return throw. Again the fruit came back to her, fast. Backward and forwards they flung it. Dora's gathering determination showed in her face. The man played the game indifferently, idly, for all the force that he put into it.

Then he reached for a second orange from the bowl and threw that too. The rhythm of their exchanges was immediately different as the two shiny oranges flew through the air. They threw them faster and harder. And faster still. What had begun casually was now beginning to look like a contest.

'Edward!' cried out Alice. 'Oh, Edward, do take care! A window could easily be broken. The furniture . . .'

At the sound of his wife's voice the man slowed down. Interest faded from his eyes. He appeared to fall into a reverie, remembering something from long ago. He continued his exchanges with Dora but slowly, desultorily. She felt forgotten and ignored. He looked tired. His mind was elsewhere.

The skivvy entered the room and announced shyly that their meal was ready to be served. The dining room at the rear of the house was also tiny. Dora found herself squashed tightly between the table and the wall. The meat was tough and dry and the vegetables were too wet. The diners ate slowly and without enjoyment. The heat in the room was almost palpable.

Yet, despite the limitations of her establishment, Alice still continued, calmly and grandly, to preside. She put a question to each guest in turn and she urged each of them to have more of this and more of that. She herself skilfully poured the coffee from a tall silver pot that seemed to reach close to the stained, cracked ceiling.

But she became vexed when her husband, who had long been silent, suddenly blurted out, 'Oh do let us go for a walk now. The heat in here is intolerable.'

And he, the furthest from the open window, did, indeed, look miserably uncomfortable. Drops of sweat fell down the side of his head and his neck into his collar. Others trickled from under his eyes into his moustache.

The two guests were plainly relieved by this proposal. And the man quickly helped them to extricate themselves from their chairs. They stood in the narrow hall, being kept waiting by Alice who was looking for her parasol with an indolence born of irritation.

Then they set off towards North Hill, that looked so high and apparently so near. Standing up from the flat land where the houses were, it looked like a mountain thrusting into the hot, deep blue sky. In that oppressive afternoon heat the bracken and gorse on the slopes shimmered swimmingly.

The group walked in two couples. Elgar had fallen in with Minnie and Alice walked with Dora. They moved slowly towards the hill through the raw new streets. One was just now being laid out and the villas were in the process of being built. Horses with long ribbons of bright perspiration on their flanks pulled the crude wooden carts that carried the shining red bricks. The labourers and the bricklayers called to each other in a way that sounded coarse and rough to the four walkers.

Elgar led them to a path that went up the hill. The climb quickly became steep. They all breathed harder. He climbed rapidly with a wiry energy. Imperceptibly Minnie fell behind and Dora took her place beside the musician. The curling path swung away to the eastern side of the hill.

'There's Bredon,' breathed Elgar, pointing away to a dark mass in the distance among the greens and yellows of the plain that stretched away from below them to the far horizon.

'And there's Edge Hill where there was the battle during the Civil War.'

He spoke to her in a kindly way now, like a father. On this hillside he was altogether different from what he had been in the hot, fetid little house. Dora thought he sounded sad, worried.

Dora wished to explain what had happened and to say something personal to him but was deterred by the sound of the two ladies toiling away behind them. She was alone with him and yet not alone. It was most frustrating.

As they climbed higher, it became cooler. There was even a slight breeze. Amidst the fern and the foxgloves there were sheep. They baaed and their bells clanked and made the man and the girl laugh. The older ladies had now fallen a good way behind.

'I am sorry that I could not come alone and for longer . . .' Dora murmured rapidly.

'But you will come again . . . soon.'

'Oh yes.'

'My wife will invite you. On your own. You will see. She will speak to you about it before you go.'

He gazed out over the wide eastern plain and said almost inaudibly, 'And you will dance for me again?'

'Yes, if you wish.'

'Do bring your dress.'

A voice that was petulant, though breathless, called to them from behind.

'Oh, Edward, Edward, do stop. Minnie and I are becoming quite exhausted . . . Look, there is a seat over there . . .'

The man and the girl waited for their companions to come up to them. The two older ladies looked pale; Alice was particularly haggard.

They all sat down on the seat. From this height they could look down into the streets of Great Malvern. They could see the horses and carriages moving and manoeuvring in the steep little cobbled thoroughfares. They could also see the roofs and gables of the houses, the green lawns and the darker green orchards and wooded gardens. At the centre of it all stood the large medieval priory with its perpendicular tower and its walls and tracery of yellow stone that to Dora's eye looked so much more bright and airy than the dark red stone of St Peter's in Wolverhampton. At the edges of this spa town there began the yellow and green fields divided by their dark hedgerows into a pattern of checks and oblongs that disappeared into the blurred bright distances of Warwickshire.

The four people were much taken with this view. They sat for some time gazing silently down. They started to recover from their fatigue.

Then Minnie grew anxious about the time it might take to return to the railway station to catch their train.

'We regret it so much that you are not able to remain with us longer,' said Alice hurriedly. And before Minnie could speak she continued, 'Edward and I have been wondering whether Dora might like to visit us again in the near future. A fortnight from tomorrow there is to be a very special event which we feel that she, as a fellow musician, might enjoy.'

Dora felt that she was being treated a child. She was being offered a treat or a surprise. There was that, and yet more than that to it.

'That is the day of the vestrymen's meeting. You would certainly have to come on your own,' said Minnie in a cautionary voice. She clearly expected the girl to decline.

'Oh, I shall be all right. Do not fret yourself,' replied Dora confidently.

Minnie looked disconcerted and reproving. Her head trembled with the upset. But she could think of nothing more to say. So in this tense fashion it was settled.

Then they all set off down the hill. At 'Forli' they found the Elgars' daughter Carice doing her homework in the hot dining room that still smelled of the luncheon food. She was a pale, shy, bridling girl whose manner suggested that she felt in the way in this house. Occasionally she glanced up and regarded her father with an unusual look of hope and fearfulness. Her parents' commitment to her father's career allowed little time for her. Dora was taken aback to see that the man had a daughter of this age. She would have liked to be kind to the girl. But Minnie was in a hurry to be gone.

They were in ample time to meet the train from Malvern. The choirmen from St Peter's appeared to have greatly enjoyed themselves on their day out. As the train drew into the station they hung out of the windows of the glistening brown and cream carriages and uttered many excited and jolly huzzas for their Rector's wife and daughter.

The following morning Dora asked her father for permission to go to Malvern again and for the money for her train fare. But the Reverend Penny, who was capable of such extended monologues on the intricacies of the Melanesian currency, was surprisingly abrupt when it came to the subject of sterling.

'I have no wish to prevent you from seeing your friends. But I do wonder if we are able to afford such frequent entertainments and luxuries. I do.'

It was after breakfast. He had come from celebrating the early morning communion and still wore his black cassock. He smiled at her in a kindly but impersonal way. She knew it to be his professional smile. She could have been anyone. She also knew from the very set of him that he would not allow her the money. He would persist in a pained doubtfulness that was the mask for an ugly, miserly obstinacy. Dora remembered other such occasions. At such times she felt a physical dislike for her father. And she was indignant. The living of St Peter's brought in £510 per annum and the house. And there was also her mother's money, which was really hers.

'Very well, father. I am sorry that I asked.' Dora's voice was low and tense. She turned abruptly and walked from the room. Minnie was shocked by this petulance.

But Dora was not to be denied her excursion. And within hours she had decided how she should manage to go.

She would travel to Malvern on her bicycle. In the weeks that had passed since she had first received the machine she had become quite expert at riding it. She was admittedly awed by the distance that she would have to cover but resolutely set this doubt aside. She would go. Her mind was made up.

When Minnie learned of the idea, she was aghast. Mrs Bayliss was even more horrified. While the afternoon tea was being served, these two ladies laboured unceasingly to dissuade the girl from her undertaking. The housekeeper was especially insistent. For all her bullying manner she was always genuinely concerned about the girl's welfare.

'And what about the weather, miss? If it rains? You can get on, yo'd be stuck. And the roads. How do you know the roads are good enough all that way? I'm not so sure as they are. And whatever should you do if you run into a tramp? A tramp under some hedge?'

The stout panting woman quivered with disgust and worry.

But Dora sipped her tea calmly and was not to be prevented. Nor did the Rector object when he came home. When told of the plan he merely nodded his head unthinkingly. The proposal had nothing of the same effect upon him that the request for money had had.

And so very early one morning a few days later Dora set off. She wore a straw hat and a linen jacket and skirt of a subdued yellow colour. Her portmanteau and oilskin were strapped to the rear of her cycle. Not that she thought that she would need the oilskin, for the weather continued fine and hot. The sky over the blast furnaces and factory stacks was a brilliant blazing blue.

An anxious little group stood by the gate to the Rectory garden to watch her mount and set off. There was her stepmother, Mrs Bayliss and Mrs Shinton. They all put a brave face on it but their worry could be heard in their calls of farewell and then in the very way they waved their handkerchiefs at the departing figure who set off, wobbling a little at first, towards North Street.

Turning left Dora pedalled slowly past the Old Mitre Inn, Pounds House and the Prebend House. The bright early morning sun illuminated the ivy on the walls of these two elegant houses of the early eighteenth century. The town streets were not yet busy. Dora was excited at the thought of the day's adventure before her. She freewheeled across the central square and moved, ever more confidently, past the Star and Garter Hotel with its high narrow gables and the 'Victoria Drapery and Supply Stores' whose proprietor, Mr James Beattie, was at this very moment supervising the lowering of the sunblinds over the windows of his shop. He made a very formal bow to the Rector's daughter, who could only manage to remove a hand from the handlebars for one brief flick of a wave. The portly businessman gazed after her in some surprise.

She gathered speed as she proceeded down the slope of this street past the shops and the fine old town houses. She came into a poorer quarter with many squalid-looking little taverns. Then she was going past the high factories built a century before. The clamour was upsetting, deafening to her. Factory hands lounging by the blackened Doric columns of the gate watched her curiously as she hastened past. Then she was among the cots of the nailers. Their dwellings and workshops, all of old maroon brick, stood at inexplicable angles under trees by little streams. And then as these buildings came to an end she found herself at last out in the clean quiet countryside among the gently glowing fields. She was on the high road to Worcester.

Dora was exhilarated. She pedalled away increasing her speed. She felt that she could go on like this for ever. She rejoiced in her freedom. She felt like singing.

She glided past large lurching wagons. Once she made the horses rear up. The older drivers turned and raised their hats to her, their respect mixed with puzzlement. The younger men regarded her more blatantly and cheekily. A girl on a cycle was no part of the forms and traditions of deference that they knew. Many had never seen a bicyclist before.

She came into the green undulating landscape of Worcestershire. There came a fork in the narrow cobbled road that ran between the luxuriant hedgerows. The left would have taken her into Stourbridge with all its glass-blowing kilns. Dora remembered the Bishop telling her how the young Dr Johnson had walked there from Lichfield to visit his cousin Cornelius Ford. But she would go to the right down a narrow wooded highway that eventually brought her into Kidderminster. She cycled straight through the centre, past the town hall and the statue of Sir Rowland Hill. Here there were a few other lady cyclists moving slowly and demurely from shop to shop. They looked with wonder and respect after the now slightly dishevelled girl who was obviously a cyclist of great distances.

The air here was troubled with the deep rumble of the steam looms in the carpet factories. There was the heavy, incessant rhythm of thud and clank and hum, thud and clank and hum . . . She was relieved when she was beyond the town and back among the fields and pastures and woods.

But now she was beginning to feel afraid. There was a tiredness in her feet and thighs that made them feel light and disjointed. Twice she had to stop and sit on a milestone to restore herself. She looked with some dismay on the decreasing but still considerable number of miles yet to cover. In all, her journey to Malvern would amount to more than forty miles.

The day was now hot and Dora perspired heavily at her brow, her waist and under her arms. A fear that she had attempted more than she could achieve grew upon her.

With legs quivering she pedalled slowly into the village of Ombersley. It was a handsome place, its main street composed almost entirely of black and white buildings. It was like entering the past.

The King's Arms was a large inn with three gables of half-timbering. It was of Queen Elizabeth's time or even earlier. It had two low wooden doors that opened straight on to the village street. A stout figure of a man in a smock lounging by the casement took off his cap as Dora approached.

'Good day to you, miss.' For all his sleeply slothful calm he was astounded to see this beautiful fair-haired girl come pedalling through Ombersley. He studied her most carefully. He had never seen a bicycle before, though he had heard of the invention. It had never occurred to him that a woman, a lady, might ride one.

'Good day.' Dora tried to summon the proper pleasantness.

'Bit 'ot, eh?' He motioned with his hand at the warm, deserted village street.

'Yes, it is rather.'

'Might I invite you to step inside and have a drink? We've ale, small beer, cordial, wine . . . dandelion and burdock, if you like . . . '

He had a kind red face. He was courteous and fatherly. Shakily Dora dropped a foot to the ground and stopped and considered. Her legs trembled visibly. The man's voice had a strong Worcestershire burr. She was far from Wolverhampton now. And she felt so very weary. But for a lady to go into a public house alone!

'I have brought some sandwiches. Might I eat th . . . th . . . them inside?'

'Of course you might, if that is your desire. Please to get down and come inside and rest yourself from the sun.'

Stiffly Dora dropped from the Dursley Pedersen which the man took from her. He studied it with the closest interest as he carried it down the two steps that led into the front room of the

116

inn. He was a stout, well-fed man and could have been a farmer as well as an innkeeper.

Inside it was dark and cool. There were ancient benches and settles around the walls and the low plaster ceiling was of the time of King James I, with mouldings of a rose and a mermaid.

'I'll just fetch my wife,' said the landlord with a simple kindly delicacy. He added, 'And what should you like to drink?'

'I should like to have some of the dandelion and burdock, if you please,' replied Dora.

The man's footsteps could be heard slowly descending stone steps. Dora sat back and rested. How she savoured the quiet gloom and coolness of this room!

The man returned with a stone bottle of dandelion and burdock in his hand. He was followed by his wife, a thin, bony-faced woman in a dark dress who hung back, surveying Dora, like one come to see a wonder.

The innkeeper poured the drink into a pewter tankard and Dora drank it up. It was profoundly and delicately cool to her mouth. It was an ecstasy to drink it. She could not recall drinking anything in her life before that refreshed her as this did. It was a restorative that drove all the heat and weariness out of her.

The innkeeper's wife watched Dora's every movement. The sudden appearance in the village of this handsome girl in her suit of such an elegant shade of yellow was to this countrywoman like something out of a fairy tale.

'And how far have you come, miss?' she enquired after a while, her curiosity overcoming both her diffidence and her sense of the respect due to a lady.

When Dora told her, the woman gasped, opening her toothless mouth and turning to her husband in surprise and alarm.

'And 'ow far be ye goin'?'

The reply produced similar expressions of shock. The girl and her shiny bicycle were almost unbelievable.

Dora enjoyed the admiration that accompanied their surprise and their anxiety. Her confidence and her energy were becoming restored.

When the time came to set off again, she mounted her cycle

with enthusiasm. She felt much encouraged by the friendly deferential farewells of the two older people.

Off she went, back into the rolling green countryside. She rode a little more slowly now. But she was calm and content. For much of the way the only sound was the distant hum of bees. She pedalled away with a sense of happiness, achievement and freedom. Twenty years on, amidst all the bitterness and pain of that later time, she would remember the pleasure of her first journey to Malvern on that warm bright summer day when Lord Salisbury was still Prime Minister and the old Queen still reigned.

Dora was much reassured when she saw the tower of Worcester Cathedral appear in the distance. As she pedalled slowly through the streets of the county town she was struck by how much elegance there was here compared with Wolverhampton. There were ladies in French hats in the Foregate, glossy prosperous clergymen in the area near the cathedral and many a handsome horse and carriage that she had to negotiate her way past with care.

She crossed the bridge over the Severn with another thrill of excitement. This was one more proud occasion in her career as a lone traveller. She thought of how it would be to return to Wolverhampton and relate her travels to the Danks. This excitement sustained her as she moved on into the countryside again down the narrow bumpy road that led to Powick. But as she moved past the large church in that village her legs were beginning to ache again in a disconcertingly shivering way. She encouraged herself with the thought that she was now close to her destination. And in less than an hour she could see the harsh red brick of the villas standing up from the rich green of the surrounding fields. North Hill was large and hazy in the heavy warm air of the late afternoon.

Wobbling precariously, unable to prevent her legs from shaking, she turned down Alexandra Road and entered the cul-de-sac that led to 'Forli'. She had done the forty miles! She dropped from her bicycle with a feeling of relief and pride. Her skirt stuck to her bottom and her face was soiled with black lines of perspiration. For all the fairness of her colouring, there was now a certain swarthiness to Dora's appearance, somewhat like that of a gypsy. She tried, without much success, to tidy her hair before passing through the garden gate.

She was taken aback to see, in front of the porch of the house, three fashionably dressed ladies. They also turned in some surprise when they saw her slowly wheeling her cycle up the path. The tallest of the three, who wore a long fitting green pelisse with a high collar and fancy revers, raised a lorgnette to inspect the newcomer. There was an awkward moment. Then fortunately Alice Elgar appeared behind the three from inside the house.

'Dora dear, how happy I am to see you . . . And to have bicycled such a distance . . . We feared it might be too much . . . How brave of you!' But the excitement and admiration were quite contained within the lethargic deliberateness of her speech. Always there was a suggestion of calculation.

Decorum also required that Dora's achievement be set aside. Alice continued, 'These ladies are certain officers of the Worcestershire Philharmonic Society. May I introduce Miss Burley.'

This was she of the lorgnette, a lady in early middle age with a large head, a big nose and nervous, uneasy eyes.

'Miss Norbury.' A more countryfied person this, with a plain dark skirt and a blouse with a Regency stripe. Her features were small and well-formed, her expression kindly.

'And Miss Fitton.' The young girl was the closest to Dora in age. She was hoydenish with a long face and a large, strong jaw. But there was a merry vitality in her eyes. She had a shock of fine chestnut hair. As she was introduced to the girl, Dora experienced a pang of alarm and suspicion.

Dubiously the three ladies shook Dora's moist, sweat-grimed hand. Then they proceeded with their departure and were driven away in a smart pony and trap.

'Oh dear, dear!' exclaimed Alice in her ponderous contralto as she watched them go. 'Now you will guess what we had in store for you. The surprise is spoiled. How very unlucky. But then, I suppose that you would have guessed very quickly. They came to decide on the last few details to do with the concert. It will take place tomorrow, you know.'

'Ah yes.' Dora was still in the dark but thought it impolite to enquire further at present. Alice had a good deal on her mind. She said no more of Dora's journey. The flesh around her eyes was moist and wrinkled. She was beginning to look very much an old lady.

Grandly Alice summoned the skivvy to show Dora up to her room. It was a tiny place at the top of the house under the rafters. In the room below a violin lesson was in progress. There was much uncertain bowing, much irritable monosyllabic comment from the man and little pecking cries of apology from the young lady pupil.

Dora took off her top clothes and stood there in her white chemise. Pleasurably she poured the cold water from the heavy porcelain pitcher into the wash-bowl and washed her face and neck and arms and the soft creamy flesh of her shoulders. She took off her cotton stockings and white garters and washed her feet and legs and thighs. What a refreshment and relief it was to do that! Then from her portmanteau she took the snake dress and put it on. She had promised to do her dance again and so must dress for it. She let down her light brown hair and brushed it up again into a tight topknot. With a thrill of daring she put the slightest of touches of rouge on her cheeks which, she thought, looked pale from her exertions. Then with her knees and ankles still quivering, she went downstairs.

Alice, she was surprised to discover, was in formal attire. She wore an evening gown of light blue velvet that was noticeably worn at the elbows and seat. The two waited in the small parlour chatting slowly. Dora could feel exhaustion seeping through her body. She was upset that she might be too tired to enjoy her first evening here. Elgar appeared at last. He also was in evening dress. He offered her his arm with all due formality and 'took her in' to dinner. The ceremoniousness belonged more to a mansion than to this small suburban villa. Dora thought that she might have laughed, if she had felt less tired. But the Elgars saw nothing incongruous.

The dull food was eaten in silence. Elgar appeared distracted. Dora was hurt. She had come all this way, to fulfil her promise to him, and now he took no interest. This moodiness made her increasingly miserable; she felt a lump in her throat. He had never been like this to her before.

But as they finished their coffee, he roused himself from his thoughts. He turned to her and said, 'Shall we do the dance?'

The voice was that of the gruff patronising elder. An impulse of petulance in Dora almost led her to refuse. But then how could she, sitting there all prepared in her snake dress? She agreed.

'What japes!' he said perfunctorily.

In the little parlour to which they now returned there was no piano. He took out a violin from a cupboard and would accompany her on that. He struck up the first few notes of the Hammersbach lullaby. Dora began to dance. But her limbs were stiff and quivering. She could not achieve the necessary undulations of the dance. Her legs and arms were tired and unsupple. Her movements were heavy and unresponsive to the music. The smallness of the room also confined her. She slipped slightly. Her balance was altogether wrong. Then she almost fell and the violinist had to hold on to the note, waiting for her. It had a comic effect. The man grinned. And as they proceeded, the dance grew less serious. It had become a parody of her dance. Even Alice was smiling. The dance had become a family joke. Dora herself was amused as she clumped, clumped about the room, unable to keep time, but she was also close to tears. Something very precious had been lost.

When the dance was finished Alice asked if Dora were not very tired. Would she not wish to retire early after so exhausting a day. Edward too should have his rest before tomorrow's concert. Dora weakly accepted the suggestion and went upstairs. As she lay down in bed, she found herself weeping. And as the tears continued to flow, she fell into a deep sleep.

But she awoke the following morning her spirits fully restored. When she went down to breakfast, she found that Elgar had already taken the train to Worcester. He would attend on some pupils during the morning. The two ladies would join him there for the concert in the afternoon.

'We do hope that you will enjoy what you hear,' said Alice in a slow voice that suggested that she had every confidence that Dora would. 'Edward was so anxious for his orchestra to be a surprise for you. You didn't know that he was organising one, did you? I am sure that it will be of help to him in obtaining his proper recognition.'

The older woman buttered her toast in a lingering, scrupulous fashion that could, Dora thought, become unbearably irritating very quickly.

After breakfast the two ladies walked leisurely in the gentle morning heat into Malvern. How beautiful it was, Dora thought. On their left and below them, a golden shimmering plain and on their right the dark mass of the hills. And after Wolverhampton, how quiet! Not for a long while had she heard so many birds sing.

The ladies continued past the long bright façade of the Foley Arms Hotel and into the centre of the little spa town. Alice wished to go to a milliner's in Belle Vue Terrace. In the shop she seated herself on a red plush chair, ordered another to be brought for Dora and then, with pleasant condescension, allowed herself to be served. Dora was embarrassed to see that at the last the visit amounted to only a few coppers' worth of business. Yet the ladies of the shop bade them good day most deferentially. On their way home Alice would stop frequently to bow to some elegant lady or gentleman who, either on foot or in a small carriage, formed part of the lively procession to and from the spa.

After a cold luncheon in the semi-detached house in the northern suburb of the town, the two ladies set off to the nearby railway station and travelled the few miles into Worcester.

The concert was to take place in the Guildhall, a large, handsome building of Queen Anne's time with Corinthian pilasters, a balustrade decorated with statues and an enormous pediment containing a baroque trophy. Alice and Dora found themselves part of a quickly moving queue of people filing through the grand doors and up the stairs leading to the assembly room. It was very full. They had only a few minutes to wait before the orchestra entered.

Dora was indeed surprised! For the great majority of the performers were not men but ladies. There must have been thirty or forty of them. They wore dark skirts and white blouses, often with gigot sleeves and frills at the front. Dora recognised the three ladies to whom she had been introduced yesterday. Isobel Fitton, she noticed, was tuning her viola with the greatest of care.

Of the few men in the orchestra the drummer was to Dora the most remarkable. He was an unusually ugly man, small and stout with coarse brown hair clipped very short on his large head. He was myopic and wore thick bottle-glass spectacles. Dora had the impression that he was eyeing her. Perhaps it was the effect of his glasses. But it made her feel uncomfortable.

Then Elgar appeared, hastening up on to the platform from a side door. He reached the desk before the applause began. Dora watched closely how he held his back in a tense curve, holding himself away from the audience. When he turned to bow, his eyes looked away and upwards. There was in him some nervous insistence that there should be no flow between him and the audience. He held himself like one who had no right to be there.

Then, with a sudden relaxation, he turned to his orchestra and swung into the music. Of the pieces performed that afternoon Dora would recall music from *Tannhäuser*, Mackenzie's *Dream of Jubal* and Schubert's *Fifth Symphony*. She thought she noticed a particular attention on Elgar's part to Isobel Fitton, who played with tense concentration as though what was demanded was beyond her powers.

The ugly drummer made his drums resound through the hall. There was no doubt that he was a highly competent, perhaps even a professional musician. He attended to the conductor with great care. The squat, gross form was aquiver with attention to the baton and to the music. And there was such a subtle rhythm and reverberation in his drums whenever they sounded! The girl had never known such dedication in a performer. Now Dora stared at him.

But chiefly it was from the ladies that the music came. How hard and carefully and obediently they worked for their conductor! They were mostly string players. And they bowed and bowed away for him, their white arms swinging lustily to and fro across their white bosoms. The nervousness of Rosa Burley was now completely dissipated. Looking up at Elgar with wide, adoring eyes, she sawed away, whack, whack, whack. A lock of hair hung down; she was abandoned to the music.

The playing was not always smooth and fluent. But there was a genuine passion and enthusiasm in it that infected the audience. When the Schubert concluded, there was an immediate crash of admiring applause. The audience rose and the clapping grew in intensity. Shyly, evasively, as if he had his eyes shut, Elgar doubled up in a bow.

'Let us slip out now, Dora dear,' whispered Alice, urgently, 'and see if we may assist Miss Hyde with the tea.'

Without further explanation she hastened away down the aisle, Dora following. Hurrying through the older quarter of the city Alice chattered on, her words coming more rapidly than usual.

'Well it was a success, wasn't it? A fine début! Definitely a success, definitely. What a fine reception at the last! Now was perhaps just a little ragged at times . . . but definitely a success, definitely. What a fine reception at the last! Now Edward has a place where he may be certain his work will be performed . . . And that of others too, of course, naturally. And you never know what it might lead to, do you? There were gentlemen present from the newspapers. Did you see? And at least one from London. No, you never know, do you?'

Ostensibly Alice was speaking to Dora but in reality she was talking to herself. There was a peculiar gurgle of excitement in the usually placid voice.

'So what do you think of our little surprise, Dora dear? Is not our Philharmonic Society impressive? Edward's very own orchestra. His orchy.'

On and on went the little lady without ever pausing for an answer.

Dora, as she hastened along beside her excited companion, was content to remain silent, though she was uneasy at being taken, apparently, to a tea party to which she had not actually been invited.

They left Foregate Street and entered one of the finest streets of old Worcester. On either hand there were large, well-kept Georgian houses. Alice entered a porch with large and immaculately white, Tuscan columns. She lifted the bright, brass door-knocker respectfully. They were admitted by a maid in white apron and cap. She led them up thickly carpeted stairs. On the first floor another smart, uniformed maid took Alice's mantle and led them into the large room where tea was to be served.

Dora had the impression of much light and spaciousness in the room. Four large, high windows looked out on to the cobbled street below. The furniture was all of light wood, oak and walnut. Many of the chairs were of the same period as the house. The sconces and candle holders were silver.

By a long table covered with a thick white cloth and bearing plates of sandwiches and a tea urn stood a handsome lady in early middle age.

'Ah, Mrs Elgar,' she cried. 'I was able to precede you then. I have only now put down my violin in the music room. Do allow me to pour you some tea.'

'Dora dear,' said Alice, 'I should like to introduce you to our most kind hostess, Miss Hyde.'

Dora shook hands. She felt shy, being here without an invitation. The lady had a long handsome face with a certain grave and intelligent cast to it. Hers was an interesting beauty, even though at this very moment in her life youthfulness was on the verge of leaving her. It occurred to Dora that many of the ladies in the Worcestershire Philharmonic Orchestra were like this. Even now they were entering the room in little groups for their tea. They looked neither young nor old. Dora felt a sadness for Miss Hyde and her characterful beauty. She could so easily imagine her as once a bride and now a mother.

The room was filling up rapidly. Alice and Dora left their hostess to her tasks. Alice introduced her young companion to a succession of people. Dora felt dismayed to discover how very large Elgar's circle of acquaintances was. She now realised how foolish she had been to think that he could have been so single-mindedly concerned with her as she with him.

The person she liked the most among those she met was a Mr Griffith, a tall gangling man in a suit of heavy green worsted that made him look uncomfortably hot. His dark hair was parted in the middle and slicked down. The mouth and chin under the moustache were a little weak. His eyes gazed out unsteadily and dependently upon Dora. He made an awkward lunging movement with his arm in order to shake her hand and somehow contrived to knock a number of cups and saucers from the table to the carpet. There was a clatter and a crash and everyone in the now crowded room turned to look at them.

'Oh dear,' said Mr Griffith, looking down helplessly and ineffectively at the cups, at least two of which had been broken. Then with a curious swimming motion of his arms and bumping heavily against a large lady standing nearby he dropped to his knees and began gathering up the pieces.

Alice shook her head. 'What a shame! Poor Mr Griffith has such a tendency to become involved in accidents. Edward rails him a great deal about it. But he is such a staunch friend.'

The large, ungainly man grunted away on the floor. Everyone now made a point of not looking at what had happened. Glancing about the room Dora recognised Isobel Fitton and Rosa Burley, whom she now knew to be the headmistress of the local public school for girls, The Mount. Carice Elgar was one of her pupils. With Rosa Burley now were two very expensively dressed girls. Each wore a blouse and a bolero and a skirt that fitted close to the figure and flared out below. The mauves and light greens that they wore looked most fashionable. But the overall effect was spoiled because both girls were broad in the hips and very red-faced. They were, Alice whispered to Dora, the Misses Tetley, a wealthy brewer's daughters from Leeds. They were two of Rosa Burley's senior pupils and well known for their good nature.

There was a commotion at the door. It was Elgar himself, in the company of the plump dwarf of a drummer, who, as he came into the room, looked to have a dark complexion, as though he were Jewish or perhaps Oriental. And he spoke German.

'Ach, Gnädigste, es freut mich so sehr Sie wiederzusehen.'

With his heavy, yellow, fleshy hand he would lift up a lady's hand and kiss it. There was something vulgar and familiar in the gesture. For though he was to some extent pleasantly clownish in his manner, there was a suggestion of bullying and domineering too. There was an ugly glint to the thick spectacles. Already he had made himself the centre of attention in the room. He reached up and put an arm around Elgar's shoulder commendingly.

'Und was denken Sie jetzt von unserem Orpheus. Ach wie herrlich begabt, als Dirigent so wie als Komponist!'

Rosa Burley, to whom these words had been addressed, turned away, her uneasy eyes flickering with unconcealed distaste. The boisterous little man with his loud complacent voice had utterly disrupted the decorum of this English house. All the notions of form, taste, tone and quiet that had been adhered to prior to his entry were now set aside. Covertly there was a shocked attention to him.

But Elgar seemed not at all offended by his loud companion. Rather he was amused and entertained. And this indulgence of the drummer had an effect on the musician himself. For despite the dignity of his evening dress with white bow-tie and silk lapels, and the gardenia in his buttonhole, he was, in the company of this little man, made to look rakish and common. There was a coarse look to his mouth and occlusion as he laughed at the dwarf's jokes and familiarities.

The pair of them approached Mr Griffith, who still looked disconcerted and shamefaced from his recent accident.

'Lieber Herr Maler,' exclaimed the drummer, 'Und was für ein schönes Ührchen.' He squinted mockingly through his thick glasses. Mr Griffith peered down at the man vacantly. Then he made a motion of the hand towards his waistcoat pocket. An expression of foolish surprise came over the hang-dog face. He felt from pocket to pocket ever more rapidly. Now he was horrified; his watch was lost.

The German lifted his fat beringed hands into the air and rubbed them together slowly as though washing them. Gradually from between his soft, thick thumbs there appeared a large gold watch.

Some of the onlookers in the room laughed; others cried out. Despite the tacit disdain for the disreputable little man they were entertained.

'Oh du Bösewicht, Onkel Klingsor,' cried Elgar rocking back on his heels with a cackle of laughter. Dora was surprised to see how fluently the German came to him. Once again he was a different person from what she knew.

The drummer threw the golden sphere high into the air. It almost hit the ceiling, spinning prettily all the time. Mr Griffith watched it open-mouthed and mystified. People laughed again.

'Onkel Klingsor?' Dora repeated the phrase in a murmur to Alice. The girl was intrigued.

'That, of course, is not his real name,' replied Alice, clearly vexed and embarrassed by the incident. 'It is Herr Ettling. He is a travelling representative for a firm of Rhenish wine merchants. He resides in Malvern.'

Alice struggled to amend her tone of apology. 'He is an excellent timpanist, as you will have heard this afternoon. Edward regards him very highly as a performer.'

But the two men were upon them. Herr Ettling now spoke English.

'Good afternoon, Mrs Elgar, my compliments.'

His attitude resembled that of a dog begging. He had to reach up slightly to take her hand. His own hand, Dora noticed, was heavily tufted with black hair on the back. His lips were on Alice's hand an instant longer than was necessary. The gesture was part of the continuing comedy that he created. Alice, try as she might, could not prevent herself from stiffening from the repugnancy she felt. She loathed being treated in this vulgar way by this man and especially in front of some of the very best society of Worcester. But her husband was greatly entertained. He opened his mouth widely, showing his uneven, discoloured teeth. There was a malicious amusement at his wife's discomfiture. Together the two men were social *banditti*, roisterers, conspiring to mock those around them.

The drummer next turned his attentions to Dora. Histrionically he took a pace backwards as though dazzled by her.

'Aber, Tet, Tet, wer ist denn diese Schönheit?'

The slow effusive exclamation was not altogether parody. But Dora herself was most taken by the dwarf's use of the familiar form of the man's name. She had never heard of such a thing before.

'May I introduce Miss Dora Penny. Miss Dora, Herr Ettling,' said Elgar, suddenly brisk.

'Dora, Dora,' echoed Ettling dwelling on the first vowel of her name and pronouncing it lingeringly in the German phonetic fashion. The large weak eyes stared attentively and insolently out of the ugly thick glasses.

'Miss Dora is a very good friend of mine,' said Elgar, stressing the first word correctly. And he took the man by the arm and turned him away towards someone else. Very definitely Elgar would not permit Dora to be subordinated to the man's insistent, wicked jocularity.

Miss Hyde came across the room in her poised, young matronly way.

'Mr Elgar,' she said, 'Father is able to be with us and I should very much like you to meet him.'

'But of course.' With this lady his voice became shy and throaty again. Herr Ettling followed on behind them.

Miss Hyde led Elgar through the groups of tea drinkers to a tall, elderly and very gentlemanly figure standing by the door. Mr Hyde, one of the most prominent solicitors in Worcester, was dressed in black in the style of thirty or forty years before. He wore a morning-coat that sloped away in front to broad tails behind. The edges of the coat were bound and there were flapped pockets at the waist. He wore peg top trousers, a dark silk waistcoat and a wine-coloured cravat. He had a mass of grey hair and a strong face which, for all its character and dignity, had a certain gentlemanly innocence to it.

He shook hands with Elgar with an easy, regal pleasantness. Herr Ettling was presented next. Perhaps because he was over-excited himself, the German overestimated the old gentleman's ease and amiability. Whirling his hands rapidly near to Mr Hyde's portly midriff, the conjuror produced an embossed leather cigar-case. Bowing, Herr Ettling displayed the object to those standing nearby. Only two or three approved or applauded. Most were disagreeably shocked. Everyone regarded Mr Hyde, who continued to look out upon the room as though nothing had happened. Herr Ettling laughed to himself and then returned the expensive case to its owner with a fulsome, obsequious bow.

Elgar smiled upon the episode in an indulgent way. But the trick had nevertheless created a tension in the room. Rosa Burley was red in the face from indignation. It was like a fever in her. Others responded similarly. One of the cathedral canons, a tall stooping figure dressed entirely in black, ostentatiously turned his back on Ettling and Elgar as these two chatted on uneasily, stridently. How apart the two of them were, suddenly, from the society of that elegant room. The two men were fleshy, loud and not confident of their manners. They could have been actors come from the theatre or even the music-hall.

The general mood of embarrassment increased when it was discovered that Mr Hyde no longer had his wallet. Politely, Miss Hyde came up to the two men and asked Herr Ettling if the removal of her father's wallet had been part of his most enter-taining act of conjuring.

'I haff not taken the vollet,' squealed the little man defensively. He was frightened and resentful.

The canon, on the other side, could be heard murmuring sanctimoniously about the incident. Mr Hyde looked dazed. His daughter questioned him anxiously. Elgar continued to stand by his friend, talking to him with a forced unconcern.

Half an hour later it was discovered that Mr Hyde had left his wallet in the pocket of another jacket. There was much relief. But the feelings of tension and distaste that had developed in that room did not altogether subside.

At last Alice felt able to suggest that they set off to the station. Beneath her customary lethargic placidity, humiliation simmered. They received their coats at the door and were joined by the others who were returning to Malvern, Rosa Burley, Mr Griffith, Isobel Fitton and the Misses Tetley. They would travel to-gether.

Out in the street Elgar was at once the leader of the little band.

'What a blessed relief to be out in the fresh air again!' he exclaimed.

Herr Ettling and Mr Griffith on either side of him murmured their agreement.

'And away from all those fizgigs!'

'Edward! How can you!' Alice's voice was unusually loud. There was indignation and long nurtured anger in it.

'Those people have been most kind and generous to us . . . you . . .' She could not express herself. She glanced along the line of ladies that walked with her. They all appeared not to have heard the exchange. The three men moved on ahead. Only Mr Griffith, lumbering on with his flat-footed strides, occasionally turned and expressed uneasiness at forsaking the ladies in this way.

The streets of the city were quiet in the early evening. A beautiful orange light glowed on the windows and pediments of the handsome old house fronts.

They arrived at Foregate station and all entered an empty compartment of a local train. The party sat in tense silence waiting for the stationmaster to blow his whistle. On the platform stood a farm labourer with his wife and young daughter. Their belongings were in two straw baskets. Beside them lay a scythe wrapped up in sacking. The man in his old corduroy trousers and coarse woollen shirt looked weary and depressed. His wife, hugging her arms to her body under a ragged shawl, stared miserably at the ground. But the little girl in her faded cotton dress did not look unhappy. She gazed inquisitively but in no way impolitely at the company of grand ladies and gentlemen on the train. She had an anaemic, but pretty face. Dora in the window seat could see the deep grime in the child's neck.

'What a very rude girl,' remarked Rosa Burley who was sitting across from Dora. She sounded very much the schoolmistress.

But Mr Griffith had become agitated by the forlorn-looking group.

'Poor beggars! Homeless they look. It's depression on the land, you know. Very bad it is. Especially in arable. And it's some time until the fruit-picking.'

Mr Griffith gulped as he spoke and shifted his body edgily in the soft upholstery of the seat.

'Not that anybody does anything about it!' he continued in an unexpected sob of anger. 'Not the landowners. Not the squires. Not this government we're blessed with, Salisbury . . . Joe Chamberlain . . .'

131

Elgar stood up and put his thumbs in the pockets of his white dress waistcoat in mocking imitation of an orator.

'Tub thumper! Radical tub thumper!' he growled. His action was a joke and yet not a joke. And it was apparent that this type of exchange was a custom between them. Mr Griffith also stood up. But just as he opened his mouth to answer back, the train jolted forward clankingly and he fell back on his seat, a part of him landing on the large, silken thigh of a Miss Tetley.

'Clumsy old ninepin,' roared the musician delighted. 'Radical rabble-rouser! Serve you right!' There was a sneer as well as amusement in the throaty laughter.

The train drew slowly out of the station. For a long time Dora could still see the figure of the child with her attractive curious face and soiled dress and body.

Mr Griffith and Elgar continued to exchange political abuse. Dora wondered again about the musician's Toryism. He believed in it passionately, spiritually. Yet how apart, how different he had been from everyone else in the Hydes' drawing room. And how different he was from all those red-faced complacent Tory squires from the villages of south-west Staffordshire who came to call on her father. This man's belief had nothing to do with his circumstances. It came from some intense, unquestioned and unquestionable personal ideal.

But now the disagreement between the two men had turned into horseplay in which they indulged, in part, for the entertainment of their fellow passengers. Elgar had put up his fists and was pretending to attack Mr Griffith like a pugilist. Mr Griffith defended himself in the same way. Herr Ettling laughed loudly at the mock fight. But several of the ladies were plainly bored by such humour. To Alice especially, this facetiousness was intolerably familiar.

The joke came to an end automatically when Mr Griffith, miming an uppercut, struck the same Miss Tetley on the shoulder with his elbow. He sat down, mumbling his apologies inaudibly.

For a while there was silence in the compartment as the slow train skirled and clicked its way through the shining evening landscape.

And then, unobtrusively at first, Herr Ettling began to do

conjuring tricks. With clever, offhand motions he slowly made a bright new half-sovereign appear and disappear. Then after a few minutes, as he sensed he had attracted an audience, he began to undertake more ostentatious, ambitious tricks. The coin flew high through the air and landed in Herr Ettling's soiled shirt cuff. Then up again it went, the coin, twirling in a graceful spiral.

Despite the oily obesity of the man, despite the ugly, large pores in his light yellow skin, Dora was now beginning to be charmed by him. There was a precise, delicate good nature in his endeavour to entertain.

Well before anyone was likely to grow tired of his conjuring he put the coin away, clasped his fat hands together on his knees and said pleasantly and briskly, 'Nun wollen wir was singen.'

Dora was amused by the quiet, gentle way in which he arrogated to himself the right to speak German. But it certainly helped to put aside the tensions among the English people. In a good tenor voice Herr Ettling started to sing:

> 'Himmel und Erde müssen vergehen
> Aber die Musici bleiben bestehen.'

Shyly, faintly at first, the English people joined in. Then unexpectedly their voices swelled. There was a good deal of emotion in the singing. Herr Ettling lifted his hand and started to conduct energetically. People smiled, for in his manner there was a subtle parody of Elgar's way of conducting earlier that afternoon.

Elgar smiled and shook a finger at the little man. But the singers grew in confidence for his leadership. Their voices sounded well as they went from repeating the couplet in unison to singing it as a round.

When they ended, with a deep off-key bass drone from Mr Griffith, there was an expectant silence. Everyone wished to sing more. And with a flounce of his hands Herr Ettling led them into 'Am Brunnen Vor Dem Tore'. Dora sang the song happily. When it came to the line about the sweet dream, she saw Elgar glance at her intensely, almost fiercely. How contented she was at this moment! It was a joy to her to be one of this group of people who shared her own passionate interest in music. She was beginning to feel an affection for each one of them. The solidarity of the singers gave her a physical pleasure in the inmost of her body. And amidst all this there remained that deferred issue between herself and the composer. What it would lead to, she could not, and troubled not, to imagine. The very anticipation was sweet to her.

The slow train rolled methodically along. With her back to the engine, Dora could, on certain curves of the railway-line, still glimpse the dark mass of the tower of Worcester Cathedral showing up black against the darkening sky. That day, that evening, would come to be one of her best memories. During and after the misery of the Great War she would like to remember how they had all travelled along through the country evening singing German songs in good, close sympathy together. Impossible that time would come to seem. And yet it had been.

They were still singing, when the train slowed down and then stopped at the station at Malvern Link. They had, sadly, to abandon a song in the middle. With some reluctance they had to leave their close cell of sound.

In twos and threes they walked to the Elgars' house. There was to be some supper before they dispersed. Dora found herself walking with Isobel Fitton. She proved to be a quiet, shy girl, very deliberate in her speech. She played the viola and this was the subject of their conversation. Quickly there developed between them a sympathy that had in great part to do with their belonging to the larger group. They would become close friends. The large, careful and very beautiful handwriting in Isobel's letters to her, Dora would regard as a startlingly perfect image of her friend's nature.

The house and also the food that the servant had put out looked a great deal poorer than what they had come from at the Hydes'. But the guests did not care at all. Here there was no constraint. They talked to each other enthusiastically about music, even when they did not know each other well. They were no longer residents of suburban Malvern, but rather *Musici* – people of the Muse. By them the stale pork pie and sandwiches and the sugary, sickly little cakes went unremarked.

As his guests chatted and ate, Elgar brought out his violin and played movements from serenades by Mozart and Brahms. Herr Ettling played with great energy upon imaginary drums. Elgar then performed a Paganini piece, swaying his body, scraping his bow extravagantly and batting his eyes. He was in high spirits after the successful concert in Worcester. He came up to Dora and whispered in her ear. She could feel the hairs of his moustache against her cheek. She was reluctant to accept his request. She did not feel easy about doing her dance before all these unfamiliar people. And besides, it would take some time to change into her dress. But the man insisted. She could dance as she was. Reluctant to go against his wishes, she at last consented.

She removed the jacket of her blue linen suit and tucked the bottom of her blouse more firmly into the waist of her skirt.

The man silenced the company with a skirl of strings and then motioned to Mr Griffith to push back the heavy table in the middle of the room. The guests moved towards the walls wonderingly. Mrs Elgar looked at her husband with some apprehension. She looked tired and old. She was far older, far less energetic than anyone else in the room. Her husband ignored her and began to play the *Bei Hammersbach* music. Dora began her dance. She was uncertain at first, being still fearful of the smallness of the room. But gradually she grew in confidence and her body assimilated the rhythms of the music. Her limbs trailed and floated with much grace. The men caught their breath and watched her greedily. To Elgar the sight of her dancing in her ordinary clothes was even more arousing than the burning memory of her in that special snake dress. How beautiful she was, with the wisps of blonde hair drooping negligently over her soft neck, her large, firm young breasts moving under her shirt, her small leather-belted waist and her finely tapered hips that her skirt draped and then revealed as she moved in her dancing.

For an instant he mistook the rhythm in his playing and Dora, now taken over by the music, missed her footing, and came near to crashing into the mahogany cabinet by the wall. Ineffectively, Mr Griffith reached forward to assist her but himself tripped on the carpet. Herr Ettling snorted. Dora surveyed the room for an instant with a look of queenly, womanly power. The possibility of comedy was instantly dispelled. She commanded them all. She resumed her dance and brought it to a conclusion with much sinuous elegance and charm.

The audience was more confident than the one at Wolverhampton. They cried 'Bravo, bravo!' and applauded her enthusiastically. They were genuinely impressed. Very definitely she had established herself among them.

By the standards of that time and place it was late when the guests started to leave. But even then Dora was not ready for this surprising, exciting day to end. When she at last went upstairs to bed in the tiny garret room at the front of the house, she could not sleep. Her head ached hummingly yet pleasurably from all the new experiences of the day. She could not control her rush of thoughts about the man, her triumph and all the new friends she had made. Restlessly she got up and went and stood by the little window. Outside a great full moon shone in upon her face and lit up the deep blue sky, the clear stars and the dark mysterious mass of North Hill.

When later that week Dora cycled back to Wolverhampton she found that her achievement as a traveller was regarded as something heroic.

At breakfast on the morning following her late evening return, Minnie sat looking at her wonderingly, admiringly.

'Well, you 'ave got a pluck!' said Mrs Bayliss, a heavy Wolverhampton sound in that last vowel. How unfamiliar it sounded to Dora after the voices of Malvern.

Mrs Bayliss breathed heavily as she moved about the table removing the breakfast things, all the time regarding Dora with a mixture of curiosity and respect. And there at the door was Mrs Shinton with her bloodshot eyes, peeping in at the prodigy. The Rector continued to read his newspaper. He had expressed his congratulations to his daughter but he did not appear to understand fully what she had done or even that she had been away.

But the women were in awe of the girl. They were impressed and also disturbed that there was so much more to her than they had realised. She was a dark horse! She had upset their confident wisdom. They had to think again about themselves and about her. What might she not do? But they could not but admire her.

Yet, despite this new respect, they were all fearful on her behalf when she calmly announced that she would again cycle to Malvern in three weeks' time. Minnie was aghast. Surely one journey was enough. Why take another risk? Dora would surely not attempt to repeat such an escapade!

But she did. In fact she cycled there regularly all that summer. She managed to attend nearly all the concerts of the Worcestershire Philharmonic, the tea parties at the Hydes' and the evenings at 'Forli'. For all that she lived forty miles away she was an established member of the set.

She also became a familiar figure to the country people of northern Worcestershire. Carters, ploughmen and tinkers camped by the hedgerows were always on the look-out for the strange sight of the beautiful fair-haired girl speeding past. And always they were taken aback. Cyclists were still extremely rare in that countryside at that time. 'Good day to you, miss,' they would say, raising their caps and hoping for a glance from her. 'Good day to you,' Dora would answer briskly and confidently as she sped on past the ripening fields and orchards. She would always stop for refreshment at the King's Arms at Ombersley, where the landlord and his wife came to be her special friends.

She wished longingly that she could live at Malvern. She grew more and more involved with the Worcestershire Philharmonic Society. How inadequate the little string orchestra she led at the Danks' now seemed! She was always wanting to be away from Wolverhampton. Isobel was becoming a close friend, Herr Ettling delighted her more and more with his jokes and clowning and even Rosa Burley, she discovered, had behind her stiff, snobbish façade a gentle, sensitive, even vulnerable nature. And there was Alice, who was invariably kind to her and always urging her to come. And above all there was the composer himself . . .

The more visits she made, the harder she found it to be away from her new friends. It was like a fever with her. At the Rectory Minnie shook her head sadly, uncomprehendingly. And Mrs

Bayliss, as she bustled about, made it absolutely clear that she considered Dora's condition a kind of madness.

Her visits continued well into autumn. But as the days grew darker and colder, she had to give up her cycling. She had to take the train. And since she had little money she could go less frequently. But her visits did continue through the winter nevertheless. She would not be prevented. She would not. Sometimes, alone in her compartment in a bleak snowy landscape, she herself wondered why she felt so compelled to go. But go she did.

On what proved to be one of her last visits to the house at Malvern Link she became fully conscious about her role there. It was in the spring of the following year. The weather was just good enough for her to resume her cycling for the first time.

After a string concert in Worcester and then the usual tea at the Hydes', a party of some seven or eight returned to 'Forli' for the usual, less formal, more boisterous conclusion to the evening. They were all much taken with the music from Gluck's ballet *Don Juan*, a portion of which had been performed at the concert. Mr Griffith hummed passages from it absently, repeatedly, almost irritatingly. At 'Forli' Dora was several times asked to dance Zerlina in the second *Andante grazioso*. She finally agreed. Her dancing was elegant, delicate, utterly unselfconscious. At the conclusion she was greeted with a burst of admiring applause.

Flushed and throbbing with pleasure she looked for a place to sit down. The only vacant chair was the one next to Elgar, who was now putting away his violin. Dora crossed the room and seated herself by him. The composer bowed to her in a gesture of appreciation of her performance.

The centre of attention in the room was now Herr Ettling who this evening was doing card-tricks. Assisting him was another German, Herr Augustus, as Dora had learned to call him. He was a reader for Novello's, the music publishers in London, and a very dedicated admirer of Elgar's work. He was a quiet man with a small head, short fair hair, a thick moustache and small, steel-rimmed spectacles. He had most scrupulous manners and was a much finer nature than Herr Ettling, who tricked and deceived him ever more rapidly with the cards, laughing coarsely as he did so and all the time looking around the room for applause and laughter.

When he sensed that the interest of the audience was beginning to abate, Herr Ettling produced a little silver tree, some three or four inches high, and started to juggle with it. It was a beautiful piece of very old silverwork. Herr Ettling flung it in the air. It disappeared. And then unexpectedly was retrieved from the breast pocket of the lounge coat of Herr Augustus who looked greatly embarrassed to be involved in the trick in this way. The little audience felt for him. A gentle spirit was being used by a grosser one. But Herr Ettling continued his performance heedless and unconcerned. The little tree would appear behind chairs, beside the coal scuttle, inside the host's violin-case. Once it was found growing beside the aspidistra in the fire-grate. Each time it was discovered, Herr Ettling guffawed with pleasure.

But then it disappeared completely. Herr Ettling himself could not find it. He hurried about the room on his thick little legs looking everywhere. But no, he could not find it. The myopic eyes glinted anxiously through the thick glass of his spectacles. Whatever had happened?

Then he fell to his knees on the floor in front of Rosa Burley. He thrust his hairy hand between her shoes lifting the hem of her skirt slightly. He recovered the silver tree from between her heels.

This brought a quick, appreciative laugh from Elgar.

'Bravo, Onkel Klingsor!' he called.

But the others in the room did not share his admiration. There was something indecorous, shocking in what the drummer had done. Rosa Burley's face was bright red. There was a silence. Others in the room sympathised with her resentment at the familiar way in which he had treated her.

Yet worse was to follow. For Herr Ettling walked to the other end of the room, bowed to Elgar and, falling on one knee, offered the silver tree to Dora. Or was it to Dora and Elgar together?

Dora accepted the homage smilingly and graciously, despite the uneasy silence in the room and the rudeness to Rosa Burley.

Precisely at that moment Dora realised that she and Elgar were the living centre of that group of people, he, of course, for his music and she, she now realised, because of her dancing, her beauty, her youth. It was strange to her that she had not realised this before. She must surely have sensed it, but only now had she said it to herself. Now she understood with perfect clarity. Herr Ettling, Herr Augustus, Mr Griffith were her devoted admirers. And she was Elgar's true consort. They sat here at this moment like a king and queen entertained by their jester. Alice, an old lady already, was but a shadowy figure hovering in the background.

For an instant Dora felt sorry for her and for Rosa Burley. But this passed, as she experienced a rushing throb of pride at her new realisation of herself.

Yet strangely this occasion marked the ending of the little court which she had now come to understand. For never again would there be this familiar, routine evening of pleasure at 'Forli'. Such parties came suddenly to an end. And Dora's relationship with Elgar took a new and astonishing course.

7

In the weeks following that last evening gathering at 'Forli' Dora
was surprised to find herself left very much on her own. She
received no invitations to go to Malvern. Elgar, she learned
from Alice's letters to Minnie, had an unusually large number
of conducting engagements with some of the great choral societies
of the provinces. He had to travel a great deal. Dora felt abandoned. She missed, with a feeling akin to that of physical hunger,
the familiar routine of the cycling, the concert and the little
party that followed.

As the spring matured into a hazy summer Minnie learned
that the Elgars were to have a holiday in Germany. They went
to Garmisch and also to Munich where they saw *Tristan, The
Flying Dutchman* and *Don Giovanni*. After weeks of silence
Dora received in quick succession two postcards of the Bavarian
Alps, one mentioning an introduction to the young German composer, Herr Richard Strauss, and both of them containing a series
of brief jolly jokes of an avuncular kind. Dora was hurt by the
flippancy of the cards. It was inconsistent of him, she thought.
She almost wept. At the same time she was angry that she
allowed herself to become so upset.

On the warm, gentle summer mornings Dora would tramp

around the town, longing to burst the confines of the place. She had long since exhausted the pleasures of the palatial new Art Gallery, the better tea-rooms, the expensive sweet shop by the Grand Theatre and Hayward's music shop in Queen Street. Once in her slightly frantic boredom she made her way into the eastern quarter of the town where the vast iron foundries stood. As she went a little way down Horseley Fields she felt as though she were in a different country. The din and vibration of the factories increased very suddenly. The dialect of the factory people was just about unintelligible to her.

The street that led to the factories had something of the character of an old, decayed village placed between the foundries and the modern town. There was a sequence of small grimy public houses with labourers in coarse woollen jackets and trousers squatting at the step. There was a butcher's shop with glossy, brown-feathered poultry hanging from a steel bar. Next door was a herbalist's with rows of brown paper packets in the dusty window. Many women of the district hung about this place. They stood and talked to each other in groups, their coarse voices expressing a crude, cynical harshness that Dora found menacing. She knew that they were looking at her suspiciously. She remembered the child on the platform at Worcester. Dora did not belong here; she was an intruder. This was a foreign, hostile place. At last she turned and gave up her excursion.

Coming towards her she saw the large stumbling figure of a red-faced labourer with his arm round a stout middle-aged woman. Both were to Dora frighteningly drunk. The man was one of the ash-can carriers and wore sooty, sweaty cotton trousers and a dirty woollen shirt. He passed within feet of the girl and Dora could smell the fetid reek of his body. But even more shockingly distasteful to her was his brutal grasping of the woman, whose kerchief had fallen away so that her breasts hung out uglily, long, papery dugs. The man slobbered lurchingly on the woman's unwashed neck.

The inhabitants of Horseley Fields were indifferent to the sight. But Dora could have retched with horror. All through her life her feelings for sexuality hung uncertainly between this image and some of the most elevated ones from the operas of Wagner.

She hastened back the few hundred yards to the stylish new buildings in the clean, broad thoroughfare of Lichfield Street.

On another occasion when Dora was engaged upon one of her aimless walks about the town, her attention, like that of other passers-by, was attracted by the sight of a large, expensive carriage pulled by three horses. Inside she recognised Henry Hartley Fowler, the Liberal Member of Parliament for the eastern part of the borough, who had been President of the Local Government Board in Mr Gladstone's last cabinet. The future Lord Wolverhampton had a heavy face, a thick beard and a wide strong brow. His expression as he now gazed out upon his constituents was smug, even smirking.

And yet his story, as Mrs Bayliss had related it to Dora, was a romantic one. He had come to the town years before as a penniless, young solicitor and had married Ellen Thorneycroft, the daughter of one of the wealthiest and best known of the Staffordshire ironmasters. Her parents had resisted the marriage most strenuously but had not been able to prevent it. Fowler had then gone on to build a great career in business and politics.

As the carriage passed by, Dora glimpsed the beautiful Mrs Fowler and her two daughters. Dora would have liked to become acquainted with them. They were said to be merry, lively young women. The elder, Mary Ellen, wrote stories and would one day become a well-known novelist. The carriage passed on, Dora looking after it sadly. They would be returning from Westminster to Woodthorne, their new mansion in the township of Tettenhall. But she was for ever divided from them by the fact of church-manship. They were Methodists and Liberals. She could never go to Woodthorne; nor could they ever be invited to the Rectory. Such were the rigid, entrenched habits of the factory towns of the Midlands and the North. Here there was no fine salon like that which, in a county town, the beautiful Miss Hyde presided over and in which a variety of people could come together. Here people were set systematically apart.

Midsummer passed. Dora felt almost ill with listlessness and the lack of stimulus. Her correspondence, her string orchestra, her many responsibilities at the church were insufficient for her energy and her imagination. She heard little or nothing from the Elgars but could not bear to face the fact that she had been forgotten. A faith in him had become part of her deepest self.

But the beautiful summer dragged on miserably for her. Her situation became even worse when Minnie had to set off at a moment's notice to tend a sister in Gloucestershire who had been taken seriously ill. She was gone for several weeks. Only in her absence did Dora appreciate the quiet, tactful companionship which her stepmother gave her.

Dora had now to be the hostess at her father's table. She quickly grew weary of the role. His wife's absence prompted the Rector to indulge his own inclinations all the more. He would sit musing over his plate for long periods or he would invite a certain few, rather toadying, Tory tradesmen of the town to dine with him. They considered it a great honour to come and would sit there in their Sunday best listening to the Rector's succession of tales of Melanesia, all of which were now insufferably familiar to his daughter.

On those occasions when the Rector fell into a dream at table, one or other of the visitors would seize the opportunity to indulge himself in a monologue. To Dora the worst was Mr Cope, who had once been a manager at Thorneycroft's, the ironmasters. Mr Cope could easily talk for half an hour at a time about the size and dimensions of the blast furnaces, the puddling furnaces, the forge trains, rolling mills, helves, and steel hammers. There was a complacent self-importance in the coarse-featured, grey-haired man as he lectured on, bullyingly, about these mechanisms. He spoke broad Staffordshire pungently and laconically. Some of his listeners were genuinely entertained by this and admired him. But everyone deferred to him, the Rector included. In some way Mr Cope compelled people to accept his parochial, inland language. It was a weapon with him. But Dora hated his pomposity. Every Sunday the old man would come to early morning Communion and the girl would feel guilty that she so disliked even the way in which he came into the church. Sunday after Sunday he was so stolid and predictable in the way he entered, knelt, sat in his pew and then went. He had made himself into a machine and was insufferably proud of having done so.

One evening when the Rector and his guests had lingered long over dinner, the Reverend Penny had a strange fit or seizure which greatly frightened his daughter. The company included the ironfounder, a tailor, a grocer, a candlestick maker and a prosperous publican. This latter was a short fat man with an apoplectic face, a high collar that almost throttled him and new shiny boots that creaked noisily. He had formerly been a petty officer in the navy and, at a brief pause in the Rector's flow of reminiscence, asked him about the usefulness of the English men-of-war in the Melanesian islands.

The question excited the clergyman.

'From a missionary's point of view,' he began, 'the presence of men-of-war in the islands is the source of much good. To the peaceable and well-disposed natives, the invariable kindness of the officers is an incentive to good behaviour. While to the lawless . . .'

Here his usually melodious voice took a surprising swoop upwards. There was a sudden stridency that suggested some strange passion, hysteria even. His eyes flashed and his mouth twisted as though he were confronting some terrible experience.

'While to the lawless, to the headhunters, you know, the headhunters . . . they bring home the knowledge that there is a power, hah, there is a power,' his voice trembled as he repeated again and more loudly, 'there is a power in existence to punish brutal outrage, which sooner or later . . .' the Rector smiled knowingly in the midst of his excitement, 'in some way or another, will make itself felt.'

He fell back in his chair. The company stayed silent. Mrs Bayliss, who was bringing the candles to the table, paused and scrutinised her employer's face carefully. She looked to Dora. In the continuing silence the girl was anxious and embarrassed. She at last attempted to engage in conversation with the guests. But the exchanges were strained and artificial. The Rector smiled emptily but had nothing more to say for the evening. After a polite interval the tradesmen left in a group together.

The following morning Dora received a letter from her stepmother saying that it was still too early for her to be able to say when she would be returning. Dora sat by the parlour window and re-read the letter miserably. Outside the bright morning sunlight warmed the old walled garden of the Rectory. There came a knock at the door and Mrs Bayliss entered with a slight and ungainly curtsy. She wore her customary black dress and in the dim light at the far end of the Jacobean room Dora could scarcely see her. Mrs Bayliss hesitated for some moments.

'I just come, Miss Dora, to ask if you'd like to come downstairs this afternoon and join Mrs Shinton and meself for a bit of tea. Nothing special you know. A few buns perhaps. A bit of company.'

Dora was much surprised by this but accepted the invitation politely. With some awkwardness Mrs Bayliss turned around and left the room. Dora sat wondering.

But at teatime that afternoon she made her way down the narrow twisting stairs to the kitchen and tapped on the door. Mrs Bayliss, wearing a new and elaborate lace collar over her dress, welcomed her in. The last time Dora had been down here, the girl recalled sadly, was with Elgar on the first afternoon when he had been on his journey to Hanley. Now the room looked altogether different. There was a rich, green velvet cloth over a third of the long kitchen table and on it stood great platefuls of fruitcake, cream cakes, buns, malt bread and sandwiches. A large furry black kettle steamed away on the hob. The wintry atmosphere of this underground room felt refreshing on this hot summer day.

'Sit you down, Miss. Sit you down. I'll have the tea med in a sec.'

Dora sat down at the long table. Opposite her sat Mrs Shinton, who looked as though she had been specially washed and brushed for the occasion.

'How do you do?' she said shyly to Dora. All the time she kept her watery, tremulous eyes on the girl as though on a princess.

'Mrs Shinton's not stopping long,' announced Mrs Bayliss, making the tea. 'Are you?' she insisted, speaking heavily into the face of the pale, retarded woman.

146

'Come on now, please do 'ave something,' continued Mrs Bayliss, pushing the large plates towards Dora. The girl took a small piece of buttered malt bread. Mrs Bayliss appeared thwarted and dissatisfied. Mrs Shinton reached over a thin bony hand and took a cream cake rapidly.

Mrs Bayliss poured the tea. 'Is your father well today, Miss?' she enquired. She looked at the girl very directly.

Dora knew to what she was alluding and for an instant she thought the question an impertinence. But she also sensed that, like the invitation to tea, it was kindly meant.

Mrs Bayliss had now entered upon what sounded like a prepared speech.

'Well, if he's poorly, or anything, you let me know and I'll give you a hand. And I know what I'm talking about. Them men as have been abroad a lot get things on them. My eldest brother (he's dead now) was out in the Crimea. With the South Staffords. When he left Sowick (that's where we come from, you know), he was as right as rain. But when he come back, he never said a word to anybody. Not a word. Just sat in his chair and read the paper. He'd go to work and come home and never say a word. Not a word. As though the tongue had been cut out of his head. Not a word.'

The last three words were spoken insistently, challengingly. Mrs Shinton nodded her narrow, toothless head rapidly to show that she believed what was said.

'No, it's a well-known thing,' resumed Mrs Bayliss with great confidence. 'They often go funny, men do, once they've been abroad. Can't settle to normal life here any more. That music teacher that takes his holidays in Germany, he's another one . . .'

Dora was outraged. That Mrs Bayliss should presume to criticise her father and Elgar virtually in one breath was an impudence not to be borne. She wondered if she ought to rise and leave the room.

But Mrs Bayliss talked on, utterly unaware of the girl's anger. The housekeeper was attempting to offer the support of her illusionless common sense, her mature wisdom as a woman as something to be invoked against the puzzling, possibly dangerous unpredictability of the girl's father and friend. Dora's anger abated somewhat as she came to understand this coarse good-will.

'So I know what I'm talking about,' Mrs Bayliss was saying, by way of interim summary. 'So if yo ever have any trouble of that kind, yo let me know.'

Dora nodded. Mrs Bayliss was a different person here below. Her Staffordshire speech came out more noticeably and also a harshness, a harshness that was concealed by an effort at gentility when she was in the parlour. Dora was reminded of the women outside the herbalist's in Horseley Fields.

Mrs Bayliss was now listing other instances of pain, madness and death in her large family. One had to do with 'a girl like you, without a mother, Miss,' and another with a niece that 'was let down by a lot of fancy friends'. Dora was again astounded at such gross, vulgar familiarity. But she did not know how to object. These allusions were just parentheses, illustrations, in the other woman's explanation of her philosophy. This held that the world was an unkind, cruel, unreliable place and that you had to 'tek no notice'. That was an expression that recurred frequently in her reminiscences. 'Tek no notice.' And once you were hard enough, there could be understanding with others based on a sympathetic sharing of the fact of pain. In Mrs Bayliss such sympathy expressed itself in the urging of cake upon the young girl.

'Go on. 'Ave some. I've bought it.'

Dora's resentments faded. The kindliness and the goodwill were not to be separated from the other. And in a way she did feel supported by this energetic, crude goodwill. But she could not accept the woman's outlook. She could not.

After she had left the lower room she paced about her bed-room restlessly. She wanted to think beyond what had been said. But this was difficult. There was more to life than Mrs Bayliss suggested. There must be. For herself and for this house and this place. She would not be smothered by loneliness, by this harsh mechanical town or by a ghoulish community of resigned unhappiness. She definitely would not!

The following morning brought another letter from her step-mother. Dora gasped as her eyes hurried down the lines of neat handwriting. Minnie had met Elgar! They had encountered each other at Hasfield Court, the mansion of Minnie's brother in Gloucestershire. In fact, Minnie had been 'taken into dinner' by the musician.

Dora raced on through the letter. At last she came to it:

'We had a most interesting, if at times rather startling conversation. He enquired about you, my dear. He said, "How is my sweet Dorabella?" I may say that I was most shocked. I have often felt that Edward was too free in his manner toward you. But this struck me as extraordinarily improper. "Oh, so it has got to that, has it?" I replied. He looked at me strangely and said, "Do you not know that that is a quotation from Mozart's *Cosi Fan Tutte*?" I had to confess that I did not. I also told him that in my view that was beside the point. I was quite severe with him. And I informed him that I should tell you of what had been said. But this caused him no dismay. He said he felt sure that you would understand.'

Dora read and re-read these words many times. She scarcely even noticed the good news that Minnie would be able to return to the Rectory in a few days' time.

Dora struggled to recall the details of the Mozart opera. She had seen it performed at the Covent Garden Theatre. She thought she could remember the passage he had mentioned. But she could not be sure. She thought and thought. It was another of his puzzles.

Feverishly she seized her straw hat and white cotton gloves and set off into the town. A mellow orange glow of early autumn warmed the still new-looking grey statue of the Prince Consort in Queen Square. Dora hurried on into Dudley Street, a narrow congested thoroughfare with many small shops, and on into Queen Street and entered Mr Charles Flavell Hayward's music shop. In her haste as usual she set the shop door bell jangling wildly.

Today Mr Hayward was here. He rose from the gloom at the rear of the shop and came forward.

'Ah, Miss Penny. What a pleasure to see you!'

Though not much older than Dora he was stooped and thin. He had soft, white, freckled skin and receding sandy hair.

Dora was breathless and to her great vexation could not speak for a moment or two.

'And what can I have the pleasure of showing you today?' enquired Mr Hayward. He was a most deferential tradesman, making a great effort to be genteel. But he genuinely admired the Rector's daughter and enjoyed her frequent visits to his shop.

'I wondered,' began Dora gaspingly, 'I wondered w . . . w . . . whether you might have a score of Mozart's opera *Cosi Fan Tutte* that I might consult briefly?'

'By all means, Miss Penny,' said Mr Hayward in his soft way. 'We have in stock all the Mozart operas.'

He was pleased to be able to help her and hopeful that they might now, as on other occasions, be about to share an enthusiasm together. Music could bring them close to each other despite the differences of class and sex.

He led her further into the shop and from a long row of scores on a shelf took down one in a handsome dark binding.

Dora sank down on to one of the shop chairs and turned the pages. Two of her ideas proved to be incorrect. But then she found it, in the eighth scene of the second act.

'E la mia Dorabella?
Come s'è diportata?'

As she read these words, the details of the opera came back to her. But how much more there was to these words than the translation which Elgar had given Minnie! For in terms of the opera as a whole they asked not merely how she did but whether she had been faithful and constant, in a complicated game of tests, trials and disguises. The message was perfectly clear to her. But all the implications were at this moment incalculable . . .

Dora did not realise how long she had been staring at the eight words. She raised her head at last to find Mr Hayward looking down at her curiously. She would have to rouse herself and ponder all this later.

'Many thanks to you, Mr Hayward,' she said in her confident well-spoken way, 'there was just one matter of detail which I wished to confirm.'

'My pleasure, Miss Penny,' he replied, receiving the score

from her. The watery blue eyes looked at her with interest, perhaps slight amusement even. What a flow of sympathetic feeling
he had for her! She was always full of ideas and questions and
initiatives about music. Her youthful spirit, which was more
energetic than his, rallied him. She brought stimulus and excitement into the dark shop with her. Her visits enriched his
life.

'I wonder,' she said, rising from her chair and sweeping her
hand from back to front around her cotton skirt, 'whether you
have any of the music of Richard Strauss?' All the consonants
in the name she uttered slowly, very carefully, in the German
pronunciation.

The son of the English Paganini rocked back on his heels,
thinking. His creased black suit showed up dully against the
shining dark wood of a grand piano.

'I really don't think that we do, Miss Penny.'

'Really?'

'I'm very sorry.' There was genuine regret in the young man's
face. This was a personal disappointment to him.

'Well, I am surprised.'

'I'm afraid there's not much call for that around here. People
like what's familiar. The tried and true, sort of thing.'

Dora thought he sounded whining and complacent at the same
time. She was for some reason reminded of Mrs Bayliss. She
suddenly felt irritable. She wanted to be outside in the fresh air
with her own thoughts.

Curtly she thanked Mr Hayward again and bade him good
day. As she made her way down the length of the shop, he
watched her go with a sneaped expression on his soft, pale face.

Once out in Queen Street Dora was immediately aware of her
abruptness. How could she have been so impolite when he had
done her the kindness of letting her see the score? She recalled
all his other many kindnesses to her. She felt most sorry. How
could she have done such a thing?

She would repair the situation, later. For the moment she was
on fire to re-read Minnie's letter and to think through all the
hints and implications in the man's allusions to her. But one
thing was simple and clear. She had been right in her trust.

There was definitely a resolution, a settlement to come to between the two of them. And she knew, without even the faintest doubt, that she would soon be invited back to Malvern in order that this might take place.

And she was right.

8

It was Alice Elgar who wrote, asking her to come. The letter arrived towards the end of October and suggested a date early in the following month.

Alice wrote: 'You will hear some wonderful and most exciting music, Dora dear! You simply must come and hear. I have promised Edward not to say a word.'

Dora laid the letter down on the oak dressing-table in her bedroom. Always a mystery! But she was relieved and happy that the invitation had at last come. Though it would mean cancelling the concert which she, the Danks and other members of her string orchestra were to have put on that day. Only for a brief moment did Dora experience a resentment that the Elgars invited her and neglected her, as it suited them. The thought had no real force; her breath quickened with excitement and anticipation.

She set off down the narrow stairs. In the parlour she found her stepmother doing some sewing for one of the missionary causes. Trying to suppress her excitement, Dora thrust the letter into Minnie's hands. The brown eyes in the lined, kindly face went over the letter with care. Meanwhile Dora moved about the shadowy room restlessly. Outside late autumn rain beat down and sodden yellow and green leaves fell upon the grass of the Rectory garden.

'Well, Dora. This will be a nice outing for you. They will meet you at Worcester, I see. You must certainly take the train at this time of the year. Do not ask your father for the fare. I shall be very happy to purchase the return ticket for you.'

The last two sentences were in a conspiratorial whisper.

'Mother, how very kind of you!' exclaimed Dora hurrying from the window to sit down beside her. She was touched by this generosity. And at that moment she also realised for the first time that Minnie must feel supplanted by her stepdaughter in her old friends' affection and interest. But Dora was too preoccupied with her own complicated concerns to pursue this thought any further.

'Whatever do you think the surprise may b . . . b . . . be that Mrs Elgar mentions?' Dora enquired. 'Do you think that they have founded another Philharmonic Society?'

'Oh no, it is not that,' replied Minnie confidently. Then she lowered her eyes as though she had said too much.

Dora was suspicious. 'I think you know something, m . . . m . . . mother.'

'No, Dora, I assure you that I cannot be certain what is meant. But you can see from Alice's letter that the Philharmonic Society is still in existence. There is indeed to be a concert on the day of your visit. Though, I was given to believe, during my stay in Gloucestershire, that there had been some unhappy divisions among the performers. Certain of the ladies in the violin section had a disagreement with other ladies who played the cello. It reminded me of the difficulties we have experienced, fortunately only very occasionally, with our choristers here at St Peter's.'

Dora regarded her stepmother closely. She thought her words a clumsy device to avoid the real question. Dora felt that she knew something. Ever since Minnie had returned from Gloucestershire she had been noticeably uncommunicative on the subject of the Elgars. Dora sensed that she was in some way 'in the know'; she was also worried, but unable to speak about what disquieted her. After a while Dora left the parlour and returned to her own room, the better to enjoy her old and her

154

new imaginings about the beautiful Malvern Hills, her many friends there, and that one special friend.

The day at last came to set off and Minnie accompanied Dora to the station. It was cold, and a delicate white frost glittered at the edge of the grimy platform. Dora had a compartment to herself but was too excited to rest. In Worcestershire the orchard trees were bare and black and squat. She caught the smell as well as the sight of wood fires eddying into the deep blue sky. She was in the country again.

At long last the train clanked to a halt in the dark shadow of the station of the cathedral town. Dora stepped down and looked about the platform; there was no one to meet her. She walked up and down anxiously. Porters were noisily unloading shiny milk churns from the guard's van of the Birmingham train. Dora was the only traveller left on the platform.

Then she saw Rosa Burley hastening towards her with intense nervous strides. She was clutching a platform ticket.

'Oh, I do hope I am not very late,' she called out from a good distance. Dora reassured her. Breathlessly Rosa Burley explained.

'Alice and Edward were detained at the concert hall at the last moment. They asked me to come to meet you in their stead.'

Dora experienced a feeling of hurt. But this was quickly replaced by one of amusement and sympathy for her companion. Rosa Burley looked strangely overdressed in a lady's Chesterfield of yellow and brown and a hat with two dead birds on it and much lace. Everything she wore looked a size too large for her. As always, she was, under her show of stern decorum and control, tremulous and ill at ease. The large mouth and jaw were clenched hard but the watery blue eyes were restlessly wary.

The two ladies made their way down a street of Georgian shop fronts. They were silent, Dora still sensing a strangeness in being met by Rosa Burley. This was increased by her companion's habit of stepping away from her as they walked, as if to survey and examine her. Why should she excite this curiosity, Dora wondered.

Painfully oppressed by the responsibility to converse, the older woman said abruptly, 'You did not join us at the Leeds Festival.'

'No, I am afraid, I could not get.'

Dora was upset to be reminded. It had been a great disappointment some months back that she had not been able to afford to go.

Rosa Burley realised that her words had been too casual and had given pain.

'We were most of us there,' she said, now very gently. The 'we' sounded as though she were speaking of a family. She added, 'And it was a great success for Edward. A great success. I am most sorry that you could not be present.' Rosa Burley's sympathy was painfully genuine and just as unfortunate as her earlier abruptness had been.

They could hear a dull but excited hubbub as they approached the concert hall. It was full. They were lucky to find two seats at the back. On the front row was Alice, her hair greyer than before, and wearing what looked to Dora like a new afternoon dress. Alice was gesticulating emphatically to someone at the side. Always and at every moment she was the little manager.

The ladies and the few gentlemen of the orchestra were busy tuning up. There came a silence. And then a loud burst of applause greeted Elgar as he approached the conductor's podium. It was far more enthusiastic than his reception at the last concert Dora had attended. Dora caught her breath, then gasped slightly, when she saw him again after all these months.

He had changed. His hair was sleeker, his face more pink, and razored. And he wore a new and well-cut coat of black. He bowed to the audience and addressed himself to the orchestra with a greater confidence than she remembered.

Dora mooned her way through much of the concert. But a series of pieces from Richard Strauss drew her notice because the very movements of the conductor's body conveyed to her his especial concern with them. There were some passages from *Thus Spake Zarathustra* and the symphonic poems *Don Juan* and *Till Eulenspiegel's Merry Pranks*. As in later years when she heard the *Salome*, Dora was roused, shocked, embarrassed and yet fascinated by this new music. She glanced around her to see how others in the audience were responding. Most sat stolidly in their chairs. Rosa Burley was in a rapture of attention, her mouth wide open and her large hat askew.

At the reception at the Hydes' the atmosphere was far more formal and subdued than before. There were many more clergymen and figures from the Close. They all talked in hushed voices. The click of a cup in a saucer sounded strident. How things had changed! And within just a few years! Dora felt uncomfortable. She wondered how Herr Ettling and Mr Griffith would be received in such company. But neither of them appeared that day.

Dora was increasingly aware that many of the company were glancing surreptitiously at herself. She was reminded of Rosa Burley's manner towards her on their walk from the station. Why ever was she such an object of interest? The girl felt uneasy.

Elgar arrived, accompanied by his wife and Herr Augustus. The company fell instantly into a respectful silence. It was as though each person was waiting to be presented to him. Attitudes had changed. Dora was again surprised. So much had changed since she had seen him last. His success at Leeds must have been greater than she had realised from the newspapers.

She was taken aback to see that he was ignoring all the people who stood waiting to shake his hand, and coming directly towards herself. Her eye was taken by a dark blue and silver cravat that she had not seen before.

'Dorabella, Dorabella, how happy I am to see you again, at last!' He took her hand in both of his. The deep-set eyes glinted enquiringly.

For all her easy poise, the girl blushed, the pink suffusing down to the neck of her dark green jacket and up to the fair upswept hair. Elgar continued to keep the girl's hand within his hands.

'Dorabella,' he said, drawing out the syllables of the new name, 'who has been away from us for a season among the dark satanic mills.' He eyed her happily, savouringly.

Herr Augustus sensed the girl's happiness and also her embarrassment. He admired her greatly and was and would always be intensely and sympathetically responsive to her.

'Edward has given you a name, my dear; you should give him one too.' There was a gentle, but definite partisanship in the German voice.

'Yes, Dora dear,' intoned Alice, grandly condoning the jest, 'you should.'

'Yes,' said Dora glancing up and looking him in the eye almost provocatively. 'I shall call him, His Excellency.'

The words and the idea just burst from her. A moment before she had absolutely no intention of saying such a thing. Some part of herself had responded automatically and her conscious thoughts and feelings for the social situation had no part in it.

'His Excellency,' repeated Alice slowly. Her eyes brightened. Then an unusually large smile took over the placid, complacent face.

Elgar regarded the girl for a moment or two with an expression that had affection and also a smiling threat of reprisal in it. Then he turned away.

'Come, Alice, let us be on our way. Remember we have something for our friend Dorabella.' Husband and wife glanced at each other briefly.

'Oh, Edward, do not be impolite. You must greet at least a few of the people who are here to meet you.'

So he did. But it was not many minutes before they were receiving their coats and descending the stairs. Once in the street Dora was uneasily aware that they were only three: herself, Elgar, and Alice.

'But w ... w ... where is everyone else?' she enquired halting, as though they had moved too rapidly ahead. She had in mind the several others who in the past had been in the habit of returning to Malvern with them.

'Oh no, Dorabella,' said Elgar, 'you are our sole guest. You will understand when you see the surprise.'

They set off again. Dora experienced a curious shyness at being alone with the husband and the wife in such unexpected circumstances.

Alice announced grandly, 'Before we arrive, I must apologise to you for the state of our house. We are to move to another house very shortly. And we have already begun to pack things.'

They were to leave 'Forli'? Here yet again was a change. So the old Malvern days were absolutely at an end. That which she had dreamed and so looked forward to, was, now that she

158

had come back to it, no longer the same. It had disappeared, without her knowing it, and all in a summer.

At the railway station they found a compartment to themselves. As they waited for the train to start, Dora glimpsed the faintest of knowing smiles on Alice's face and on her husband's.

Then a man threw open the carriage door noisily, bustled in and sat down beside them. He wore a fawn Raglan overcoat and a brown bowler. His manner was jaunty and irritating. He had a newspaper which he folded and refolded and smacked and punched. He made grunts and groans and exclamations as he read. He looked about the compartment insolently. It was clear that he wanted to enter into conversation with them. He had a rabbit's eyes and mouth. Dora thought him very vulgar.

At last the man burst out. 'Have you seen the latest? Have you? Those radical johnnies are trying to have our men ordered back from the Upper Nile.' (It was the time that English and French troops came to a confrontation at Fashoda.)

There was an underlying scream of self-righteous indignation in the man's voice. There was also a theatrical quality to it.

Dora had expected that Elgar would treat this ill-bred interloper coldly. But she was disappointed. For he immediately agreed and sympathised with him.

'The deuce they are,' he replied. 'It is a pity they cannot be sent out there to do the fighting themselves.'

Elgar dropped his lower lip below the thick moustache in that panting sneer that Dora always found so distasteful. The unexpected conversation between the two men slowly and surely gathered momentum. Their contempt for those who opposed the expansion of Empire was expressed in very physical, gargling outbursts. They muttered bitterly about the conduct of the Liberals, they spoke with confident, knowledgeable calm about the staunchness and reliability of Lord Salisbury and there were spasms of deference when they alluded to Her Majesty the Queen.

After a while Dora followed only the sounds and not the meanings of their exchanges. They embarrassed her and made her anxious about being with Elgar when he was in this mood. Dora gazed through the window on to the platform, where in the dusk the lamplighter was lighting the gas lanterns. Vividly Dora recalled the shabby little girl who had once stood on this same platform. The men's voices went on and on in gnawing contempt.

At last the train started to move. In the darkening countryside, Dora was surprised to see, great fires were burning. In one village they went through there was a high red fire about a hundred yards from the church, illuminating the square western tower. Children could be seen moving to and fro, rapidly in the flickering red light. Farm labourers and their wives stood back to watch. Of course, it was bonfire night! Dora looked more attentively to see the next village fire. The country air was filled with the smell of burning wood.

Even Elgar was for a moment distracted from his insistent conversation by the recurring amber brightness that would shimmer into the compartment on to their faces.

'Guy Fawkes Night!' he exclaimed in mild surprise. 'Guy Fawkes! Now there's a chap who might have saved us from all this political bosh!'

How ugly that last syllable sounded in his mouth. He had such stores of bitter contempt. Even the man in the brown bowler appeared startled by the force and passion in these last words.

When they descended from the train at Malvern Link, Elgar fell silent. Alice was making a point of not speaking; she was keeping a secret. Dora felt unnerved to be walking along with them in the dark in this mood of silent suspensefulness.

Elgar unlocked the door. Furniture was piled up in the hall and the stair-carpet was in the process of being taken up. So, definitely, 'Forli' would soon be a thing of the past, this house which, for all its shabbiness, she thought of as so glamorous. Dora experienced a sharp pang of loss.

When they had removed their top-coats the three of them went into the parlour. Some of the chairs had been turned upside down and strung together. Elgar took the poker and roused up the fire, which had been covered with slack to burn slowly. He rose again, red in the face.

The three surveyed each other for a moment. Then Alice said melodiously, 'As you will see, Dora, we are packing and I feel rather tired. I think I will retire now. But you stay. Stay up with Edward a little longer. I know he has something to show you.' The words sounded rehearsed. Alice smiled benignly. Then, after another brief glance at her husband, she quickly left the room.

Being suddenly alone again with the man was to Dora a physical shock. This it was then to which everything that had gone before had tended! She found herself trembling. She felt chill.

He looked at her diffidently for some time. He appeared to be considering how to phrase something.

When at last he spoke, his voice was altogether different from that which she had heard on the train. It was now kindly and urgent and warm. There was also a certain stuttering humility to it.

'Will you go upstairs with me, Dorabella?'

Years after Dora would remember that unique state of unthinking acquiescence in which simply and unhesitatingly she had said 'Yes'.

She followed him from the room. He carried a lighted candle. Their boots scratched noisily upon the uncovered timbers of the stairs. He opened the door to his work-room and lit the gas.

'Do sit down,' he mumbled thickly.

In the cast of the lamplight she noticed the new grey in his hair. The thin, fine stuff of his new suit hung down from his shoulders. He had an elderly shambling look as he moved about the room.

'Y . . . y . . . yes, Your Excellency,' replied Dora uneasily but with a determined brightness.

She seated herself upon the worn leather couch with books spread upon it. She was most interested to see the room, because never before on any of her previous visits had she been invited to enter it. There was an upright piano against the wall and on a low Indian table two violin cases were lying open. The threadbare carpet was covered with music paper which, as Dora knew, Alice had always lined for him, in order to economise on expenses.

The man was uncertain as to how to proceed. He was restless.

He sat down on the piano stool, rose, and then sat down again.

Not looking at her directly he said, 'I have written a piece of music. It is to be entitled *Dorabella* and it is for you.'

Dora had no reply. She had no idea of what she had expected in this room; certainly it had not been this. Then she began to feel shy that he had written something about her. But he spared her embarrassment by twirling around on the stool and starting abruptly to play her music.

The first section was a little dance tune, fluttering, scintillating, but hesitant. She flushed. He had caught something that was very much her, her stammer perhaps, or one of her styles of dancing, or the agitation produced in her by her peculiarly intense nervous energy.

But then under this there appeared a song that on a later occasion she would hear played by a single viola and then by a chorus of violas. There was in it a swell of sensitive, mooning and yet profoundly womanly feeling. She was amazed that he should represent her in this way.

Then after a repeat of the dance figure, which now reminded her of the times she had danced the *Bei Hammersbach* music, there came yet another beautiful melody. It was music for two dancers in the ballet; it was poised, elegant, graceful.

Dora felt the vibrations of the piano beating on her hand and arms and her breasts. She was almost overcome by the music. It revealed her to herself in a way that she had never known before.

Fortunately the bright, lively music of the opening now returned and this gave her some relief. It now suggested to her some of Dorabella's agitated music in the opera.

But now the melody of mature graciousness also returned and she had to turn her quivering face away lest he should see her. As she would tell the many enquirers in future years, she felt, at that instant, a whirl of pride, pleasure and almost shame that he should have written something so beautiful about her.

This moment she would remember as the supreme instant of her life.

The piece ended, as it had begun, with the dance of fairy-like brightness. At the very last it trailed off echoingly into the silence.

Elgar jumped up and came towards her. He was anxious and apprehensive.

'Did you like it?' he demanded, searching her eyes intently.

'Oh yes. Oh yes.' There was a catch in her voice. At any moment the tears might come.

His face relaxed. 'I am so glad, dearest, dearest Dorabella.'

He came forward until he was standing over her. She expected him to sink down on to the couch beside her or to let his arms fall upon her.

Then the door opened with a loud creak. Alice surveyed them both with a look of indulgent, maternal affection.

'Isn't it beautiful, dear Dora?' she murmured slowly and suavely. 'I do hope you like it.'

9

THE following morning when she awoke, Dora was instantly seized again by the same joyous, excited amazement of the night before. In fact, the throbbing happiness had pulsed through her sleep like a fever. There was a warm ache in her muscles. She felt slightly feverish, as she dressed herself.

When she went downstairs she found that Elgar had already set off for Oldham where he was to conduct an oratorio. And she would have to go back to Wolverhampton before he returned home. At first she was bitterly disappointed, but then she discovered that it was a relief not to see him. What had passed between them was yet too little understood and assimilated for her to resume it with him over the bacon and eggs.

Dora passed the time until her departure in a daze of happiness. Occasionally she was aware, mistily, as though at a distance, of Alice asking her about the music. But the girl was bored, even irritated, by the indolently nagging, patronising questions. Dora resented her as an intruder. Her music should not be open to the prying questions of the older woman. It was something that concerned herself and its composer.

Upon her return home Dora found an unfamiliar energy released in her by this new happiness. She worked away at her own musical activities enthusiastically and passionately. She introduced some new and difficult pieces for her string orchestra to play. She felt confident enough now to accept solo soprano parts for the Wolverhampton Choral Society. She was happy that she had not to see Elgar in the immediate future. She took a warm anticipating pleasure in this present suspension of their meetings. She must first understand what was meant by the music he had written for and about her. In the meantime her own music-making was especially important to her. This was the right way of making her life close to his. Amy Danks was swept along, uncomprehending, by this new passionate energy.

Dora's little orchestra performed very successfully with the local choral society in concerts at the Agricultural Hall. Dora was fascinated to hear the sheer passion that now entered into the singing. The members of the choir who looked such sober lugubrious citizens of the town sounded intoxicated or exalted with their singing on these special occasions. As she conducted them with quick graceful movements of her arms, Dora wondered if she had misjudged these people. She stood on the very spot where some three-quarters of a century later and in a different building another band of musicians from this borough sang to their groupies and their fellow townspeople of their hero, that man who says he can, time after time . . . Dora walked home in a daze, feeling herself close to Elgar, as if he were walking beside her.

During the next few months Dora's life fed on such secret excitement. This throbbing memory of her music meant much more to her even than the letters he wrote to her. These were, in turn, gruff, avuncular, joking, in his usual way. But they were peripheral to the real issue between them.

In the spring Dora began to wish to hear her music again. She wanted to see him and to have her memories confirmed. And, at precisely this time, there arrived a letter from Elgar inviting her to come and stay with them at their new house. So on a beautiful morning in early May she set off on her bicycle once again, to pedal the forty miles to see him.

When she arrived in the northern outskirts of Malvern, she had to stop and consult the comic map he had drawn in his letter. She cycled on slowly through the centre of the town, past the Priory, and down the Wells Road. On her right was a succession of large villas, their wooded back gardens moving sheer up the steep hillside into the sky. It was like Italy. Below the road, on her left, the wide valley of the Severn extended to the distant horizon, the pale green fields shimmering in the warm spring light.

Dora at last identified the house from the freshly painted white Gothic letters on the front gate. 'Craeg Lea' they had named it. There were two wide bay windows and a high timbered gable. The roof was of bright red tiles with several high-standing chimneys. The front garden that swept up from behind the low wall and the holly hedge had mature trees in it, cypress and ash. At the back of the house where the garden climbed on up the steep hillside there was an immense pink rhododendron in flower. The place was almost an estate. How very grand it all was after 'Forli'!

Considerably intimidated, Dora opened the gate and lifted her cycle up the steps and on to the fern-lined path that swung around to the front door on the left-hand side of the villa. On the wall beside the door was a sumptuous pink and mauve clematis as high as the door. In the hillside garden at the back Dora could see white lilac amidst the gloom of the green trees.

Hesitantly she prepared to knock the door. But at that very moment it was thrown open and there was Alice welcoming her with a slow, deliberate enthusiasm.

'I thought it was you, Dora dear, I did. I said so to Edward, when I heard the gate click. But then he never heeds anything I say these days . . . But come in, my dear, come in. You must be tired . . .'

Diffidently Dora stepped into the large white hall. She could hear Elgar in conversation with someone in a nearby room. She was relieved. For she was now shy about seeing him again for the first time after that intimate evening of her music. Dora listened attentively as Alice closed the heavy door behind her. Yes, it was. It was! It was Mr Griffith. She recognised the growling mockery of the voice. She could not have wished for a more appropriate fellow visitor. With him here everything would have to be light-hearted and easy.

Elgar appeared at a door to the right. He wore a sporty-looking Norfolk jacket of light green.

'Welcome, welcome, dearest Dorabella. Welcome to our new house.'

'Thank you, Your Excellency.' She could not look him in the eye.

He clasped her hand in his and led her into the room from which he had come. Alice was left with the cycle.

The room was large, spacious and had high ceilings. The walls were painted a bright, clean white. The Elgars' furniture, which had always looked too large for 'Forli', here appeared rather small. The carpet by no means covered the floorboards and the long high walls were for the most part uncovered. There was a spareness and a frugality to the room with its large, wide windows that struck Dora as in some way very German. Yet it also accorded well with Elgar's nature, she thought.

Mr Griffith rose from his chair by a shiny grand piano that Dora had never seen before. It was surely brand new. He crossed the room stumblingly and shook her hand with excessive enthusiasm. He peeped at her shyly from under his eyelids. In this clean, light room he looked even more the unkempt bachelor than usual. The bottoms of his trousers were ragged and there was a button missing from his frayed worsted jacket.

'What a very grand house!' exclaimed Dora, looking to the three of them in turn. 'And what a lovely cool room.' She hurried over to the large windows. 'And such magnificent views.' Her admiration was genuine but there was also something theatrical and calculated in the way in which she moved and spoke and made herself their centre.

'Mammon of unrighteousness, if you ask me,' grumbled Mr Griffith, rolling his head from side to side. He sat down again and peered at the carpet as though seriously distressed by some impropriety.

'Oh don't listen to the silly old ninepin,' snapped Elgar.

'You can get on,' whined Griffith sanctimoniously.

'He's just a small-town atheist,' explained Elgar wearily.

Mr Griffith shook his head again as if he were grieving over some appalling instance of moral decay.

'Highly profitable, this sanctity business you know,' he said sarcastically. 'Cantatas, sacred songs, oratorios, that kind of thing. The market's very good just now. Just about replaced Gilbert and Sullivan, you know.'

'Be quiet, you pot-bellied pagan you!' retorted the musician.

'If you ask me,' Mr Griffith mumbled on, 'his best music was written for the band at the Worcester asylum. Very tuneful it was. You won't remember that, Miss Penny. He was very poor in those days. Maestro Elgar and his lunatic orchestra, that's how he was known then.'

The sneers and insults continued and Dora laughed at the sparring. A stranger might easily have thought the animus genuine. But she enjoyed the accelerating exchanges, in great part because she knew they were put on for her.

Alice rang for some tea for Dora and it was brought by a haughty servant in a black dress and starched white apron. Then Alice asked the two visitors if they would like to see the new house. She could hardly control her excitement at the prospect of showing it to them. The house was a pride and a confirmation for her.

So off they set, up the wide stairs and through the many large bedrooms, at least two of them completely unfurnished. Everything that Alice pointed out, with her unconvincing air of modesty, Dora and Mr Griffith looked at respectfully.

They came at last into the large front bedroom and Elgar led them to the window. He was their guide now. He pointed out some of the distant hills standing out in the sunny green flat lands of the Severn valley. They were dark mounds upon the bright plain. Directly before them was Bredon. And there was Oxerton and there Woolstone Hill. His voice quavered. The shimmering land below them exhilarated and enraptured him.

'My oh my,' murmured Mr Griffith in mock humility. 'This is by far the largest artist's garret that I have ever seen.'

Elgar was roused from his trance-like searching of the green horizon.

'Art requires a grand view,' he said, in a tone that suggested that Mr Griffith was an exceptionally obtuse schoolboy.

But as they returned downstairs and settled again in the

drawing room Mr Griffith proceeded, undeterred, with his special manner of indignation.

'And do you know what?' he continued, addressing Dora but not looking at her. 'He has the impertinence to inform me today that he no longer has the time to continue with my piano lessons. Too grand for that now! Glad enough to do it when he was the struggling artist. Very keen to teach me then at a shilling an hour. Not that he was ever very good at it. Most of what I know is self-taught.'

The dark, hang-dog eyes now brightened with an idea. 'I'll show you, if you like.' And without waiting for an answer he rose, crossed the room and seated himself at the new piano.

After an abracadabra flourish of his large hands he began to play. The piece was recognisable as one of Elgar's early compositions, but only barely. Mr Griffith played it too slowly, he was often flat and he hit about one wrong note in every three. And he thumped, thumped away at the piano as though it were lacking the proper volume. Thump, thump, thump, bang, bang, bang, he went, with all the time a pleasantly gentle, ruminative look in his eyes. Dora was at first shocked by this presumption, then she wanted to laugh. It really was a very good joke, a joke on Elgar, on his music, and above all, on his expensive new piano.

Throughout the course of the thumping the composer sat with his legs crossed and his head thrown back and supported negligently and elegantly by a large white hand. It was a very creditable impersonation of someone unaware that the piano was being played at all, of someone sitting alone thinking.

Mr Griffith concluded his programme (it was a lullaby) with one last, heavy smash at the piano. Then he shambled back to where he had been sitting.

'Virtually all self-taught,' he murmured plaintively. There followed several minutes of silence. Then Alice, much offended on her husband's behalf, smoothed down her dress and announced, 'We will go in to dinner in about three-quarters of an hour. Perhaps now might be a very good time to retire.'

In her room Dora's suppressed, guilty laughter released itself into a fit of the giggles. What a card Mr Griffith was! And for

Elgar who was not, for once, his usual commanding self but rather the butt of the joke, she felt an amused yet especially cherishing sympathy.

She suddenly wondered, and for the first time consciously, if she might be in love with him. Hiccoughs now set in.

She changed into a dark maroon dress. She examined herself in the gilded oval mirror above the grate. She looked older, she decided, no longer a girl but a woman.

She was the last to return downstairs. She had spent longer looking into the mirror than she had realised. Mr Griffith 'took in' Alice to dinner and Elgar escorted Dora to her chair. His fingers splayed out tightly, almost painfully on the flesh of her inner arm.

Like all the other rooms at 'Craeg Lea' the dining room was large. The little company was constrained by it. There was not the intimacy of 'Forli'. For a while Elgar and Mr Griffith argued roughly about the Boer War that was just then developing. Mr Griffith took the part of the Afrikaner farmers and was heartily denounced by his host. But the discussion did not proceed very far. Their voices echoed in the room and each person felt self-conscious as though they had no right to be there.

Their mood improved when they returned to the drawing room at the front of the house. Elgar went and stood by the new piano. He regarded it proudly, rubbing his hands with anticipation.

'At least here we have room for a real piano,' he said. 'We can now have house-music just as they do in Germany.'

'Would you care to entertain us again?' he continued, turning courteously to Mr Griffith.

'I fear I am unable to,' was the reply. 'I did not bring my music with me.' Mr Griffith gazed gravely and sadly at his boots.

Elgar sat down at the piano and began to play. First came some of his early, light pieces. Then he stopped and said, 'Here is something that I have recently completed. Can you think of a title for it?'

Slowly, quietly, he began a gentle, grave melody. As it developed there came into it a hint of melancholy but also a quality of resolution. Dora was surprised and pleased to discover that she could identify the subject of the music. Yes, there again came that opening phrase that suggested to her a viola player crossing the strings. She contained herself, waiting for the pianist to complete the piece. It ended on a single, protracted note, very like the sounding of a horn.

Dora burst out, 'Why that's Isobel, Isobel Fitton.'

Elgar nodded, a pleased and rather knowing smile on his face. Alice nodded her head complacently but Mr Griffith merely continued, with a pessimistic air, to gaze at the floor. Was he bored or just somnolent?

'What is the title for this then?' continued Elgar.

It was solemn, dignified music but there was also an under-tone of merriment to it. Dora was definitely reminded of some-one she had met, probably at one of the Hydes' receptions. She thought and thought. But she had finally to give up.

'It's Richard Arnold,' said Alice, surprised, perhaps indignant even at Dora's failure to identify him. Dora thought it strange that they should expect her to know their large circle of acquaint-ance as well as they did themselves. But she remembered the man now. He was the son of the poet Matthew Arnold, and himself a person of literary interests. He lived hereabouts. In fact on one of her visits Dora had attended a reception at his house. He was very gentlemanly but had a strange nervous laugh which Elgar had caught very accurately in his music.

'Now, how about this one?' asked Elgar. He was becoming caught up in the game. Mr Griffith appeared to be asleep with his eyes open. But Elgar did not care. He began the next sketch.

It started with a heavy drum-roll and then continued hastily and impetuously. It sounded like someone hurrying around busily and clumsily. There was a good deal of bluster in it. The music now suggested a loud, coarse argument. It swept on and on insistently and clamorously and came to a sudden, gauche con-clusion with, yes, the sound of braying in it.

There was no difficulty at all in identifying the portrait. Its accuracy was shocking. But also comic. Yet Mr Griffith con-tinued to gaze down at the floor, apparently quite unaware that this was he. Dora could hardly control her laughter. She put her fingers in her mouth and looked away. Her face grew red and tears hung on her lower eyelids. She simply could not get over the way the piece had ended with a banging sound that brilliantly parodied Mr Griffith's piano-playing earlier on.

The subject of the work blinked his eyes; his mind was far away. Alice tittered decorously and secretly behind a white lace handkerchief.

'Shall I play it again?' asked Elgar, suavely wicked. He clearly savoured his revenge. And without waiting for a reply he hurried again into the raucous, obstreperous piece.

Mr Griffith now noticed the button missing from his coat and pulled at the broken threads with a vague, childlike interest. Dora bit her lip hard. Her jaw was unsteady. Elgar smiled dreamily as he struck the keys; he enjoyed his effect upon her.

The piece came to an end and there was silence in the room. Dora gradually controlled herself.

'They are all part of a series, you know . . .' began Elgar now, for some reason, mumbling shyly.

'How many sketches are there?' asked Dora politely.

'Oh, a dozen or more . . . They are for the orchestra.'

Alice intervened enthusiastically, 'Oh they are wonderful, Dora, when you hear them together. Quite the best thing that Edward has ever done, in my view. They are to be performed at this year's Three Choirs Festival. It will be in Worcester this time, you know. Oh you must come down and hear it. Your music is a part . . .'

Dora caught her breath. 'Oh, I will, I will. I will try.'

'I shall write to Minnie and tell her about it,' announced Alice. 'She must come too. She will find it amusing, since she knows all the originals. Some are very old friends. And she will admire it I know.' The grey-haired lady seemed about to burst with pride and managerial purposefulness. She surveyed the young woman and her husband with heavily indulgent eyes.

Dora found the mood in the room oppressive now. She felt that more admiration was called for. But what else was there to be said? To her relief there came a knock at the front door. The grand parlour-maid led in Herr Augustus who had arrived on the evening train from London. The little man entered the room smiling. He kissed Alice's hand and then Dora's. Next he shook hands with Elgar and Mr Griffith, each time bowing his head.

He looked tired and pale. But his presence exuded a special warmth and kindliness into the room. He wore a neat blue suit, the style and cloth of which were not English. His shirt had a creamy celluloid collar and his tie was of an unusual yellow pattern. The maid brought him some light refreshment on a tray. He ate the food neatly and delicately.

Comparing the fastidious German with the baggy figure of Mr Griffith who sat nearby, Dora was struck by the idea that they were plain opposites and yet, at the same time, Elgar's two closest friends.

'The passages which you have sent me . . .' began Augustus, 'wonderful . . . wonderful . . .' His English was insufficient at this moment but his eyes blazed with admiration as he looked at the composer.

Elgar glanced about sideways and grew embarrassed. He suggested hoarsely that they might play the passages in question the following day. Dora was intrigued by this friendship, by the German's emotional directness and Elgar's awkward evasiveness. Friendships were hard to understand. And whatever had happened to Herr Ettling? She had neither heard nor seen anything of him for months. What could have happened to him?

'Let's play the sonatas that we tried out last time you were here,' mumbled Elgar under his moustache.

Augustus looked surprised for a moment or two but then seated himself at the piano and gave Elgar the note to tune his violin. Then they began to play Beethoven sonatas for the two instruments. They concluded with the *Kreutzer* and the *Spring*.

How beautiful and stirring that concert was! Dora felt her very body touched by the power of the music and the close and enmeshed reverberation of the two instruments. Below, in the Wells Road, a gentleman on horseback and a young couple in a pony and trap halted to listen to the compelling, bright sound issuing from the lamplit room high above them and eddying out strongly over the darkening Severn Plain.

With Augustus as a fellow guest there was no immediate oppor-

tunity for Dora and Elgar to be alone together or to talk about
her own music. Perhaps the arrangement had been made for this
very reason, she thought. In any case the girl was very happy
during her stay. She greatly enjoyed the company of the German.
Her pride and confidence were reassured by his kindly regard
and affection for her and by his thoughtful attentiveness. He
was a genuine, gallant and in no way problematic admirer.

On the following evening Elgar played some more of the
sketches. Without saying anything he began to play her own
music. She saw that Augustus was studying her attentively as she
listened. But she was happy to find that she experienced none of
her former embarrassment.

The intermezzo came to an end. Augustus took Elgar's place
at the piano.

'Will you, please, to dance it for us?' asked the German
humbly.

And without any hesitation or ado, she did. How altogether
natural it was to swing about that large room in her simple white
blouse and dark skirt, responding with her whole body to the
quiet, delicate rhythms of her own music. She pattered and
swayed and yearned across the open floor without in any way
planning her dance. The music led her along. The light leather
soles of her shoes scratched on the uncovered floorboards with a
sound like that of mice. Yet the sound fitted in with the especially
gentle, fairy-like way in which Augustus played his friend's
music. Her audience was in thrall to her. The music fitted her
and she it; she abandoned herself to it and was carried by it.

'Bravo! Bravo!' exclaimed Augustus as the final, quiet notes
fell away under his fingers. Alice and Elgar clapped their hands,
still captivated by the youthful grace of the dance. Thinking
about it afterwards Dora was surprised that she had not before
suspected how perfect her music was for her dancing.

On the following evening she danced again, so that when, on
the morning after that, she had to return to Wolverhampton,
her music which had once been a difficult emotional issue between herself and its composer was now something social, even
familial. As she pedalled thoughtfully through the countryside,
Dora judged this to be a relief. But also a loss.

Within three weeks she was back in Malvern. Elgar had invited her to visit them at the little cottage in the woods where, in their growing prosperity, they now spent the weekends. The July was blazingly hot; the air felt vibrant with sunshine. Dora was sweating and uncomfortable as she stopped, north of the town, to consult yet another amusingly drawn map which he had sent her. She leaned her cycle against an ancient oak by the roadside, took off her straw hat and fanned herself with it. The brim was wet and her white blouse and long green cotton skirt stuck to her body. She stood listening to the low hum of insects in the green hedge. When she was cooler, she set off to the right up a narrow and steep woodland path which she thought, not altogether confidently, was the one indicated on his map. The way was stony and often she had to lift and carry her bicycle. But she was grateful for the shade and the quiet gloom under the big trees. Even the texture of the moist green ferns as they brushed against her skirt seemed refreshing. After a while she came to a junction of four or five narrow paths. The map made no mention of this. She stood wearily, miserably, wondering what to do.

Then she became aware that this glade, like the whole hillside wood, was full of birds and their song. Why had she not noticed the din before? Birds flew low among the branches. Small nestlings were making their first attempts at flight. There was incessant chatter and whistling and calling, from tree to tree and from glade to glade. The woods were raucous with birds.

As she continued to ponder her direction, Dora caught the sound, amidst the noise of the birds, of the notes of a piano. It was faint, very faint, yet definitely distinguishable. She wondered if she were dreaming the sound in that remote wood. But no, there it was, a piano playing, re-playing, sometimes changing slightly, the same lyric theme. Dora thought she could tell the direction from which it came, so that was the way she decided to set off. And, sure enough, as she climbed further, the sound of the piano grew louder. Then came a moment when there was a balance, a startling complementariness between the sound of the birds and that of the instrument. Dora paused for a while to listen. She had never heard anything like it before.

She resumed her climb up the steep dirt path, up and up. At

last, with a quick curve, it led out, broadening, on to a small patch of well-tended grass, behind which was an old red-brick cottage. 'Birchwood' was the name on the gate. This was it! And there, by the low front door sat Alice under a large sun parasol. The sounds of the cottage piano now boomed loudly from an open window.

Alice rose to greet the girl. She took the cycle rather gingerly and, after some struggle with it, leaned it against the front window. She called inside to Elgar and the piano ceased, leaving a strange, heady buzz of silence in which even the sound of the birds was reduced.

Elgar appeared at the door. He wore an alpaca jacket, white flannels and a white shirt without a tie. They were very much clothes in which to relax on a hot summer's day yet they looked incongruous on him. His eyes, his posture, the set of his head were too intense for the new fashion of 'weekending'. He still held his pencil between his teeth.

'La Mia Dorabella,' he shouted jollily.

'Your Excellency,' she replied, bowing her head in ostentatious respect.

'Oh, you poor girl, how hot you are!' He stood surveying her.

'Come in. Come in and rest and have something to drink.' He led her up the path to the front door. Inside the cottage it was cool, almost chill. They sat down in the kitchen that had a pleasing, red-tiled floor. The ceiling was so low that the man had to stoop. Dora noticed his hair. Today it was combed back sleekly, close to his skull. She was reminded of an animal's head and muzzle. From the dark larder he brought a stone jug of lemon water that Alice had made that morning. Dora drank a glass of it at one go. The two older people watched her attentively.

Then Alice brought out an uncut Gloucester cheese, a fresh loaf of farmhouse bread and some tomatoes. Dora grew cooler and her energy returned to her. She asked if she might see the cottage. She could never understand why the Elgars always found themselves in houses so different from everyone else's. She was shown two low-ceilinged bedrooms that were reached by the smallest of winding staircases and also the oak-beamed sitting room where the upright piano stood. This room was littered with sheets of music paper, some written upon and some not. Elgar was anxious to be gone from here. They returned to the kitchen and sat down. There was a silence.

'Shall we walk in the woods?' said Elgar to Dora haltingly, unexpectedly.

'Oh yes, do go, the two of you,' said Alice quickly, as if on cue. 'I do not wish to walk. It is too hot for me by far. And besides I have some sewing that I wish to finish.'

The man glanced at his wife irritably. He was much irked by having his invitation placed so obviously under his wife's auspices.

But Dora politely nodded her acquiescence and the two set off into the heat. After a while they came to a shimmering mossy glade where Elgar, coughing, suggested they sit down. They sat close together, their backs against the trunk of a tall, shady tree. Dora took off her hat and placed it by her green skirt, which spread out about her revealing her shoes of soft leather and her ankles covered by her long white cotton stockings. They sat in silence for a while listening to the many sounds of the wood. He was much taken with the rhythmic rise and fall of her firm bosom just inches below his head. He looked at her legs, slightly apart and stretched out under her thin skirt. With his foot he could have touched her foot. The sunshine burned down in bright patches through the high interlacing of branches and greenery. They were very solitary in this remote place. Normal constraints could easily, quickly fall away.

His body stiffened with desire for her. Then he noticed that he had absent-mindedly brought a sheet of music paper with him. He had been holding it in his hand all the time. He put it down among the dark coiling roots of the tree.

He turned again to look at her. Slowly he moved his eyes down her body from the topmost wisps of her hair down to the buckles on her shoes. He saw that in one place her shirt had come away from her skirt top and he could see her bodice. Her eyes were shut. How vulnerable she was! There was something childlike in the untidiness of her shirt. She could have been his daughter. Almost. Not really. His desire steadily infused his whole body and his head and his mouth. But how could he ever touch this girl, this child?

The birds of the wood hopped about them. After a time he said, in what he intended as a kindly way, 'If we are perfectly quiet, perhaps someone will come and talk to us.'

As he spoke his tongue and throat were dry with desire. Right away he was intensely angry with himself for talking to her in this foolish, childish way. He was a sentimental, cowardly fool. Why could he not be direct, forthright in his desire? Like the Prince of Wales? Years ago he had accompanied his father when he went to tune the pianos at Witley Court, the great house just a few miles down the road, and he well recalled the stories that were told in the servants' hall of the Prince's many adventures. Phrases, details roused him still.

Yet at this exciting dizzying moment he could think of nothing to say or do. There was a protracted silence.

And then, to confirm his earlier prediction a plump robin came hopping towards them through the trees. It stopped and cocked its head enquiringly just two or three yards from their outstretched feet. The girl opened her eyes and turned to Elgar with a smile of enchantment on her face. For a moment the man's bitter frustration was in abeyance. With a sceptical shake of the head the robin turned and hopped away and disappeared among the trees.

The man and the girl continued to recline there against the tree in the sultry gloom of the clearing. After a while a field mouse appeared, moving towards them jerkily, in quick spurts. The little, bright-eyed creature came close enough for Dora to have been able to touch it. She gave a cry of delight. The mouse fled.

Again she turned to smile happily at her companion. They continued to sit. Her head swayed drowsily. She was content, he knew. But did she even think of another contentment? It was for him to put this to her with an action, gesture or words. It was for him to lead her or fail her. If he did not act he would fail her. For he was fully aware of his ascendancy over her. He knew that no one would ever replace him. He knew all this. The knowledge brought a feeling of desperation.

His eye fell again on the patch of white stocking below the hem of her dress. His will was gone; he felt suspended, arrested in tension.

He lowered his head and saw the sheet of music paper by his side. His wife had patiently ruled the lines for him, to save a few pennies, as she had always done, since the time they were poor together. She did so much for him. She had even allowed, encouraged, managed this very walk with the girl. And she had known he could not act. She must have. She had merely arranged to further her own designs for him. His wife controlled him in ways he only occasionally surmised. He was grateful to her, certainly. But also bound to her, enclosed by her. At times he loathed her. And the young girl she also controlled.

If only he could move those few inches to the dozing girl in her light cotton clothes. But his good wife whom he loved, depended upon and resented was another scotch upon his desire.

He sat for a good while in this state of heightened consciousness, this sense of a decisive time, yet fully aware that he was suspended in inaction.

The tension did not disappear but gradually grew less violent. The girl, he noticed, had gone to sleep. His desire turned sour. How undignified, how absurd he was! What a fool! With a bitter set to his mouth he dozed away into sleep.

They slept there against the tree together for about two hours. They were awakened by the tonk-tonk-tonk of a sheep-bell nearby. Each was instantly awake and they laughed aloud at the comic sound and at having slept.

'It's tea-time,' exclaimed Elgar guiltily, consulting his pocket-watch. They scrambled up, dusted twigs from their clothes and set off to return to the cottage. Dora felt refreshed and happy. She was now quite recovered from her long bicycle ride. But her companion was silent and involved with his own thoughts.

'Wouldn't you like to be able to live here all the t . . . t . . . time?' she asked buoyantly.

'I would,' was the quick, definite answer. After a moment or two he went on patronisingly, 'But this is not where the audiences are and the concert-goers are, is it? This is not where life is led. I have to go to Burslem and Huddersfield this week. And you to Wolverhampton.'

But Dora would not be made miserable. She went loiteringly down the bracken-lined path, trailing her hat. She loved to be alone with him in unspoiled country like this. She remembered White Ladies. She could imagine no greater happiness. It was a loss in her life that she would not have, or even imagine, a further happiness.

Over tea Elgar was withdrawn. He was filled with self-doubt and self-loathing for his failure earlier in the afternoon. He was a nincompoop, he thought. An old fool. He went more and more into himself. Alice talked on blandly and melodiously to Dora about trivial things.

After tea she took out the archives, the large confused collection of all the reviews and comment ever printed of her husband's compositions and performances. It was her ambition to place in chronological order everything that had ever been written about him. It was an immense task and one for which Alice had the will but not the ability. All the small cuttings were too much for her; they hurt her eyes. And in any case her many powers did not include the necessary secretarial skills. But Dora took to the work immediately. Her slender fingers moved rapidly as she helped the older woman to arrange and paste the cuttings in the large leather volumes. They worked away patiently until the darkness came. The man sat on a chair in a corner, smoking a cigar and gazing moodily through the window.

Throughout the following day he remained in the front room working over certain passages at the piano. At meal-times he was distant and occasionally uncivil. Dora wondered if she were to blame. In her mind she went over everything that she had done and said but could think of nothing that might have offended him.

The weather grew oppressive. The brilliant sunshine of yesterday had turned into a cloudy sultriness. It was building up to a thunderstorm. Dora decided that she would leave early, before the Elgars returned to Wells Road. But Alice detained her while she finished an enthusiastic letter to Minnie.

'And do urge her to come to the Three Choirs. I know she will enjoy it. I wonder how many of the sketches she will recognise? And you have definitely promised to come, Dora dear, have you not?'

'Yes, I shall come.' The girl spoke falteringly.

Alice finished the letter, sealed it with a regal gesture and handed it over. Dora wheeled out her bicycle.

'Dora is leaving now,' cried Alice outside Elgar's door. After some moments the piano fell silent and he came out.

He said, 'But you will be caught in the storm that is coming.' His manner was only apparently solicitous. Underneath it was guarded and steely.

'No, I have decided to ride only as far as Worcester. Then I shall put my bicycle in the guard's van and t . . . t . . . take the train.'

She shook hands with them and wheeled her cycle to the top of the hillside path. The air in the woods was intensely humid and sticky. She thought he might have helped her down to the road and was hurt that he did not. He merely waved to her once from the top and then returned to the cottage. He treated her as though she were only an acquaintance. As she struggled down the steep, difficult path with her cycle, she felt tearful to think that she had offended him.

She pedalled all the way to Worcester in a frenzy of self-questioning. She must also race the storm. The hot, heavy, moist air struck her like a blanket. The first large raindrops started to fall and the lightning cracked across the sky at the very moment she entered the Foregate station. She carried her bicycle up the high stone staircase to the platform just as her train steamed in, the black boiler and cab and tender and the cream and brown coaches all streaming with sheets of rain.

As the kindly old guard with the walrus moustache helped her stow her cycle on the train, it occurred to her to wonder whether the Elgars might worry about her. She hastened to the metal kiosk, purchased a postcard of the cathedral and addressed it to them. It would just be in time for the evening post. The only message she could think to put down were the words: 'High and dry'.

Then she settled down wearily in the train. As she travelled on through the lurid rain and thunder of that summer evening, her mind echoed with the phrases that the man had played at the piano whilst she had conversed with Alice.

Over breakfast on the morning after her return home Dora preferred to inform Minnie of very little of what had happened on this visit. Instead she entertained her by telling her yet again of Mr Griffith's music and the incidents relating to it. Her stepmother was much amused by what she heard of the musical sketches of her old friends and she required no persuasion to go to the Three Choirs in order to hear them performed.

As the two women chatted on, they were astonished to hear murmurs from the Rector at the other end of the table. He interrupted them to announce that he also would attend the Festival. A concert of sacred music, he intoned, would be a source of spiritual strength to him. The two women opened their mouths in surprise at this announcement.

The Rector was more plump, ruddy and apopleptic-looking than in former years. And increasingly his custom was to spend meal-times in preoccupied silence, whilst his wife and daughter talked quietly to each other. There was no discourtesy in this. It was accepted, established habit. So it was a shock to hear him address them. It was more like a pronouncement. He had made it and did not refer to it again.

So off they set, the three of them, one bright morning in early autumn. Mrs Bayliss waved them off as their hansom clopped off down Horse Fair. She was sad; she would miss the family. She waved away until the cab was out of sight and then returned to her underground kitchen, to express her many doubts about this excursion to the uncomprehending Mrs Shinton.

On the train the Rector sat stolidly, staring through the window, seeing everything, remarking nothing. Dora might have laughed at him. But for some reason she was much irritated by the large and, to her, ignominious umbrella that he held and twisted between his knees. The beautiful fruit orchards passed by their window. He saw nothing. Dora felt constrained by his presence. He signified an imprisonment to her. She would not be able to go to 'Craeg Lea' as usual. Instead she must stay with her parents who put up at a fusty hotel that was near the cathedral close and much patronised by visiting clergy. Yet she was somewhat comforted by the thought that she was invited to the reception at the Star Hotel that the Elgars were giving after the concert at which the sketches were to be played.

The next evening when the three of them set off for the concert, Dora wore a new suit of soft green wool and a hat of the same colour that dipped becomingly to the side and had a veil in the new French style. Though it was a pleasant, sunny evening the Rector brought the large, flapping umbrella to use as a walking-stick.

At the great door to the cathedral, a portly, self-important sidesman took their tickets and led them slowly to their places. There was an unusual atmosphere of suppressed excitement in the sombre medieval interior. Dora was immediately aware of the buzzing attention she attracted as she walked the length of the high echoing nave. The whispering hubbub intensified as people turned in ways they considered unobtrusive, to look at her. She had had some suspicion that this might happen, for the sketches had been played, some weeks earlier, in the St James' Hall in London under the famous German conductor, Hans Richter. So she knew that her music would be known to some. But she had not realised how many. And she had not known at all how self-conscious and uncomfortable she would feel to be recognised in such a large assembly. She lowered her eyes, blushing, and fixed them on the worn stone flags of the floor.

Her seat was on the edge of an aisle. And when at last she had managed to recover some of her composure, she glanced surreptitiously about her to see who had come. There was Mr Griffith near the alabaster pulpit in what was clearly his best suit. He was attempting to look debonair. But his tie was alarmingly awry; he looked as though he had been cut down from a hanging. Nearby sat Rosa Burley with a nervous cough and a continual shake to her head. Alice and Augustus sat together at the front. Three rows behind them was Isobel Fitton looking pale and alarmed; she turned and gave Dora a shy wave. Dora wondered if

Herr Ettling had come. It was strange to see all these people whom she associated with the Hydes' salon and with 'Forli' in this vast, solemn and imposing cathedral. Dora was intrigued by the strange pink cast to the ancient walls. Her eyes swept up to the arcade and the dim, mysterious triforium. All the old, easy friendships took on a new seriousness.

The cathedral was now full. By some inexplicable act of the general will the whispering subsided and was replaced by a mood of silent and intense anticipation as the audience waited for the members of the orchestra to settle themselves under the crossing tower by the chancel arch. Then the music began. Despite everyone's expectation it came as a surprise. It sounded loudly through the high building, booming and resonating.

The first item was a Handel anthem. There followed a cantata of the early Victorian period. Dora found this piece dull. But then after a brief, hushed pause the orchestra started to play Elgar's new work. How different this sounded from what had gone before. It was the more atmospheric, lighter, more flowing music of the end of the century. Dora was dismayed to see a supercilious, even contemptuous, expression establish itself on her father's broad face. But the girl and her stepmother were quickly caught up in the novelty of the music. Those sketches which Dora had heard played on the piano now sounded altogether different as the sounds of the orchestra rang up and down the stone tracery and high vaulting of the cathedral. Occasionally Minnie and Dora would turn to each other with amused, shocked expressions when they were able to identify one of the subjects. Dora noticed that other members of the audience were behaving similarly, talking, as it were, with their eyes. One of the sketches even made Minnie open her mouth wide in a scandalised way, her eyes fearful and uncertain, as though the music had said too much.

But when the great ninth section began, the faces in the audience grew still. The listeners were set back and awed by its ambitiousness, by that mood of noble aspiration which was established and then developed and borne along by the insistent course of the music to the almost unbearably splendid climax. Dora remembered that evening when Elgar and Augustus had played

184

the Beethoven violin and piano sonatas together. And she knew without doubt that it was to the generous, loyal German that this stirring passage alluded. As the section came to its quiet conclusion, as the notes vanished one by one into the high dark roof, Dora nearly wept at the gentle dignity of it.

And then, almost before she had realised it, the orchestra was well into her own music. She was greatly taken with the sound of the viola. But she blushed bright red as she sensed that people were identifying her. The Rector noticed her flushed face and his eyes glittered angrily. Dora's mind went into such a whirl that she could only listen distantly to her music. Her hot self-consciousness prevented her from concentrating. She was actually glad when it ended and the next sketch began. She was now able to attend better. She knew that the present section had to do with Mr Sinclair, an organist, who was a friend of Elgar's. It was an amusing passage. Mr Sinclair's bulldog could be heard barking.

The sketches followed on fascinatingly. Dora had no idea how many there were to be. But with the proud commanding gesture which the fourteenth quickly made she knew that this would be the conclusion. She also felt instinctively that this was Elgar speaking not about some other person, but about himself. The gravity, the idealism and the carefully measured pride that swelled in this music she had always known to be in him, under the shabby suit of the country music teacher and the ostentatious formal dress of the successful conductor. She was reminded of that evening, all those years ago, in Wolverhampton, when she had asked him about himself. This now was her answer.

The music compelled her. She was losing control of her emotions. She felt she might in some way break down. To what nobility the music built! At last there came the exaltation of the final chords. They beat about her. They swept up into the lancets of the high east window. Their intensity made her feel deaf. She could not hear them fully. It was more than she could receive.

The next item on the programme she was too unsettled to attend to. She sat in a slumber, her ears exhausted and her mind moving slowly over her impressions of the earlier work, especially his own music. For some reason she kept thinking of the story of Whewall, the dandified miner.

The concert ended and she had to rouse herself. She was by no means ready yet for the social world. But the three of them had to set off for the Star Hotel where the reception was to be held. As they walked through the now quiet streets gently lit by the orange evening sun, the Rector was full of bitter criticism of what he had just heard.

'That such frivolous, modish, worldly music should be heard in God's house! God will surely judge this country!'

He was greatly appalled. The bitter voice rasped on and on, while they slowly made their way across College Yard and Deansway, down the High Street and into Foregate. As if distantly Dora was aware of the column of black-clad paupers moving across the Queen Anne courtyard of Berkeley Hospital. She was also taken with the bright red and very French façade of the Hop Market Commercial Hotel that was just now being completed. But for the most part her mind was oppressed by her father's harsh, insistent voice; it jarred on her nerves and made her feel sick. She was relieved when they reached the Star Hotel, one of the large old coaching inns of the city.

The reception in the banqueting room was grander than any Dora had ever attended before. Standing complacently in a corner and the centre of attention was the Bishop in his purple cassock. There were many other high dignitaries including the Dean of Worcester and the Lord Mayor of the city in his ornate gold chain. The gathering was an important civic occasion. Every year, it seemed, the Elgars moved in different, more elevated circles. Dora felt uncomfortable. This was all so far removed from her normal experience.

She felt very much on her own in that large assembly. She looked about her for someone to stand with and to speak to. Her stepmother was happily engaged with some old friends and her father had joined a group of dull-looking clergy. He stood among them, his eyes cast down upon the floor, not attending to what was being said.

And there beside the window stood Elgar also within a group

of people (all of them ladies in large and elaborate hats) and similarly distracted. How alike the two stances and attitudes, Dora thought. How apart they both were from the hats and spats of the Worcester burghers, the Kidderminster carpet-makers, the Birmingham enamellers and the Wolverhampton ironmasters who made such a showy occasion of coming to the Three Choirs. Each of the two men stood there in his dream. Yet how utterly different their dreams were!

Dora continued to edge about the crowded room looking for someone she knew. She was aware that strangers were looking at her. She assumed a rather forced air of indifference. (It was to grow into one of the characteristics of her later life.) At last she came upon Rosa Burley in a large green cloak that looked more appropriate to the opera house than to the cathedral. The two shook hands and then did not let go. They recognised that they very much depended upon each other at this moment. Dora enquired if various acquaintances were present. But Rosa Burley had seen no one as yet.

'Will Herr Ettling be coming?' asked Dora. 'I haven't seen him for ages. It must be years. I do hope he will b . . . b . . . be here.'

Rosa Burley's unsteady eyes regarded the girl uneasily. Or was it critically? Then she said with some relish, 'Oh, didn't you know? Ettling has been dropped.'

Dora could not take it in.

'Oh yes. They dropped him some time ago. I should have thought you would have known.'

The pale, nervous face of the schoolmistress shook with pleasure as she announced the dismissal of the enemy who had been so very distasteful to her. But soon her expression became more reflective. She looked at Dora questioningly. At that moment both women were confronting the shocking possibility of being dismissed from this very society in which they now found themselves.

As well they might. For within a few years Rosa Burley would be dropped. And some fifteen years later when Dora, in her middle age, acquiesced apathetically and half-heartedly in a dull marriage she too would be neglected ever after. When he first encountered her as a married woman, the composer would cut her in the street.

But this was years ahead, at the time of all the other suffering of the Great War. The present, disturbing silence shared by the two women was now ended by Elgar himself.

'Ah, Dorabella. At last I've found you.' He stood at a slight distance, admiring and appreciating her. He looked elegant in his evening dress; he wore jewelled cuff-links. Poor Herr Ettling could not be this man's companion.

Dora was much relieved that he was no longer resentful and displeased with her as he had been at their last meeting. He was most jovial. What accounted for the change?

He stepped up to her, grasped her firmly by the arm and led her away. Dora felt that they were being rude to Rosa Burley. But Elgar was very purposive.

'Come,' he said briskly, 'you must meet your fellow variations. Oh, and there's something else I have to tell you.' He mumbled into his moustache. 'Something between you and me.'

But first came the introductions to those others in the new music whom she had not yet met. They were all either squires or ladies from the local gentry or country musicians such as Elgar himself had once been. Dora felt an immediate sympathy with each of them and they, she was sure, with her. They had been made to belong together. They were like a family. Elgar had taken them and put them in a pattern together so that their lives would never be the same again. The famous music would give Dora status as a local celebrity. But, far more important, her place in the music would give her a feeling of profound and intimate involvement in the lives of others whom actually, socially, she did not know well. Some forty-five years later, when the factories and outskirts of Wolverhampton were levelled by German bombs, Dora, as an old lady, would grieve more deeply for this family than for any other. She was the youngest of the fourteen and she would be the last survivor.

Finally, Elgar led her up to Augustus and made a grandly formal introduction, as though they had never met before. The German bowed, then kissed her hand, his lips lingering affectionately on her fingers. Dora could have thrown her arms around him, so heady she felt with affection and excitement. Augustus, the other variations and Elgar made her heart palpitate and her breath quicken. She was even more atremble now than when she had heard the music in the cathedral.

Then Alice made her way over. She whispered emphatically, bullyingly in her husband's ear. Regretfully and with the briefest of nods to Dora and Augustus he followed his wife across the room.

Nor did Dora have an opportunity to speak to him again that evening. He was so taken up with well-wishers and admirers. Finally Minnie summoned Dora to rejoin her father, who in his own grandly obsequious fashion was speaking to the Bishop and his circle of British commercial activities in the South Seas.

'In the final instance,' he was saying, 'in the final instance, contracts with the natives could be enforced. Enforced.'

When she was back in Wolverhampton Dora pondered a good deal about what Elgar had intended to say to her. His changed attitude suggested that something new was afoot. He seemed determined about something. But what? Always the mystery. She could but wait as usual. She knew that he would write to her.

Instead there came a telegram: 'Alice ill. Can you come?' Instantly, without consciously deciding to go, Dora went and changed into her travelling clothes. She felt as though she were being hurried along, without her willing it, as in a dream. In her haste she was quite indifferent to Minnie's many questions, her frightened eyes and her nervous, tentative hints that there was some impropriety in her going.

On this occasion Dora was able to afford to take the train and she arrived in Malvern in the early afternoon. She found a weak, haggard Alice in the music room struggling tearfully and inadequately with the archives. She had a high fever. There was perspiration on her sallow brow and her teeth clacked together so loudly they could be heard from the other side of the large room. Dora tried to persuade her to go upstairs to bed. Reluctantly the old lady at last agreed. Though, invariably, on those few occasions when she was able to focus on Dora, there came a hard, sceptical glint into her eyes. But at last the young woman was able to get her to bed. She brought her her favourite Indian tea and a compress and finally left her in an uneasy sleep.

During all this time Elgar himself had been in the music room too. He sat in his shirt-sleeves going over some of the proofs for his new oratorio. He was very cheerful, winked a good deal at Dora and was utterly indifferent to his wife's illness. He had sent for the doctor a few hours before but that was the extent of his concern. He even appeared to take a pleasure in his indifference. Dora was slightly appalled by such callousness.

When she returned downstairs from settling the invalid, the afternoon post had come bringing more proofs of his latest work, the great oratorio. There was also a long letter from Augustus suggesting many revisions. Elgar thrust the letter into Dora's hand.

'Here, you read it. I find it difficult to make out that German handwriting.'

He spoke gruffly, almost bullyingly. Then he lay down on a chaise longue, letting his left arm trail to the floor and supporting his head in a dandyish, negligent manner with his right hand. But the carefully adopted posture now had the effect of making him look stout and older.

'Begin.'

Obediently she started to read. But each paragraph was punctuated with a snort from Elgar.

'Impossible. Ridiculous. Shan't change that, for him or for anyone else.'

Dora stopped reading, hurt. What was the point, when everything in the letter was so rudely dismissed?

He sensed her upset and jumped up. 'I'll show you what I mean,' he said, more reasonably. 'He really is asking me to change some of my better things. I'll play it to you, if you like.'

He hurried over to the window with the wide green prospect of the Severn Plain. Dora expected him to produce his violin. But his eye fell on a shabby trombone-case standing in the corner. He hesitated then took out the instrument and glanced across at Dora with a mischievous look.

'This is the passage to which he refers,' he said gravely. 'You see if you don't think I'm right.'

And he started to blow on the instrument. It sounded like a distressed donkey and was immediately, irresistibly comic. The foolish, braying sound was so strange and out of place in this room. Dora had prepared herself to listen to passages of solemn music but she found herself in a violent fit of uncontrollable laughter. 'HEE HAW, HEE HAW', blared the trombone. This was more like something for the circus than for a cathedral. 'HEE HAW, HEE HAW'. The player was swelling his cheeks and yes, rolling his eyes. Dora's body shook from head to foot with giggles. Elgar now marched about flat-footedly, occasionally lifting his knees up high. He was like a clown in some ludicrous oompah band.

Often he would hit the wrong note or the trombone would produce a shrill squeak or a vulgar grunt. It all sounded like some strange bad-tempered animal that could squeak like a mouse and roar like a bull. Dora was now beginning to lose control of herself; she grew more and more susceptible to the outrageous sounds. She could no longer prevent her laughter from convulsing her and weakening the muscles in her lower body. Her face was red and wet with tears. She took out her lace handkerchief and held it to her mouth and eyes but this did no good. The laughter took her breath and shook her ever more violently. 'HEE HAW . . .' Dora thought she might be becoming hysterical.

The man stopped and eyed the flow of spittle trickling out of the instrument. He looked so foolishly surprised by what he saw. Dora was winded by a whack of laughter that made her hang her head down from the side of her chair. She sobbed and sobbed.

He turned on her pompously. 'How *can* you expect me to play this dodgasted thing properly if you laugh so?'

Dora sobered briefly. The adjective was perilously close to blasphemy. She hiccoughed.

With a flourish he resumed his playing. 'HEE HAW, HEE HAW'. But more and more the music degenerated into a series of coarse, flatulent explosions, each one eliciting an oath from the performer.

Dora was again in a fit. She could not shut her mouth, her hair had come undone and hung down on her shoulders and her body palpitated violently. Sometimes she would sit forward in her chair and try to control herself. But then the next piggy grunt from the trombone would set her rolling back in her chair. At last, almost incontinent, she darted from the room and went up and sat on the topmost landing by the attic.

It was well over half an hour before she had recovered herself and was able to return to the room. Elgar had now gone back to his piano and would occasionally play and re-play passages from the proofs. He was preoccupied and did not speak to her. Though peculiarly weary, Dora busied herself with the archives that poor Alice had left in such a jumble.

Dora and Elgar had dinner together. Sitting across from each other in their formal dress and served by the prim housekeeper in the heavily starched apron they could have been man and wife. Sometimes they could hear Alice weakly calling to them from upstairs. When she went to tend her, Dora found her full of anxiety. Dora suspected that the older woman feared that she no longer had that ultimate control which she had had on those other occasions when she had allowed, or arranged for her husband to be alone with the girl. Alice struggled to rise but she was too weak. She fell back tearfully among the twisted sheets.

Afterwards Dora and Elgar went to the drawing room together. She drank coffee and he played the piano for her. His mood had changed again. He was kindly and gentle with her, and between items he talked to her of what he had played. He started to speak of his ambition to write a violin concerto, but then stopped guiltily. He talked of his great interest in the opera, especially Mozart. He gave her a brief intimate smile and then talked on. Never before had he been so direct and forthcoming about music as now. But there was a hard, tense set to his jaw. And beneath the pleasant, charmingly intimate manner she sensed again that new purposiveness and determination in his bearing towards her of which she had been aware at the Three Choirs.

Something would happen, she knew. But for the moment she relaxed in the comfort and glamour of the evening. Into the high-ceilinged room with its bare walls there drifted the white light of the half-moon standing above the shadowy, broad plain outside. The darker white of the gaslight from the street lamp cut across the pale moonlight in thick wedges. Dora in her loose crêpe dress of light blue studied this pattern of light as she listened to her concert. Elgar played some Beethoven sonatas, some pieces by Brahms and some new things by his friend Richard Strauss. He put together a sequence of some of his own early pieces and then played the *Sea Pictures* in full. This was followed by some passages from the new oratorio and from the Cockaigne overture. For some reason Dora was reminded of the child on the station platform at Worcester. Then Elgar fell to improvising for a while; he was thoughtful and musing. The two of them shared a peaceful contentedness.

Then Elgar roused himself and started to play some of the sketches from the Variations. The first was that of Mr Griffith. They both laughed aloud, heartily and happily, as Elgar thumped away at the keys in the conclusion. He went on to play several others and asked Dora whether the subjects had recognised themselves and how they responded. He was both curious and ignorant about the effects of his work. He greatly enjoyed what Dora could tell him. They talked on laughingly, like two happy gossips.

He played another of the comic sketches and made Dora laugh. And then, well before her laughter had subsided, he suddenly began playing, very quietly, her own music. She stiffened in her chair, her loose sleeve fell back from her arm. She was affected by the music as on that first occasion. Uncannily, she felt as though she were back in the upper room at 'Forli' where he had first played it to her.

When the last notes had sped away, she could not look at him. She gazed into the dying ashy fire.

She heard him rise from the piano stool. His footsteps were moving slowly across the room towards the armchair in which she sat. A shudder went over her body; he had taken her two hands in his. His fingers grasped her wrists. He lifted them so that she was forced to come into a position that was neither sitting nor standing up. She was shy, fearful, yet intrigued. Only slowly could she turn to look at him. He gazed at her intently, his eyes bright, his lips apart and his breath much quickened. He gripped her wrists tightly, holding her in the same, unusual, unsteady position.

'And how do you like yourself, my dear Dorabella?' His voice cracked. He moistened his lips quickly with his tongue.

For a time the girl was speechless. How could she begin to put into words what she felt? But she must say something. So there came a rush of banalities. It was wonderful . . . beautiful . . . It was marvellous to be a part of the work w . . . w . . . which was acclaimed by the world as his greatest work . . .

She broke off, feeling foolish and embarrassed at the pathetic inadequacy of what she had said. Her eyes conveyed her utter dependence upon him at this moment. He looked into her face searchingly.

'You dear . . . child,' he broke out throatily with a difficult hesitation before the last word. Then he started to bring his mouth down on hers. Down, down he came. She wondered how his moustache would feel upon her lips.

At the last he lifted his head jerkily and his hairy mouth descended on her forehead. The kiss was heavy and lingering.

Abruptly he let go her hands so that she dropped back into the armchair. He turned and strode from the room.

Some time later she could hear him pacing about upstairs. The haughty parlour-maid came and asked if she should extinguish the lamps and bank the fire. Absently Dora agreed and herself went upstairs to bed. For a long time she sat in a chair thinking and waiting to become calm again. She thought and thought about what it all could mean. But to no avail. Her knowledge and confidence were not enough.

When she awoke the next day, it was late. She hurried downstairs to find that some breakfast had been kept warm for her. Elgar could be heard at work in the music room. Alice was up but still very weak. She wore an old dressing-gown of heavy Indian silk. She was laboriously preparing a shopping-list. Dora remembered that she had agreed to go into Malvern to do some necessary shopping. The errand was welcome. She was glad that she would have something to do other than reflect on the incident of the previous night. Energetically she helped Alice to complete the list and then went and hung out the Union Jack over the garden wall. (This was the Elgars' way of stopping the two-horse brake that plied the hillside road between Malvern Wells and Great Malvern.)

When she went back into the house to see how Alice did, the older woman regarded her curiously. She said slowly, 'My dear, I wonder if you would just knock on dear Edward's door to see if he requires anything from the shops.'

A reasonable enough request, yet Dora detected malice in it. Her face coloured.

Reluctantly the girl went up the stairs and prepared to tap on his door. She was stifled with embarrassment to have to approach him after his departure last night. She touched the door lightly.

'Come in.'

Breathlessly she told him that she was going on some errands for Alice and could bring him anything he needed.

'Come in and close the door!' he barked irascibly. He was wearing a dark worsted suit and looked very much the head-master.

Dora quailed. 'I really must hurry. Must hurry. I've put the flag out and the brake will be here any moment. I m . . . m . . . must go.' Her voice trailed away; her liquid eyes were again painfully susceptible to him.

But he was now brusque and harsh with her.

'I can't see what is the good of your coming all the way from Wolverhampton if you go and spend half the day in Malvern directly you arrive.'

She was hurt by the unreasonableness of his attitude and by the nastiness, almost viciousness in his tone. But she could think of no answer to make.

'There's the brake!' she cried, hearing the brief, sharp trumpet-call. And she turned and rushed from the room, down the stairs and out of the house.

In Malvern, amidst all the other stately, fashionable ladies, she slowly completed the shopping. She felt her lack of sleep as she walked along. Her mind would not think things through very far. All the changes and inconsistencies in his attitude to her were more than she could manage to understand.

She returned to 'Craeg Lea' to find Elgar gone to an engagement in Birmingham. The two ladies sat quietly together. Alice took long, slow pleasure in announcing to Dora that she was much impressed with the girl's work with the press cuttings and that, with Edward's consent, she would be prepared to offer her the position (honorary, of course) of Keeper of the Archives. It was a joke like all the many other names, nicknames and titles in this household. And yet at the same time it was not a joke. It was an honour and a solemnity. Dora accepted quickly and with laughter but also with genuine gratitude.

The next morning Alice's condition had deteriorated. In fact, she was as ill as she had been two days before. When Dora went to see her in her room, she found her feverish and mithered. The girl insisted that she stay in bed and receive another visit from the doctor. But the poor wan figure struggled pitifully to rise.

'But I must. I must,' she gasped. 'Edward must be at the station by ten for his journey to Leeds. He is to conduct there tonight, you know. It is most important. Most important to his career. I must go and help him make ready . . .'

Dora repeatedly assured her that she would take care of everything for her. And at last, unconvinced but exhausted, Alice fell back weakly among her pillows.

For the invalid's sake Dora was glad that she had prevailed. But now she felt daunted in having to approach the man again. She went to the drawing room where she found him playing Bach fugues on the piano. He wore only his black dress-trousers and a newly laundered white shirt. She had never seen a man with so few clothes on before.

She stood in the doorway hesitating, a little ashamed. Then she announced faintly that Alice had suffered a relapse and that she had come to do what she could to help him to get ready to leave.

Full of shrill petulance he snorted, 'I'm not going; I'm going to stop at home.' He continued to play the piano forcefully.

The girl lingered. What was to be done? How ever could she report this decision to Alice? So how was he to be humoured?

Then fortunately he relented. 'Oh very well, bring over the things, I shall change in here.' Still playing, he motioned to the collar, tie, studs, waistcoat and other clothes on a nearby table. Gladly she carried them over to him.

He looked up at her and said, 'You can jolly well do some work and dress me. I'm not going to stop playing.'

What strange idea was this? She didn't know what to say. He stared at her in truculent defiance. She hesitated. He continued to play. It seemed definite that either she must dress him or he would not go. And she would be to blame.

With hesitant steps she approached him, a very unsure handmaiden. She inserted the front and back studs in the white collar and gingerly started to attach them to his shirt. It was a shock for her fingers to touch the back of his neck under the hairline. It was almost like a burn. The hair was greasy under her fingers. She managed to get the collar fixed at the back. It was more difficult to do the front stud, under his chin. She pushed and pulled at it with her finger-ends. All the time he played on. What would anyone think, seeing the two of them now?

As her fingers moved over the stubbled skin of his throat and Adam's apple, he started to chuckle, not in an amused way, but more in a pleasurable, voluptuous way. The sound deepened; there was a rattle in it. And it was infectious for as she started to knot his silk tie, Dora found herself laughing too.

Then she had, one by one, to lift his hands from the keyboard and put them through the armholes of the waistcoat. She laughed even more at the silliness of it all. Her hands moved across the dark silk back of the waistcoat, smoothing it. She caught her breath at the feel of it. The man chuckled all the more deeply and Dora laughed wildly, fearfully. It was all a game, a joke, but also in some way shameful.

They each grew hot with their uneasy laughter. There were small stains of perspiration under the arms of his clean white shirt. For an instant she was vexed, but then laughed on with him in some abandonment. He grew more visceral; she more shrill. She was shocked, ashamed, surprised to have touched him. He regarded her insolently; the piano boomed on.

Their laughter fit started to slow down when she was putting on the very last items, his jewelled cuff-links. Slowly it abated, and when she stepped back to judge her work, they were only breathing hard. He looked well. She took a pride in her skill at dressing him.

He played one last chord on the piano, stood up, put on his jacket and overcoat, picked up his case and hastened from the room. She heard the front door slam. Not a word of farewell had he said to her.

She sat for a good while in the drawing room. She felt chill and abandoned. She gazed and gazed at the now desolate piano and piano stool where he had sat.

10

SHE did not understand the laughter. Even less did she understand the old, sour anger that was a part of it. But over her many years of reflection upon these times she would come to surmise it. Her education began on her next stay at 'Craeg Lea'.

That was the frightening occasion on which, in a fit of tired, bitter frustration, he struck her.

This visit did not take place until many months after the last one. In the interim she encountered him at concerts and festivals, but only infrequently.

Once, unexpectedly, he and Alice appeared at a concert of the Wolverhampton Choral Society at which Dora and Amy Danks sang duets. She did not have an opportunity to speak to him on this occasion. And she was glad, for she feared she might have looked ridiculous standing on the platform beside her ungainly, carbuncular friend who was so much taller than she, well over six foot tall.

On other occasions Dora would invariably encounter him in large gatherings of people, people who were increasingly unfamiliar to her.

This was the time of his great recognition and success. That very year he received the doctorate from Cambridge and three years later there came the knighthood. He was now surrounded by many new friends and acquaintances, some of them titled and very wealthy. At times Dora found herself surprised that she knew such a person. At other times she felt wounded that she was for so long neglected and that the puzzling but genuine bond between them was never developed or acknowledged.

Paradoxically, though apart from him, she was at this time fully integrated into the circle of admirers. She had been right those years before to call him 'Your Excellency'. For he now presided over a court in which everyone had their title and function. The protocol was clear and strict. Dora was the Keeper of the Archives and as such would be invited to join the inner group of twelve or fifteen followers as it made its way each year into the opening concert at the Three Choirs: Gloucester, Hereford, Worcester. When she came to look back on her life, Dora would see her youth spinning away rapidly to this rhythm of cathedral cities and ever more select tea-parties and evening receptions. She was one of several women who, odalisk-like, were privileged to follow on behind him at these great festivals.

In a way this was a pleasure to her. She was ever more widely known as a figure in the famous music and as a friend of Elgar, an Elgarian. This conferred upon her a certain social position. She was invited by church groups at Walsall, Wednesbury and West Bromwich to give talks on his music. And she was listened to with great respect. As the light, fair down above her upper lip coarsened and her complexion became ruddier and her waist thicker, she came to be something of an institution in these inland counties. Gradually she developed a dame-like, presidential manner. Her quick, virginal energies were hidden behind this public exterior. Her stammer too had slowly disappeared; it had been part of her youth.

But the old loneliness was still there. Often she would sit musing in her oak-panelled bedroom, wondering how it had all come about. She could recall so vividly that very first day when they had gone to the football match together. But it must be more than ten years ago now. How fast that time had gone! How casual, easy, even pert, her attitude had been then! Yet that coincidental meeting had determined her life. The relationship which had been so fluid, so full of merriment, excitement and promise had now solidified and she was defined by it. However perplexing the underlying uncertainty, her life had been made what it was by that first meeting. She had her position, her post, her title, her fame. But as the years had gone by the original quick of sympathy had been slowly covered over, lost sight of. And now the established social forms that had been produced from it were the more important. Incessantly she asked herself how this had happened. This question was the main subject of her most intimate thoughts during the months, indeed years, early in this century when her visits to the Elgar household were suspended.

One likely answer was that early in the new King's reign the Elgars had moved from Malvern to an even larger and more imposing house on the north-eastern side of Hereford. The greatly increased distance from Wolverhampton would, they would think, make it impossible to cycle over. The archive materials were sent to her by post every week. She dealt with them and returned them promptly. Sometimes she felt like a mere official, or functionary, though Alice did occasionally enclose a personal note listing Edward's most recent successes.

This same year marked one of the highest points in Elgar's fame. In March there was the Elgar Festival at Covent Garden. Three evenings were devoted exclusively to his music. And at one of the performances King Edward himself was present. To her intense dismay Dora was prevented from accepting the invitation that was sent her to attend. And always thereafter she felt that her absence on that occasion might have been one of the things to create a break between herself and the composer. She who had known him during his time of struggle was not present to see him at his moment of triumph. This might well explain both his continuing neglect and his later, shocking act of cruelty to her.

It was the Rector who was responsible for Dora's absence. She had informed him of her invitation and of her intention to go to London one morning, when the household was returning to the Rectory from early morning communion. She regarded what she had to say as mere information that would be of only passing interest to her father, if even that. For he attended less and less to his daughter. So she was taken aback when he halted, stepped back under the branches of one of the ancient yew trees in the churchyard and glared at her in a passion of anger.

'Are you mad? Are you mad to think of attending entertainments in London at this time?'

His face grew red, his eyes bloodshot. In the course of the years his once handsome face had taken on heavy jowls. The flesh shook. The skirts of his cassock smacked loudly against his trousers in the cold spring wind.

Dora faltered. Never before had he spoken to her so harshly. The dull steam hooters could be heard sounding from the factories in Horseley Fields.

'What is amiss with this time . . .?' the girl began.

Her father turned away his florid face in disgust.

'Are you forgetting, Dora dear,' intervened Minnie quickly in a low voice, 'that it will be the period of Lent?' She glanced nervously from father to daughter, patting the grey hair under her bonnet. She had long renounced her ambition to minister to them. Both were beyond reach of her gentleness. Her best hope was in that acquiescing in everything that her husband said or did, she would not give offence to Dora or to others.

Despite a moment or so of fear at the strangeness of her father's behaviour, Dora spoke up for herself.

'But, father, there is to be sacred music.'

'Sacred, you call it?' A bitter sneer.

'The words are sacred, father.'

'Some of that Gerontius music, I suppose.'

'Yes, father, parts are to be played.'

'He calls it a dream. I should call it a nightmare.' The Rector laughed throatily to himself and looked around the little group for applause.

Minnie stared at the gravestones; her eyes moved slightly like those of a wary bird. Mrs Bayliss breathed heavily; she was developing something of a heart complaint. But Dora knew that the housekeeper's sympathy was entirely with her and against her father.

He went on in a passion of disgust.

'The man's music is decadent. Decadent. It reeks of incense.'

His voice skirled viciously. Over the years in the borough he had become ever more crudely conservative, ever more pre-occupied with his own inner concerns and ever more contempt-uous and dismissive of anything else. His snobbery was almost an illness. Ever since the time at Worcester he had recurrently expressed his dislike for Elgar's music. He found it distasteful, even sinister. Sometimes Dora wondered if he might be jealous of her friendship with the musician. Could there be such an emotion under that lifetime of tortuous pondering? Incorrectly, but justifiably, she decided that there could not. She could only see that Elgar was an affront to her father's proprietary, Anglican idea of the world. He was simply one more occasion for the Rector's many feverish, often tormented imaginings about power, humiliation and vengeance.

He pulled his long black cloak about him and moved towards her.

'I merely say this. It is the period of Lent. If you forget God and go after your own vain amusements from morning to night, you will assuredly make shipwreck in the end. I forbid you to go to London. I forbid it.'

Brusquely he set off again under the dark sooted trees, the women following behind.

During the next few days Dora thought of defying her father. But at the last she was unable to deny what was considered her duty to her father and the proprieties of churchmanship. She belonged in her father's world as well as the musician's. Such was the time.

And Elgar, she felt, never forgave her that she had not attended his triumph.

It was during her visit to Hereford in the following year that he hit her.

This terrible, unforgettable episode occurred just months before Dora's path crossed, quite coincidentally, with that of the young American poet who was to became famous for his dedica-tion to the art of the troubadours. Dora was in Malvern on a visit to Isobel Fitton. And as she was passing down the road by the Ash Wood she saw the striking young man come slithering down the bank, leading a dishevelled young woman by the hand.

Earth clung to their clothes and their faces were flushed, their eyes dilated in the aftermath of passion. This poet was, of course, to become a noted polygamist. (Though that is another story, of another time.) But Dora scarcely noticed the unusual couple, still so dejected and preoccupied she was with that ugly episode of the previous November. All these months later, long after the actual bruise had disappeared, she could feel his blow upon her body. It would always be a vivid physical memory. It echoed through her limbs.

She had at long, long last been summoned to Hereford by Elgar himself. The visit was briefly proposed in a letter that was principally concerned with politics. He greatly feared, and rightly, that in the forthcoming election (it took place in the following year) Mr Balfour, whom he much admired, would be defeated by the Liberals. Subsequently he cited the political condition of the country as one of the reasons for his depression, upset and untoward behaviour to Dora.

When the girl arrived at 'Plas Gwyn', the large white villa with Regency ironwork among the hills above Hereford, Alice it was who opened the door to her. She was fashionably dressed in a suit of dark green plaid but she still looked ailing and anaemic. She moved about fretfully giving the impression of one trying desperately to remember things. She seemed not to have expected Dora.

'Oh . . . oh . . . dear Dora, I am so glad that you could come . . . But His Excellency is extremely busy. How long have you come for? I am afraid it will be rather dull for you.'

Under the courtesy Dora sensed the development of a feline irritability. This, even more than the new expensive house, made her feel a stranger. Did Alice, after all these years, no longer wish to see her? Dora forced herself to put this thought aside and to ignore the lack of welcome.

With strained cheerfulness she said, 'Oh that will be all right. I can keep you company then. And there is lots to be done with the archives . . .'

Doubtfully Alice led her up the wide staircase. They sat down in a large sitting room that contained much new, leather-covered furniture. Dora was shocked by the obvious expensiveness of it all. It was out of keeping with the man as she knew him.

'He's been hard at work on the new oratorio all morning. He ate scarcely any lunch . . . The music is beautiful.'

Alice whispered this information, virtually to herself. But her solicitous tone made it quite clear that Dora was not to intrude or distract him.

Alice fetched a large envelope of press cuttings and handed them to Dora. The girl worked away at the archives for several hours. She was obediently silent. The only sound was that of the piano overhead. The rumbling notes sounded as though they were coming down the chimney. The phrases rang with a strong, if hesitant grandeur. Alice took up a piece of embroidery, but always her ear was cocked attentively to the music above.

Dora worked on, long after she had grown weary. A maid wheeled in afternoon tea on a trolley. Alice whispered, 'When His Excellency is at work like this, I never have a bell rung for meals and I require that everyone be as quiet as possible. But then, of course, you will remember . . .'

The two ate their tea in silence. Alice filled a thermos with tea and put sandwiches and biscuits and covered muffin-dishes on a tray. This she bore out of the room and up the stairs. The climb made her breathe heavily. Dora followed her, not knowing what else to do in this unknown house, with its unfamiliar regimen.

Alice set the tray on a mahogany chest outside the room in which the piano continued to sound. Dora was childishly glad to see the chest; it was one of the Anglo-Indian pieces that she remembered from earlier times at 'Forli'. As such, in this house, she thought of it as an old friend.

With a finger to her lips Alice motioned insistently to Dora to descend the stairs with her. In the sitting room they returned to their earlier activities. Some two hours later the silence was interrupted by the maid who reported that the master had not touched the food that had been put for him.

There was a further period of silent activity. Then Alice announced, 'It is well past time to dress for dinner. It looks as though it will be just the two of us. But it cannot be helped you know.'

As she spoke Alice assumed an aggressive, take it or leave it attitude. She was plainly bored with the girl. Miserably Dora wondered what, during her many months of absence, could have changed Alice so. She thought of poor Rosa Burley.

Some time later, just as the two ladies were preparing to go in, a door was flung open at the top of the house and the man's pale face could be seen peering down from the top of the carved banisters.

'Where's dinner?' he demanded abruptly.

'It is ready now, my darling. We were just going in.'

He looked down upon Dora indifferently and said as though mildly surprised, 'Hullo, you here?'

The two ladies went into the dining room and sat down to wait for him. The several maids peered out to see if he had come. Everything was stiffer in this house than in the others.

Dora wore a new dress of orange gauze, the sleeves of which fell back to reveal her wrists and shapely, white, lower arms. She wore also the thin bracelet of old silver that had been a gift from her real mother.

At last Elgar hurried in, his dinner jacket and cravat rumpled and awry. The servant brought the soup and immediately, without looking to anyone else, Elgar began to eat.

Not a word did he say throughout the meal. When he was not eating he gazed distractedly at the wall in front of him. The pale flesh of his face was drawn; he looked tired.

Only at dessert time when Dora reached out her hand to take a fruit did he appear to become aware of his present circumstances.

This was when it happened.

As her soft hand moved back and then rested on the table-cloth, his jaw trembled and his whole frame was shaken. It all looked involuntary, as though some motion of his physical nature.

Dora had not the slightest suspicion that the fit of rage had anything to do with her. Then the blow came.

Her plumply modelled forearm lay along the table's edge; the light, diaphanous sleeve had fallen back. Elgar swiftly reached over his arm and in a peculiar, ugly, slashing gesture, brought his hand down on her arm. It was a heavy, powerful blow; it made her cry out with pain. At the centre of the burning violent impact she could feel the hard, harsh finger-ends of the violinist's left hand.

She pulled up her arm. Tears came instantly to her eyes and fell in rapid drops down her cheeks. Her arm throbbed and ached sickeningly. There was a thick red weal above the filigree bracelet just half way between the elbow and the wrist. Dora felt suddenly faint with the hot pain of it.

Elgar stared curiously at the wound for a moment. Then he rose, pushed back his heavy chair with a clumsy motion and hurried from the room. He could be heard mounting the stairs swiftly. He banged his study door and turned the key in the lock. The piano began again.

Alice surveyed Dora with impartial interest.

'Oh, dear Dora, look at your poor arm! That was wicked of His Excellency, really.' The sympathy was suave and utterly false.

'It is not as bad as it looks,' gasped Dora, rubbing her arm. 'It will soon be better.'

She strove to preserve that convention of jokes and humour that was one of the traditions of her relationship with the couple. Even though her arm throbbed painfully and she was only a second away from weeping at the brutal malice of his action.

Alice said no more about the incident. After a while she suggested that they retire to the sitting room to continue with their earlier activities. It was as if she were challenging Dora with monotony. But the guest was only too glad of the privacy which work on the archives allowed her. She could nurse her arm and what was more difficult, try to overcome her tears and her misery.

Towards eleven or twelve o'clock Alice broke the long silence to enquire politely if Dora would like to go to bed. But she preferred to stay up. Amidst all her pain and confusion she was aware that some old-established right of hers was here involved.

Alice stood up, smoothing out the rear fold of her dress irritably.

'When my husband is engaged upon his work so far into the night, I often make tea. Should you like some?'

Dora simply could not understand Alice's chilly manner to her. This was almost as bad as the blow she had received.

Submissively she accepted the invitation. And the two went down to the kitchen with its whitewashed walls. The servants had long since gone to bed and it was an adventure for the two ladies to be preparing the food by candlelight. Dora's spirits improved slightly.

Again they took a tray upstairs and placed it on the chest outside the study. They ate their own sandwiches in the sitting room. And yet again they returned to those same activities that they had pursued through the day. The piano boomed above them intermittently. However would this visit end, wondered Dora beginning to grow fearful. At times she thought she caught Alice dozing. Then she found herself waking, with a cold start, to hear the grandfather clock in the hall chime one o'clock. She herself had slept. And she was appalled. Never before in her life had she been up so late. The piano went on. Alice, she saw, had been out and brewed some more tea. Dora was grateful for a cup. It helped to wake her.

And then the door was suddenly flung open and Elgar hurried in. His complexion was still pallid and his eyes tired and sunken but there was a new bounce and vitality to his step.

'Hello. Are you still up? And Dorabella too? Capital. We can have a bean-feast.'

He was altogether different from the man who had sat at dinner with them. There was a boyish excitement in him as he gallantly offered around the remaining sandwiches and biscuits. With comical flourishes he poured the tea from the large pot. He ate hungrily. In his present high spirits he appeared to have quite forgotten the incident at dinner.

But Dora had not. She watched him warily. She would dearly like to trust this new mood. But she no longer could.

'Should you like to come up and hear what I've been at?' he asked them with a simple humility and modesty. And there he was, at that late hour, ushering them up the stairs to his room.

It was far more impressive than the work room at 'Craeg Lea'; there were several heavy wood chairs, an armchair, a grand piano, pictures on the wall and shelves of expensively bound books.

Intently he sat down at the piano. 'Come and turn over the pages, Dorabella, just as in the old days, you remember?' His words astonished her. How could he behave to her as he had done, if the past meant anything to him?

He played the piano for almost half an hour, becoming more and more interested in the music than in his listeners. It was powerful, exalted music that touched Dora deeply. It must have been the upset and her tiredness that made her so susceptible to it.

'It is after half-past two, Edward dearest,' intoned Alice quietly at the first pause. 'I think we should all go to bed now.'

'You go on then,' replied her husband cheerfully. 'But I want Dora to stay and talk to me.'

Alice looked surprised, even betrayed, by this. Her eyes searched his reproachfully.

'Oh . . . Oh . . . very well,' she said, humouring him or taking a hint.

He strode to the door and opened it for her. Her weary langourous steps could be heard moving away down the hall.

He hurried back to the girl and took her hands in his.

'Fancy you staying up all this time – why ever did you?'

His manner was that of some child conspirator. Dora was afraid of him. She had not wanted to stay here alone with him but had not known how to leave. She still felt the blow. Her fear showed in her eyes.

'I wanted to see you,' she heard herself saying. She was confused; she had not meant to say such a thing.

His eyes moved from her face to her body. 'You do look charming in that frock. When I saw you . . .'

A thought hurtled through her mind: the way she had dressed had in some way offended him. She interrupted him, 'I wish that I had brought something a little darker and more sober.'

He answered her with a hiss. 'Don't you dare to bring any dingy, dark frocks, when you come to stay with me . . .' He paused, breathless. 'I want you always in beautiful things . . .'

His eyes were shining, his lips moist and apart. There was in him a hectic excitement coming from fatigue. Dora remembered a similar occasion in that other study in Malvern. She felt very weary now. She knew that nothing more would happen.

Suddenly he was a reproachful child. 'And you only looked at me twice during dinner,' he grumbled.

'I was afraid,' she explained truthfully, with gentle candour. 'I imagined you were thinking about something. I didn't want to put you off your stroke.'

He said simply, almost foolishly, 'At first I hoped you wouldn't and then, as dinner went on, I hoped you would.' There was something pathetic in his explanation of his moodiness. He went on, 'Finally you'd won. That was why I hit your arm. Did it hurt? I meant it to!'

He looked at her with a defiance that lacked conviction. He went on, 'And also because you've never appreciated what I feel for you. Never. Never.'

These words were more genuine, more adult, more passionate. They were spoken with a bitter sob that much disturbed the girl. This reproach was more painful than the blow itself. Only after many years of pondering them would she recognise the self-pity in them.

He put his fingers on her arm, lifted her loose sleeve and considered the thick mark he had made. It was now more extensive than it had been but less red and burning. She looked at him. His fingers moved slowly and delicately on the soft underside of her arm.

In that instant Dora could have said exactly what would happen next. And it did. The study door was slowly pushed open and Alice murmured, 'It is nearly three o'clock, my dears. Surely it is time to go up now . . .'

The following day Sir Edward was pleasant, amusing, but for the most part dreamily preoccupied. Perhaps this was due to the lack of sleep.

When Dora awoke, the blow and the images of Alice's unkindness rushed into her mind. As the day went on they would not leave her. So she found a pretext to cut short her stay and returned to Wolverhampton.

11

THIS, so it proved, was the end of Dora's ten years of peculiar intimacy with His Excellency, though she was not to realise it consciously and fully until some four years later. During this period he might occasionally call in at the Rectory on his way to some engagement and Dora paid a few infrequent visits to Hereford. But always they encountered each other, and remained within, a larger group of people. They were polite, kindly, even sometimes teasing in the old way, but always at a certain distance from each other. His letters to her were fewer and shorter. She thought she was relieved, because she would not have known how to be alone with him after what had happened. In retrospect his action came to seem worse than it had done at the time. Yet still, in a secret part of her mind she continued to wonder what else might occur between them.

Then one day in the hot summer of 1909 there came a brief letter from the Lady, inviting Dora and her friend Amy Danks to come to Hereford for the day in a fortnight's time 'to attend something very special'.

Dora walked to and fro on the bright green lawns before the Rectory and pondered this latest mystery. The sky was perfectly blue and the sunlight was intensely and liquidly hot within the old brick walls of the Rectory garden. There was a heavy scent from the garden flowers, the usual acrid smell from the nearby factories and the smell of horse manure from the street outside. Dora felt hot and uncomfortable. She was irritated with herself that she felt intrigued, even a little hectic, at the prospect of going. The years had taught her nothing. But what was it all about? She had not heard from them for many months. And why ever had they invited Amy Danks? She felt a little insulted that she was relegated to the status of an Amy Danks, that Amy was offered the same privileges, the same intimacy as she. Perhaps she would refuse the invitation, very politely. But she also thought that it might well be a kindness on the Lady's part, an act of real and generous hospitality to her lonely friend. And again Dora thought that the presence of Amy Danks might be calculated to serve one of the Lady's shrewd, delicate manoeuvres. And perhaps these in turn were an outcome, a furthering or a combating of some of His Excellency's own. What a puzzle! She gasped a little as she speculated on why such a manoeuvring should be necessary. The bees worked away feverishly at the purple clematis that grew high up the outer bays of the beautiful dark brick Queen Anne house. Dora walked around the hot, humming garden, wondering. When Mrs Bayliss called to announce that lunch was prepared, Dora was angry with herself that she had allowed the letter to take up her whole morning.

Two days later Dora encountered Amy Danks at the ladies' weekly Bible reading at St Peter's. It was a lengthy meeting and when the two stayed behind to stack the prayer-books in the cupboard in the vestry, it was already quite dark. They worked away together in the dim orangey glow of the newly installed electric light. When they had finished and Dora was locking the cupboard door, she told her friend quite casually of the invitation to Hereford.

For a moment or two Amy Danks was disbelieving.

'What a surprise! . . . How kind . . . But are you sure there is no mistake? I have only met them once. They scarcely know me. You are sure that it is I they have in mind?'

The dark eyes moved shyly and anxiously. There was the characteristic slight tremor in the large, sallow face.

'But, of course,' replied Dora with easy, insistent confidence.

'They mention you by name. I shall be happy to show you the letter if you wish.'

'Well how very kind . . . how very good of them . . .' The dark eyes examined Dora's face nervously, as if searching for more information.

'You will come, won't you?' There was a very slight edge to Dora's voice that made her sound not altogether urging or even encouraging.

'Well, yes. Yes. What an honour!'

She smiled gratefully, opening her wide mouth in her unsure way. Dora nodded almost curtly, and turning to the new bright brass switch, put off the light with a loud snap.

On the morning of the day proposed the two set off to the station together. The bright August sun warmed the imposing buildings on Lichfield Street and gave a pretty roseate tinge to the long glass awnings over the entrance to the Grand Theatre. The two ladies made a striking couple. Amy Danks walked along in her peculiar striding way, her knees always lifted unusually high. She was a good head taller than her companion. Dora walked more calmly and attractively, carrying, in a very poised elegant fashion, a small luncheon hamper. She was plumper and her face a good deal ruddier than when she had first gone to meet Elgar at this same station all those years ago.

On the train they sat at the window and waited expectantly for all the drab factory walls and smoke-stacks and gasometers of the Black Country to recede. Soon they came into lush countryside of green and golden fields and leafy woods and coppices shimmering greeny-blue in the warm haze. And whenever the train braked to a squealing standstill at country stations, they would listen for the bright clear song of the birds. After a while Dora grew pleasantly drowsy. Quite sensuously she recollected setting out on all those other southerly journeys through this same countryside and the many excitements of them. How she had rushed off! On her bicycle, by train, in a brake, anyhow! Now she was aware of savouring, and of consciously repeating, and somehow more slowly, one of her most choice experiences.

Suddenly and a little anxiously Amy Danks suggested that they should eat their lunch. They were already more than half way there, she said. They spread a heavy white linen napkin on the sun-warmed seat by Dora and set out the sandwiches. Amy Danks leaned over and munched away hastily, Dora more modestly.

Then Amy Danks became worried about their arrival in Hereford.

'I do hope I shall not be intruding,' she twittered. There was alarm in the dark restless eyes. 'I do not feel that I know them very well.'

'But they invited you. By name.'

'I feel a little peculiar about entering their house.'

'But they are accustomed to receiving many people whom they do not know intimately.'

'How should I address him, do you think? . . . Sir Edward, that is . . .'

'Just as you did on the previous occasion. He is Sir Edward and she is Lady Elgar.'

As she confirmed these names and titles, Dora was struck by the utter simplicity of her friend's relationship with the Elgars compared with her own. As the friendship grew more tenuous, which of all the names she had once used should she herself now employ?

Outwardly Dora was quite calm as she reassured her friend. But her mind was increasingly aquiver with excited curiosity. She struggled to control it. Pride and common sense required that. The agitation showed only in the way she kept attending to her clothes. They were her very best: a blouse of fine white lace high at the throat and a suit of lime-green linen, quite tight at the waist and at her now full hips and at her bosom. Beneath her skirt her shoes were a delicate light brown and very dainty. She continually rearranged her skirt, pulled at the collar of her blouse and flicked specks of dust from her shoes with the wrist end of her white gloves.

Amy Danks, in her hot-looking, grey woollen suit, could not but serve to emphasise the light elegance of her friend.

When the train came into the dark coolness of Hereford station, Amy Danks grew very nervous at the time that Dora took to arrange her large, flower-covered hat and to correct her hair at the mirror above the seat in the middle of the compartment. At last she stepped down, just as they were banging the doors of the train in order to resume the journey.

In the sunny square in front of the station there was much manoeuvring of hansoms, victorias, landaus and motor-cars. Dora knew from the letter of invitation that it would not be possible for them to be met. Nevertheless, at that instant, she still could not help feeling disappointed that there was no one there to receive them as there had so often been in the past.

Resolutely Dora waved to a cab and started to walk towards it.

'But . . .' piped Amy Danks, looking wonderingly from Dora to the tramcar. Dora shook her head decisively. That was no longer the way to approach the house. She was no longer a girl.

She shepherded Amy Danks up into the cab, climbed in herself and gave the driver his instructions briskly and brightly. She sat back in the cab with great confidence and prepared to enjoy the view from the window. Occasionally she made further adjustments to her blouse at the collar and the wrists.

The cab clopped away through the narrow streets of the city. There were glimpses of fine black and white inns and Georgian houses and then beyond the roof tops the great cathedral by the river. What a contrast with Wolverhampton it was! To Dora this old city reeked of hay and corn and farm produce. How clean and earthy it smelled. In the streets she could see farmers in their frock-coats and gaiters and shepherds in their smocks, carrying their crooks.

The cab reeled as they took a turn to the left and the horse began ploddingly and labouringly to pull them up a long hill. They were soon in a cool, tree-lined road with large villas in spacious gardens on either side. At a corner, a little before the top of the hill, the cab pulled into a driveway and halted before the high steps of the porch to 'Plas Gwyn'.

The two ladies alighted. Dora carefully counted out the coins for the fare and for something extra. Then they mounted the steps to the door and raised the heavy knocker. The door was opened by a parlour-maid in a sparkling white apron and cap. The girl was new. Dora had never seen her before.

'I am Miss Penny and this is Miss Danks,' explained Dora. 'We were invited to come here this afternoon by Lady Elgar.'

Indifferently the girl admitted them and closed the door.

'There's tea and dainty sandwiches in the dining room, Miss,' the girl recited dully as if she were tired of repeating the same words, 'or you can go straight on into the drawing room, if you wish.'

'I should very much enjoy a cup of tea. Shouldn't you, Amy?' Dora replied graciously. They followed along behind the girl to the dining room at the rear of the house.

But as they passed the door to the drawing room, Dora's curiosity was sufficiently intense that she could not resist peeping in. There stood the Lady looking abandoned and rather helpless amidst a large and confused array of wooden chairs. She glanced up and saw Dora.

'Good afternoon, Dora dear!' she called. 'I am so pleased that you could come. Do, please, come and assist me with the chairs. We are due to begin in less than half an hour. And the chairs are not yet arranged. Higgins has gone to borrow some more from Lady Brewster across the way. And I am left to put these in order on my own.'

The Lady appeared preoccupied and strangely helpless.

Dora stepped into the room and was followed by Amy Danks. The Lady eyed this second visitor a little uncertainly.

'Good afternoon, Miss . . . I am so pleased that you were able to come, Miss . . .'

'Danks. I am Miss Danks.' Two pink spots flushed into the wide, pale cheeks.

'Ah, yes,' said the Lady, almost understanding now, but still very grand.

'How are the chairs to be arranged?' enquired Dora, bustling into the room and confronting the difficulty in her old way.

'They should be in rows . . . in a semi-circle,' explained the Lady. 'That will be the most suitable for the performers.' She pushed ineffectively at one of the large Indian chairs of dark wood. She smiled at Dora slyly and curiously.

'I imagine you have guessed by now what the surprise is to be?'

Dora shook her head and she and Amy started to heave and

pull at the chairs. The Lady imitated her husband's manner with his mysteries but in a way that was less easy, less casual, and less subtle. The heavy jaw made it all more like a challenge, a confrontation. Dora was a little irritated. The Lady had aged noticeably even in the months that had elapsed since she had last seen her. Of course, she must be well into her sixties now. Her face was becoming puffy. The strong bones of her skull showed through more clearly and her skin was wrinkling in many new places and becoming powdery and rough and coarse. The face looked very worn and weatherbeaten.

The Lady wore a dark blue dress of heavy silk that trailed on the carpet. There was lace at the narrow cuffs. She also wore a deep red velvet necklace with large pearls at the centre. And the rings that she wore on the last two fingers of both hands were heavily jewelled. She moved around flittingly after the two girls making a few minor changes to their positioning of the seats.

Despite her fit of vexation with the Lady, Dora did wonder what the entertainment might be. In front of the first row of chairs there was just the grand piano and a music-stand. It could be anything. In the early evening sunlight she was becoming hot with this heavy physical work. But on she went with it, with great determination. Amy Danks, she could see, was already perspiring a good deal. A thin lock of her dark hair lay plastered to her pale glistening brow.

At last, the chairs were in order.

'Thank you so much, both of you. That was most kind,' crooned the Lady in her mannered, singing way. 'You must be very hot. I can see that you are. What a shame! Do come to the dining room and have some tea. It will refresh you. Follow me please.'

Unhurriedly she led the way through to the large dining room.

In the hall the front door was being opened regularly to admit newcomers. Very few of them were known to Dora. These were all new friends, it appeared. There were none of the old.

From the study, Dora caught the occasional, brief sound of the violin and the small piano together. What could be happening?

In the several groups of people in the dining room there was, again, no one whom Dora knew very well. She and Amy stood together to drink their tea. The Lady hurried in a preoccupied way from group to group. Dora and Amy conversed with each other a little self-consciously.

When they had finished their tea, Dora was aware of Amy looking to her for the next initiative. For want of a better idea, Dora suggested they return to the drawing room. They made their way back through the still busy hall to find that some of the chairs were already taken. Dora motioned Amy to two chairs in the middle, just two rows from the front. Vainly Dora looked about again to see if there were anyone she knew. Gradually the room filled.

Suddenly the Lady bustled in. She was quite agitated.

'I simply do not know how we are to manage. I do not. I am sure there will not be enough chairs. It turns out that Edward invited another party of people and forgot to inform me. Oh, I do hope there will be room.'

She gazed at the seated people helplessly, appealingly. Then the anxious blue eyes settled on Dora and Amy.

'Dora dear, and er . . . er . . . er . . . Miss Danks, yes . . . Could you move down to the end? And then some of the newcomers might slip in here. Yes, that's right. Straight to the end. Yes, yes. Thank you so much.'

Dora and Amy now found themselves in chairs in a corner behind the large marble mantelpiece which partly obscured their view of the piano. The Lady also asked other people to move down so that seats nearest to her and in the centre were left vacant. She regarded the chairs doubtfully for a moment or two and then hurried out.

The reorganised audience sat quietly and waited. Minutes ticked away on the large, noisy clock on the mantelpiece just above the two ladies from Wolverhampton.

Dora heard a very aristocratic-sounding lady seated immediately behind her whisper to the gentleman who accompanied her, 'What is the reason for the delay, do you suppose?'

The stout man wheezed breathlessly as he began to reply.

'All part of the mystery, I should imagine. You know Ted. Don't you remember his jape on the journey to Windsor to dine with the King?'

Dora opened her eyes wide at this familiarity. Who could this be who would dare to speak of Ted? Certainly a man of high station in life. And from the south, from London. But what impertinence! Dora looked around the room and marvelled at all the friends His Excellency had. And she knew so very few of them now. Not many appeared to know each other. All that they had in common was their acquaintance or perhaps their friendship with him.

Suddenly there was a slight commotion at the door. The Lady appeared, anxiously leading a group of some half-dozen people or more who walked in a very casual, dignified, even haughty way down the side of the semi-circle of chairs. Most of the men in this group wore dark frock-coats with waistcoats and wing collars. But two of the younger men wore strikingly jaunty weekend suits. One was in pale blue, the other in a check mixture of light brown and canary yellow. It was almost vulgar, Dora thought, much intrigued. It would definitely have been, a few years ago. But now, she conceded to herself, it was stylish, the height of style even.

Still more arresting and interesting than these fashionable younger men was the one lady who was with them. She was tall and stately and wore an unusual and beautiful long dress of light purple that was diaphanous at the top of her white arms and shoulders. She had also a small straw hat that cast shadows on the little blonde curls that hung from her hair where it was taken up at the back. She carried a parasol that was of the peacock colours of blue and green. She had beautifully calm, almost indolent blue eyes, a fine and delicately shaped nose and chin and full and very mobile lips. She moved like a queen, but utterly unassumingly. Her companions stood aside for her; the Lady deferred to her most conspicuously as she indicated the chairs that had been left empty.

Unhurriedly the lady with the parasol moved to one of the chairs and, at last, with a great, beautiful billowing of her purple dress, sat down. Her male companions then proceeded to arrange themselves on chairs nearby.

The eyes of everyone in the room gazed at the unusual, purple figure, and at the simple straw hat that must surely be French.

Intentionally or not, this beauty made the other ladies in the room look somewhat dowdy. Even Dora, perhaps after this new-comer the most handsome figure in the room, was made to feel that her green suit looked a little dull, a little unfashionable. She was sure that she looked a sight after becoming so hot, whilst moving the chairs.

'Who is that person?' whispered the inquisitive lady who sat immediately behind Dora.

Her companion began his low wheeze. It was clearly an indispensable preliminary to his hoarse whisper.

'That's the Stuart-Wortleys. Been friends of Ted's for a good while, I believe.'

'Who are they?' hissed the lady. Her whisper suggested her snobbery. It sounded as though not only information but also proof of the social acceptability of the fellow guests were required. And all this in a whisper.

Her companion began his prefatory wheeze.

'He sits for Sheffield Hallamshire. Tory you know. Very wealthy. Very wealthy indeed.'

'Oh . . . And that is his wife?'

'Yes. Quite a high-stepper, eh?'

'Who is she?'

'Alice? Daughter of Millais, the painter fellow.'

'Really?'

'Perhaps you're a bit too young to remember, m'dear. All that to do with Millais and Ruskin and Effie.'

'But of course . . . how interesting . . .'

The lady's curiosity was greatly excited. She could be heard shifting on her chair to see the figure in purple more clearly. Amy Danks also craned her longish neck to obtain a better view of the beauty. Dora wished that she would not.

Then Elgar appeared. He strode into the room, his head held tensely to one side. He looked pale but his eyes were bright and intense. Dora knew him well enough to sense the suppressed excitement within him. The strong, arched nose appeared to thrust forward from the long, high brow, driving into the room. He wore a suit of fine grey wool that Dora had never seen before and a reddish silken tie with a rounded white collar.

He was followed into the room by a slightly shabby, diffident young man who carried a violin and a bow and a sheaf of hand-written music. Elgar stood by the piano and surveyed his audience with tense, unseeing eyes.

'I am so very pleased that all of you could come . . .' he began in a deep rumble. His eyes moved around the room uneasily. Only for a brief moment did they come to a halt. And Dora saw that it was upon the grand beauty in purple that they rested.

Disconcertingly, without saying another word, Elgar sat down at the piano stool. He ran his fingers along the keys. The young man came and stood beside him and adjusted the tuning of the violin slightly. Dora was sure that the young man was Bill Reed, a violinist from the London Symphony Orchestra whom she had heard Elgar speak of on previous occasions. He was an unpretentious, slightly gangling figure. He held the fiddle and the bow down by his knees as though they did not belong to him. Dora found him attractive. He had bushy light brown hair that was parted in the middle and puffed up softly at the sides of his head. He had a largish nose and quick, lively eyes that were shrewd and perceptive. He wore a faded Norfolk jacket. He could have been the young Elgar himself, Dora thought.

She heard Elgar speaking in a low voice to the young man.

'You are not going to leave me all alone in the *tuttis* are you?'

The young man smiled largely.

With a start Dora understood that this must mean that they were to hear the violin concerto which he had hinted and talked about years ago. It was finished then. How he surprised her always! Once again he had completed a work to be set beside, and compared with, that of the great musicians of Germany. Tears started to come. There was something historic, in a way sacred, about this moment. She looked around her but no one else gave any sign of appreciating the importance and the memorability of these seconds as they passed. She craned her head a little to obtain a better look at him and saw that his eyes again dwelt upon the lady in the light purple dress. Then he averted them suddenly as though from too bright a light and immediately began to play the concerto.

Dora was instantly caught up in the music. As on other occasions when he had played to her alone, he contrived to make the piano sound like a whole orchestra. The piano, and even more the violin when it entered so quietly and unobtrusively, spoke to her of such intensely personal things that she was overwhelmed and could not assess them. She heard catches in the breath, un-certainties and repressions, together with sudden quickenings and nervous withdrawals. It was a music of renunciation. Then sud-denly came the beautifully confident singing melody which she at that first hearing understood as the most delicate and sensitive of caresses.

From where Dora sat the young violinist who screened Elgar from the audience appeared to address his music to the grand lady in the straw hat. He bowed away at his instrument con-scientiously, carefully and with dedication. But his body and his movements in no way expressed the passions in the music. It was as though the hunched intent form behind him banging, banging, banging away on the piano were speaking through him. Dora again turned her head to see if she could obtain a view of this lady from whom Elgar was concealed but to whom the music, Dora was absolutely certain, was addressed. Dora could just see her. The beautiful face and the brilliant blue eyes gazed down at the floor.

Dora felt a hot spurt of jealousy come over her. This woman then had replaced her. This foolish Trilby figure. This was her successor! And of course Alice had arranged for her to have the best place in the room. Alice, whose task it was to purvey people to her husband! Dora was chilled with disgust. With them. And with herself. And as this feeling slowly abated she was reminded of the time he had struck her.

But when she started to hear the delicate music of the Andante, she was pleasantly surprised to be reminded of her own music. Dreamily and contentedly she recollected their walks together at Boscobel and North Hill and all that they had talked about. It was all so long ago now. Fourteen years at least, it must be now since she had first met him. Augustus was of that time and he was dead.

When the great, tense cadenza of the final movement began, she realised calmly and without further pain that this was not her music. It did not ignore her or forget her but it was not of or for her. She recognised a part but not all of what was being said. The intensities and the sadnesses considered and lingered over here, the memories of repressed love and of suffering recollected and resolved, referred to her definitely, but to more than her.

The dull orangey light of the early evening slanted through the high windows on to the dark wood of the drumming piano and on to the heads and hats of the listeners. In her corner next to Amy Danks, Dora sat back and listened resignedly and happily, as though from afar, to the urgent, ecstatic music of the fiddle. It spoke of something that was both familiar and unfamiliar to her. It was another woman's music, from another place and another time.